# A Concoction of Lies

*A Novel*

PATSY C. ROBERTSON

This book is a work of fiction. Although some references to people, places, and events were the products of intensive research and used to enhance the story, the most significant references to historical events, real people, or places are fictitious. Other names, characters, places, and events are products of the author's imagination, and any resemblance to actual events or places or persons, living or dead, is entirely coincidental.

*I want to thank my husband, Ned,*
*for being the wind beneath my wings.*

# *Reviews*

Patsy Robertson took me on a roller coaster ride in A Concoction of Lies. It was jam-packed with action and filled with lies, murder, and betrayal. The suspense kept me on the edge of my seat, turning the pages as fast as possible. There was a great variety of characters, each with a unique background. The chapters alternated between the main characters in which their pasts and present were discussed. The writing style was engaging and held my attention from the first page until the last. The story was fascinating, and I kept wondering what would become of Chance after he was kidnapped. I could never predict what would happen next and was guessing until the end. I enjoyed reading this story, and my expectations were exceeded by far.

*Reviewed by Alma Boucher for Readers' Favorite*

# 1

# CHANCE

Chance Moore awoke from a nightmare, blinking rapidly to dispel the darkness from his vision. Hot sweat trickled down his face. Within seconds, fear gripped him. This wasn't a nightmare; it was reality. His heart pounded as if trying to escape his chest, and he felt as though he were suffocating. Each gasp for air brought fabric against his face, and it tugged against his shirt when he moved his head.

*Don't panic. Focus. Control yourself. It's a hood.*

Methodically, he controlled his breathing by slowly counting to one hundred. Then he began a top-down physical assessment. He was in full-body restraints: handcuffs linked to a wide belt around his waist, which in turn was connected by a chain to ankle cuffs. The restraints were secure but loose enough to allow circulation. Although he was stiff and sore, there were no broken bones. The vibrations against his body suggested he was in a moving vehicle.

Indistinct noises assaulted his ears, making his head feel like it would explode. Suppressing his terror, unable to see his surroundings, he breathed through his open mouth. But his stale breath that mingled with the oily, chemical scent of the hood made him want to gag.

As a former cyber security expert in the FBI's Cyber Crimes Division, stealing money via the dark web was never meant to be a second career. Rather, it was a temporary means to extricate himself from a horrendous financial scandal, clear his name, and fade quietly into obscurity.

It was the middle of February 2020. The cool temperatures and a six-day hike on California's Pacific Crest Trail had offered the perfect respite from the relentless media coverage of the COVID-19 virus. His modest house was in a small town sixty-five miles north of Los Angeles. A nondescript white van swerved into his driveway as he unloaded camping gear from his Jeep. Within seconds, three men jumped out, wrestled him to the ground, and injected him with something that rendered him unconscious.

Now restrained and being transported to an unknown destination, Chance's mind raced. The abduction had to be tied to a heist—but which one? He and Mack had executed their final hack on Christmas Eve, and he hadn't heard from Mack since. They were among the FBI's best cyber experts and meticulous coders; their multiple layers of encrypted security should have protected their online identities. So, how had he been found? He dreaded meeting his kidnappers.

Finally, the vehicle halted, and the door opened. The change in the air washed over him. Two male voices conversed in Spanish. Chance lay still, eavesdropping. The men spoke freely to one another, wrongly assuming he didn't understand the language. Someone else was coming for him, and they were running late.

Then came pounding on the vehicle floor.

"Hey, are you awake?" a man with a heavy Mexican accent shouted in English. "Say something. Are you awake?"

His mouth parched, Chance croaked, "Yes."

"Good," the man replied. "We're bringing you out. Don't try anything stupid, or you'll regret it. Just follow instructions, and you won't get hurt, understand?"

Intimidated by the man's tone and ashamed of his trembling voice, Chance said, "I understand."

The men yanked him out by his ankle cuffs. They tried to stand him up, but his head pounded mercilessly, and he felt too weak to remain upright. His legs wobbled, so they lowered him to the ground.

"Get him some water," the first guard ordered, struggling to keep Chance from falling over. He quickly removed the hood from Chance's head and held him like a baby in his arms, holding a water bottle to Chance's lips and forcing him to drink.

"I'm good; that's enough," Chance finally said once he could sit upright without assistance.

"Did you call them?" the first guard asked his accomplice in Spanish.

"They're on their way. They should be here in ten minutes," the second guard replied, nervously scanning the dark road.

Chance looked around as he sat on the hard, sandy ground. The men had turned off the van's headlights, leaving only the crescent moon and stars to illuminate the vague outline of hills and the arms of saguaro cactus plants reaching toward the sky. They were in the desert; the night air was chilly but refreshing after the hot, stifling van. Except for the men's voices, it was eerily quiet until a ringtone broke the silence.

The sound of an approaching truck reached them before its headlights pierced the darkness. The first guard went to the front of the van and signaled with a flashlight. A large box truck stopped, and two men hurriedly exited the truck's cab. The passenger rounded the vehicle, lifted the back door, and lowered a ramp. The truck driver walked to the van and talked with the van's driver while the other two men lifted Chance into the back of the truck. They pushed boxes to the side to make room and then made him sit as they repositioned them to hide him from view. Finally, they slammed the door closed, plunging him into darkness.

# 2

# VONNIE

It had rained during the night, and the sun peeked over the lush, rain-drenched rainforest canopy. Mosquito nets draped over the four-poster bed billowed as a balmy breeze flowed through the open French doors leading to the balcony.

Vonnie Hollister slowly pushed herself up, mindful of the pain in her lower back, hips, and knees. Howler monkeys, perched in the treetops, called to their troops; birds and other critters, hiding among the foliage, added to the chorus of awakening wildlife.

She lethargically slid her feet into bedroom slippers while clicking the TV remote. A cheerful weatherman stood before a map filled with numerical temperatures, happily repeating the same dialogue every morning: "The day is going to be hot and humid with a chance of rain in the afternoon."

Vonnie was a Belizean African American who had temporarily moved to Belize to sell the two-thousand-acre Cavendish banana plantation she inherited after her father died. The property had been in the family for over 150 years and was currently one of the country's largest and most profitable privately owned fruit producers.

Throughout her life, Belize had been her second home; The place for weekends, summer vacations, spring breaks, and holidays. But it was an inheritance she had no intention of keeping. The sooner she sold it, the sooner she could return to North Carolina and move on with her life.

The house she lived in was nicknamed The Big House and was built in the 1800s by the original English plantation owner. The white, three-story, five-bedroom, Victorian-style house stood atop a sloping hill. Elaborately carved cornices, turrets, and other architectural embellishments enhanced the beauty of the historic home.

A wide driveway stretched from the highway, forming a circle in front of the steps that led to ornately carved double doors. A large screened-in back porch overlooked the activities that kept the massive plantation running like a well-oiled machine. At night, strategically placed landscape lighting made the house glow.

Vonnie padded across the bedroom and stepped onto the balcony as she combed the tangles out of her hair. From this vantage point, she could see the brightly painted houses of the plantation's residents. Clothes fluttered on clotheslines, chickens pecked in yards, and vegetables sprouted in small, neat gardens. Fruit trees and brightly colored tropical flowers surrounded the houses. The scene was enchanting and picturesque in the early morning sun.

Beyond the colored houses lay a small cinderblock medical clinic and an assortment of buildings that made up the physical plant: the administration offices, utility buildings, garages, repair shops, and processing and packaging areas. Further on, a vast grove of banana trees stopped four miles from the Belize border, and a wild, undeveloped rainforest stretched deep into Guatemala.

The main entrance to the plantation was beyond the driveway to The Big House, farther down the highway. A gravel service road with connecting branches divided the property into organized blocks.

While tying the belt on her robe, Vonnie watched an intermittent stream of workers leave their houses, call out greetings to one another, and walk toward the groves. On the service road, migrant workers scrambled from white vans. Cars and pickup trucks stopped to let people exit, and other vehicles continued to the employee parking lot.

The pace of the day's activities was picking up.

Her bedroom was on the house's third floor, which wasn't an issue when she was younger. But now, with arthritis ravaging her joints, the stairs had become a dreaded nemesis. Tightly gripping the railing with her right hand and bracing her left hand against the wall, she slowly lowered herself down the stairs one step at a time to start her day.

The warmth of the steam and the fragrant aroma rising from the locally grown coffee soothed her as she settled into her father's rocking chair on the back porch. The plantation had a rhythm and dance that everyone followed, consciously or unconsciously. Slowly rocking and sipping, she continued watching the morning's dance unfold.

Her knees resisted when she stood to return to the kitchen for a refill, but she was drawn into the dining room instead of immediately returning to the porch. Wide, intricate crown molding adorned the top of the walls. Long-outdated navy-blue velvet drapes, restrained with ornate, tasseled ties, were accented by raised-patterned wallpaper. A highly polished mahogany dining table with seating for twelve stood atop an enormous Persian rug. Sunshine filled the room, and a spectrum of rainbow colors reflected onto the table from the chandelier hovering above a crystal vase in the center. Though most of the furnishings in the house were custom-made or imported, the overall decor represented an ancient, bygone era. It was as if time had stopped throughout the house, and the entire structure seemed as sad as she was.

As she settled back onto the porch, children of various ages dressed in black-and-white uniforms streamed from the houses. They laughed and teased each other as they rushed to board vans embellished with the Hollister Plantation logo, which transported them twenty-five miles to schools in Punta Gorda.

Slowly shaking her head from side to side and releasing a long, sad sigh, she watched the vans with the children move down the service road toward the exit gate.

*I can't run this place, it's too complicated, and I don't want the responsibility for all these people. What am I supposed to do if I can't find a company that wants to keep them here? Relocate them? Where? Punta Gorda can't absorb them. It's too much to think about now. I'll cross that bridge when I come to it.*

With her second cup empty, Vonnie returned to the kitchen and placed the cup in the sink. Today, she was flying to Belize City to meet with Mr. Benjamin Turay, president of the National Bank of Belize and one of her father's closest friends. The small plane that would take her to the city was leaving from Punta Gorda's airport in two hours. Standing at the bottom of the stairs, she looked up the stairwell, took a deep breath, and prepared herself for the painful ascent.

The sequential deaths of the people she loved most in the world had all occurred in three short years. First, it was Russ, the love of her life. Then nine months later, heart failure unexpectedly took her mother. And finally, almost one year after her mother's death, her father suffered a fatal stroke.

His death was the straw that broke the camel's back.

For the past two years since his death, she had tried everything to keep from drowning in an ocean of grief and paralyzing depression—psychiatrists, inpatient and outpatient therapies. When they had all proved ineffective at keeping the darkness at bay; antidepressants, prescription painkillers, and alcohol became the life rafts that kept her afloat.

During the two years when the depression was at its most acute, she had put off returning to the plantation, knowing she was mentally and emotionally ill-equipped to face her life's most significant and complex decision, which was letting the plantation go. But even though a dark cloud hovered over her daily, and a complete recovery was still a distant prospect, she was at least functional.

That's why she waited until New Year's Day to return. Five years of mourning was enough. 2020 would be her year of new beginnings, but there were hard decisions to make, and they all terrified her. Afraid she would change her mind after arriving in Belize, she put the plantation on the market before leaving North

Carolina. It was an anchor holding her in the past and preventing her from healing.

The tie had to be severed.

# 3

# ELOY

Rivulets of water streamed down the windowpane, blurring the view. The dark, rain-soaked night deepened Eloy Vasquez's despair as he stood at his bedroom window, hoping to see the lake below. Now, on its sixth day, the downpour had raised the lake so high that the boat dock was submerged.

But a drowning dock was the least of his problems.

Leaning heavily on his cane, the seventy-six-year-old patriarch of the Guatemalan Vasquez Cartel slowly moved away from the window, flopped down in an upholstered chair, and turned on the TV.

He rubbed his head, and several strands of hair clung to his fingers. Puzzled, he examined the thin white wisp. Hair loss was a new symptom of his illness; he would soon be bald. Dry, scaly skin covered the bones and veins of the hand holding the hair. Not long ago, his hands and fists had been hard as rocks, capable of breaking a man's nose or jaw with a single blow. But those days were gone. He was dying.

His body was betraying him when he needed it the most. Baggy green pajamas hid his shrinking body. Eating had become an ordeal due to mouth sores; solid food irritated his stomach and passed through his gut like water. Even minor activities drained his energy. Some days, his mind was sharp, but then, when he least expected it, confusion set in. Fragments of old memories intruded on current thoughts, or he lost track of time, days, and events. Moreover, unrelenting pain consumed him and disrupted his sleep.

Eloy clicked the remote, switching from one channel to another. Dire reports detailing the disastrous effects of the worsening economy and the spread of COVID-19 dominated the news.

Suddenly ill-tempered and irritable, he turned off the TV. A gust of wind rattled the window; thunder rumbled in the distance. The rain continued to stream down the pane. With a shaking hand, Eloy wiped the strands of hair onto the arm of the chair.

A decade ago, the river of money flowing in from all directions had dwindled to a mere stream. Like a pack of hyenas his enemies surrounded him, nipping at his flanks tearing off whatever they could. His empire was falling apart.

He had tried to groom his sons, Aapo and Humberto, to rule in his place one day, but both had proven inept in leading the cartel. They had failed miserably at expanding the organization, halting its decline, or protecting what little remained. All he received from them were excuses.

His mood darkened. He grabbed his cell phone and forcefully pressed the code connecting him to New York. With each unanswered ring, his anger escalated. Finally, just as he was about to hang up, Aapo answered.

Aapo's voice was groggy with sleep. "Papa, is everything okay?"

"What took you so long to answer? Are you with a whore instead of figuring out why we're losing money?" Eloy growled.

"What? It's six in the morning here; I was asleep."

Eloy's agitation grew; sweat beaded on his forehead, and his breathing became heavier. "I don't care what time it is. I've been waiting for you to call me, and I'm tired of waiting."

"But we spoke yesterday. Papa, it's four a.m. there. Why are you awake? You should be resting."

"I was in Guatemala City yesterday and haven't heard from you in weeks," Eloy retorted.

"Papa, you're confused. You've been at the lake house for over four months. Where's your nurse?"

Embarrassed by Aapo's question, Eloy slammed the phone down. Black spots appeared in his vision, and he began grinding his teeth, his hands clenched into fists. Struggling to stand, he looked around the room.

*I need fresh air. A walk, yes, I need to clear my head. I'll walk around the lake.* He scanned the floor. *Where are my shoes?*

Minutes later, a male nurse in blue scrubs cautiously entered the room, syringe in hand. Eloy's eyes widened in fear as the nurse approached.

"I don't want that; leave me alone," he protested.

But the nurse was quick, restrained him in seconds, and quickly plunged the needle into his arm.

"HELP, HELP!" Eloy screamed, struggling.

Spiraling into delusion; old, painful, suppressed memories flooded his mind.

* * *

*He was seven, orphaned and homeless, living in the slums of Guatemala City. It was late at night, but a full moon and fires in the garbage dump made it possible for him to see. He should have been in his hiding place instead of rifling through the mountain of garbage but gnawing, relentless hunger made him reckless. Suddenly, he was being dragged through the muck and filth by one of the men who hunted for children at night. "HELP, HELP, leave me alone!" he screamed, terrified. Unfortunately, his resistance was futile; he was too small and the man too strong.*

* * *

In Eloy's bedroom, the nurse wrestled him into bed, quickly maneuvering him into a bear hug and pinning his arms to his sides.

"Let me go. HELP, somebody, help me!"

The nurse quickly pulled up the side rails and locked them in place as Eloy mumbled incoherently, tossing and turning, lost in his delirium.

* * *

*Eloy tried desperately to free himself from the man in the garbage dump.*

*"Let me go! Let me go!"*

*Then, like ghosts, a gang of teenage boys appeared out of the shadows and silently surrounded them like a pack of wolves. Frightened, the man immediately dropped him in a puddle of filthy water, and Eloy scurried behind a pile of garbage. Peering out, he watched the brutal attack. When it was over, the predator lay dead, his blood streaming into the black, putrid water.*

*An older boy slowly approached the garbage bags where Eloy was hiding, stooped down, and looked at him with compassionate eyes. "Are you all right?" he whispered.*

*Traumatized, Eloy couldn't speak but nodded his head up and down.*

*"Would you like to come with us?" the boy asked. "We have food and will give you a safe place to sleep. No one will hurt you." He stretched out his hand, and Eloy took it. From then on, the gang became his family and his protectors.*

*Seven years later, he was their leader, and seven years after that, his reputation for fearlessness, cunning, and raw savagery was unmatched. As the years passed, he transformed the ragtag slum gang into one of Guatemala's most powerful organized crime syndicates.*

* * *

By six that evening, the clouds of confusion were lifting, but Eloy remained in bed, listless and drained of energy. The drapes were closed, a Tiffany lamp across the room emitted a soft glow. Barely audible symphonic music played from hidden speakers. Puzzled and uncertain, he eyed the mobile tray table a few feet from the bed. A metal top covered a plate on the table.

*Did I eat?*

The thought of food sickened him. A foul odor rose from the blanket as he shifted to make himself more comfortable; his lower body was sticky and wet. Calling the nurse could mean another shot or pill, and then maybe it was best to remain quiet and think while his mind was clear and the pain tolerable. But after an hour, unable to bear the itching and stench any longer, embarrassed and humiliated, he pressed the buzzer for the nurse.

# 4

# ALEX

In 1961, the Guatemalan government and leftist rebels were embroiled in a fierce civil war that led to the indiscriminate massacre of more than two hundred thousand people and the mysterious disappearance of an additional forty thousand to fifty thousand.

The chaos caused by the war, coupled with a corrupt and dysfunctional government, created a lawless environment where drug cartels thrived. Cartels seized control of farms and violently coerced farmers into growing poppy and coca plants, the raw materials for heroin and cocaine. In addition to the military conflict's devastating effect on the population, the cartels murdered, kidnapped, and raped thousands, leaving over 80 percent of the country's population brutalized, impoverished, and illiterate.

During this period, two teachers, Dante Martinez and his wife, Adriana, fled the violence in Guatemala City with their three children. They moved one hundred and fifty miles to Dante's grandfather's farm, located twelve miles north of the village of St. Helena.

Educated and outspoken, Dante railed against the inept government and corrupt law enforcement officials who failed to protect the citizens from the cartels. Within two years, he rose to a leadership position in the community. During a series of secret meetings, he convinced the local farmers to form a militia for self-protection.

The militia fought for their lives and land and became adept at thwarting the cartel gangs that wreaked havoc in the countryside. Although successful in their initial efforts, they were ordinary farmers and not experienced hardcore killers. Nevertheless, they were a small band of men bravely paddling a canoe in a tsunami.

Alex Martinez was fifteen when soldiers from the Vasquez Cartel raided his family's home in the middle of the night in search of his father, Dante. Cartel soldiers kicked in the front and back doors while spraying bullets from automatic rifles into the ceiling and walls. The noise was deafening, and the tiny house rattled and shook under the barrage of gunfire. Yelling and cursing, the invaders destroyed everything in their path as they advanced upon the terrified family members.

Dante awoke instantly, grabbed a pistol from under his pillow, and shot the first man to enter the bedroom. He pushed Adriana off the bed; she fell between the bed and the wall. He continued firing as more men stormed into the room.

Hearing the commotion, Alex threw off his bedcovers and scrambled to reach the rifle under his bed. His younger siblings, Bruno and Catalina, who shared the tiny bedroom, screamed and huddled together in panic. Alex aimed at the door, ready when a large man burst in. He fired, but the intruder fell on top of him, pinning him to the floor. As Alex struggled to free himself, a second man entered the room, grabbed him by his pajama top, and punched him twice in the face, knocking him unconscious.

Within minutes, Dante was severely beaten, dragged outside, and tossed into the back of a pickup truck. Before leaving, the cartel soldiers torched the fields, the orchards, and the family's truck.

After a harried and sleepless night, the following day, black and blue bruises covered Alex's swollen face. His left eye was bloodshot, his right eye swollen shut, and a yellowish pus oozed between the lids. A broken nose, swollen lips, and loose teeth made it difficult to breathe and eat. Adriana insisted he visit the doctor. Alex groaned at the thought of riding the family's donkey twelve hot, dusty miles to St. Helena.

After leaving the doctor's office, he noticed a crowd gathered in the village square as he was untying the donkey from a post. Curious, he approached the group. The onlookers noticed him, became quiet, and shuffled aside, allowing him through. The mutilated bodies of two militia members lay on the street. Beside the torsos were the decapitated heads.

The crowd watched him, mumbling among themselves. Alex turned, walked to the donkey, and rode away, straining not to show any emotion. The ride home was slower and more tedious because the thought of telling his mother about the bodies filled him with dread.

As he entered the yard, Alex's gaze lingered on the damaged front door, the broken windows patched with cardboard, and the bullet holes in the wood on the front of the house. He stopped beside the charred remains of the pickup truck. The dark, skeletal trees in the fruit orchards and blackened rows of garden vegetation lay desolate in the afternoon sun. The burned smell of what had been a thriving farm hung heavy in the humid, tropical air.

The cartel soldiers would return; they always did. And then they would take the land and do whatever they wanted with his mother, Bruno, Catalina, and him. Without his father, the family was defenseless and vulnerable.

Upon hearing Alex enter, Adriana hastily entered the living room, looking haggard from the lack of sleep and anxiety. Her hair was uncombed, and her dress was dirty and stained.

"What did the doctor say?" she asked, wiping her hands on a towel.

He saw suspicion in her eyes as he took her hand and led her to the sofa. "I'll be all right; he gave me some medicine."

"Alex, what is it? What's wrong?"

Tears stung his damaged eyes as his mother howled like a wounded animal when he told her about the bodies in the village square. She trembled with despair as Alex wrapped her tightly in his arms.

They both knew that if Dante wasn't among the dead in the village square, it could only mean one thing: he was still alive, but the cartel wasn't through with him. As the leader of the resistance against the cartel, Dante's punishment would take longer and be more severe. And after his death, the cartel would send a warning message by horrifically displaying his body for all to see.

That night, sleep was impossible as Alex held his mother's hand long after she had dozed off into a fitful sleep. He seethed with hatred for the cartel. His father was a courageous and honorable man who deserved dignity and respect in life and death. There would be no exhibition of his desecrated body for the cartel to take pride in. Regardless of the consequences, he was determined to bring his father home, dead or alive.

Before sunrise the following day, Alex crept from the house, hitched the donkey to its cart, and tossed in blankets—either to make his father comfortable on the ride home or to cover his dead body.

Fifty miles north of St. Helena, an old, abandoned sugar mill served as the Vasquez Cartel's regional outpost. Everyone, including the police, knew its location, and rumors of the atrocities committed there were legendary.

It was late afternoon when the donkey cart stopped at the gate of the dilapidated sugar mill. A tall brick wall overrun by vines and old-growth vegetation surrounded what previously had been the mill's administration building. An assortment of vehicles—some functional, others junked—littered the overgrown front lawn. A cracked and crumbling concrete driveway extended from the gate to the building, blocked by a locked ten-foot chain-link gate.

Two men in a dusty pickup truck were about to exit on the opposite side of the gate when they encountered Alex in the donkey cart. The driver, a gruff-looking man with a long scar on his cheek, leaned out the window. "Get the fuck out of the way," he shouted, waving his arm.

Sweaty and dusty from the long, hot ride, Alex climbed from the cart and walked to the gate. "I want to talk to the captain," he yelled.

"People in hell want ice water; now move!" the driver shouted in frustration. The man on the passenger side laughed and pushed a black cowboy hat up on his forehead.

Alex didn't want the men to see his nervousness, so he gripped the chain-link fence and shook it vigorously. "I want to talk to whoever is in charge," he said, insistent.

The driver immediately stepped out of the truck and stomped to the gate. "And, who the fuck do you think you are to come here and demand anything?" he growled.

Defiantly lifting his chin and looking the man in the eyes, Alex said, "My name is Alex Martinez, and I've come to get my father, Dante Martinez."

When he heard that comment, the passenger came to stand beside the driver, removed his cowboy hat, scratched his head, and peered closely at Alex. "Isn't that the little fucker who shot Jesus the other night?" he asked the driver.

"How should I know? It was dark; a lot was going on," the driver said, fuming and squinting at Alex.

"I think it's him; look at his face. I helped pull Jesus out of the room. Man, this kid has balls," he said, turning to look at the driver. "What are you going to do?"

The driver exhaled. "We need to talk about this; come on," he said, motioning toward the truck with his head. The men drove back to the administration building, and fifteen minutes later, they returned to the gate. The driver snarled at Alex while unlocking the gate. He led Alex up crumbling concrete steps through old metal double doors into the foyer of the administration building. The fading sunlight barely penetrated the dirty windows of the gloomy interior. The air was stale, musty, and smelled of mold and decay. Cobwebs hung from ancient light fixtures, and thick dust covered everything. Cartel soldiers loitering in the foyer watched them suspiciously as they passed. Finally, the driver knocked on a door at the room's far end.

An impatient voice yelled from the other side of the door. "What is it?"

The driver opened the door and stuck his head inside the room. "I have the Martinez kid I was telling you about."

"Bring him in," the voice bellowed.

A stern look crossed the driver's face as he leaned down to whisper in Alex's ear, "This is the captain; show him respect."

The driver opened the door wider and motioned for Alex to follow him. They sat together on two wooden chairs against the wall opposite a desk. A cartel soldier stood, shuffling his feet, and timidly spoke to the man behind the desk.

A sheet of paper quivered in the soldier's outstretched hand. "Forgive me, Captain, but I asked everyone. Two men could make out some of the words but didn't know what the other words were or what they meant. No one can tell me everything it says," he said, gently laying the sheet on the captain's desk.

The captain was a big, burly man of about thirty-five, with long, black, greasy hair pulled back into a ponytail. An unkempt mustache hid his upper lip, and bushy eyebrows topped a set of angry eyes. Papers spilled from a brown leather pouch on top of the desk.

Outraged, the captain jumped to his feet and hurled a large, thick glass ashtray filled with cigar butts and ashes at the soldier, hitting him in the chest. The soldier doubled over in pain and crossed his arms over his chest.

"Idiots," he shouted at the soldier. "You killed a reporter before finding out what he had written? How stupid can you be?"

"It... it was an accident," the soldier stammered. "The men didn't mean to kill him, just rough him up. But when he fell, he hit his head; there was nothing we could do."

Glaring at the soldier, the captain asked, "Now what am I supposed to do? Out of twenty-seven men lying around on their asses, not one of the worthless, ignorant bastards can read what's on these papers. Get the fuck out of my office!" he bellowed.

The soldier bowed and hurried from the room, rubbing his chest.

Exasperated, the captain dropped heavily into his chair and folded his arms. Then, he shifted his focus to Alex.

"What happened to your face?"

"One of your men hit me," Alex responded, quickly walking toward the desk. He lifted his chin and straightened his posture.

The captain looked amused. "So, you're Martinez's son?"

"Yes, sir," Alex responded.

The captain raised his eyebrows and looked even more amused.

"And if I understand what my men are telling me, you want to take Martinez home; is that right?"

"Yes, I want to take my father home."

In disbelief, the captain dropped his head and shook it from side to side. "No one has ever come here and asked me for something like this, and you aren't even a full-grown man. You're just a boy." He laughed. Then, his tone became sinister. "Your father is my enemy; I can't release him. How would it look to people? No one would respect me if word got out that I released him because his little boy asked me to." His dark eyes flashed, and his nostrils flared. He slammed his fist on the desk and scowled at Alex. "Martinez is mine."

"Hand me my ashtray," he barked at the driver, who immediately picked it up from the floor, laid it on the desk, and sat back down. Then he took a cigar from a box on the desk, snorted, leaned back in his chair, placed his feet on top of the desk, and lit the cigar.

Alex could see his time was running out; the captain was losing patience with him. Then, noticing the papers spread across the desk, an idea flashed through his mind.

"What if we made an exchange? Take me and let my father go instead."

The captain threw his head back and howled with laughter. "Exchange? Exchange him for you? You can't be serious. I have no use for a child. Go home; you've taken enough of my time," he said, puffing the cigar until it glowed. "Get him out of here," he snapped at the driver.

The driver grabbed Alex by the arm and pulled him toward the door.

Desperate, Alex strained against the driver. "But I can read."

The captain immediately removed the cigar from his mouth and sat up. His black eyes squinted menacingly at Alex. "Prove it," he said, forcefully sliding the same paper delivered by the soldier across the desk.

Alex cleared his throat and read the page aloud in a shaky voice. Then he took another sheet from the captain's desk and read it. "Now, will you take me in exchange for my father?" he asked. "I am more valuable to you than another dead farmer."

The captain leaned back in his chair and puffed on the cigar. "You make a good point; I'm impressed," he said, blowing out a long stream of smoke. Then he asked the driver, "Is Martinez still alive?"

The driver approached the desk. "I don't think so, but I haven't seen him today."

"Go down, check on him, and let me know if he's still breathing."

Beads of sweat dotted Alex's forehead, and his heart pounded while he waited for the driver's return. However, he kept his chin up and maintained his posture.

After ten minutes, the driver finally came back, scratching his head. "He's still breathing, but I can't say how long he will last."

Alex's head swiveled from one man to the other, uncertain about what would happen next.

The captain blew smoke toward the ceiling and leveled a threatening gaze at Alex. "Take your father home. Then come back after burying him. I own you now you belong to me."

The donkey trudged through the night, its reins limp in Alex's hands as they transported Dante's damaged and disfigured body home. Sobs racked Alex's chest as he cried uncontrollably. Breathing was difficult, and the tears blurred his vision.

Dante died the following evening surrounded by his family.

Alex stood stoic on the second day after his return home, supporting his mother during the funeral services. Villagers came in droves; the church couldn't accommodate all the flowers and the large crowd. The procession of mourners walking behind the horse-drawn wagon carrying the casket stretched for over a mile. Adriana was so distraught that a doctor administered a sedative and put her to bed.

Lost in a torrent of emotions, Adriana didn't adequately question Alex about what he did to bring Dante home, and for this, Alex was grateful. Explaining his arrangement with the cartel would only heighten her anguish. She would never accept an alliance with the men who had killed her husband and the father of her children.

But what he had done was necessary. It was more than a matter of honor to preserve his father's dignity; it was essential to protect the family. The cartel took care of their own, and now that he was a member of their organization, his family and the farm were safe.

During the night, Alex silently slipped into his mother's room, placed a letter on her bedside table, left the house for the final time, and went to the cemetery. It seemed as if every star in the galaxy was lit. The glow from the full moon was so bright he could see the surrounding tombstones adorned with bouquets, small statues, and mementos left by loved ones. Finally, standing at his father's grave, weak with sorrow, he dropped to his knees as tears cascaded down his face.

Then, sniffing and wiping his nose with the back of his hand, he said, "Papa, even if it takes the rest of my life, I promise you they won't get away with what they've done; I will see justice for our family."

* * *

Due to decades of civil unrest, the literacy rate in Guatemala in 1974 was less than 30 percent, and it was even lower within the various cartels. Therefore, literacy was a highly prized commodity.

Manuel, the regional Vasquez Cartel captain, presented Alex to Eloy Vasquez, the lord and master of the Vasquez Cartel, as one might present a child with a prize pony. Manuel had Alex demonstrate his reading, math, geography, and science skills in Eloy's presence. And in exchange for his extraordinary gift, Eloy happily tripled Manuel's territory.

By the age of eighteen, Alex had become indispensable to Eloy. As the years passed, when Eloy asked for a glass of water, Alex was the one who gave it to him. When Eloy walked, Alex was the shadow that followed. He saw and heard everything, forgot nothing, and his hatred never wavered.

# 5

# CHANCE

A confusing mix of sounds, voices, smells, and emotions engulfed Chance as he cycled in and out of consciousness. The fog in his mind slowly cleared, only to be replaced by creeping terror. He lay still, watching and listening, not wanting the men across the room to know he was awake. His body was still restrained, and he had no idea how long he had been unconscious or where he was.

He lay on a dirt floor in the corner of a one-room shack dimly lit by several oil lamps. The door was open, allowing the night air into the stifling little room. An older woman with two long gray braids hanging down her back was cooking on a wood stove. His two guards sat at a makeshift wooden table in the middle of the room, their faces practically in their plates as they gulped down food. The woman turned to place a bowl on the table and saw Chance watching her.

"He's awake," she whispered in Spanish as she set the bowl down.

The heads of both men instantly shot up from their plates as they looked at Chance. Then, with jaws bulging with food, the first man spoke in English.

"Are you hungry?"

Chance peeled his tongue from the roof of his mouth and croaked, "No." His gut was twisted in knots; the last thing he wanted was to eat.

"Water?" the man asked.

The second man turned to his plate and resumed eating.

"Yes, water."

"Give him some water," the man barked at the woman before returning to shoveling food into his mouth.

The woman shuffled over to Chance, squatted, and gently lifted his head so he could drink from a large plastic cup. She didn't speak, but her eyes showed sympathy.

The men spoke Spanish while they ate, and although most of their conversation had nothing to do with him, Chance learned there would be another handoff.

Stiff, sore, and utterly miserable, he strained to stay conscious. But the sedatives coursing through his system, the overly warm room, and the aroma of cumin, cilantro, and chili peppers floating in the air lulled him back to sleep with memories of a better life and time.

*  *  *

It was May 1983, and Chance was finishing his sophomore year at Virginia Polytechnic Institute and State University (Virginia Tech) in the Blue Ridge Mountains of southwest Virginia. At twenty years old, he was attending summer school and looking for a part-time job when he saw a postcard tacked to the bulletin board in the Student Center. A doctor at the university was seeking someone for yard work. He called the number and scheduled a meeting with Dr. Conswaylo Hernandez, a thirty-year-old Mexican professor in the Foreign Languages Department.

Chance drove to the small, rural town of Shawsville, twelve miles from the Virginia Tech campus. Unfortunately, the directions were confusing, and he almost missed the turn into the dirt driveway. Trees and overgrown shrubs obscured the view of the doctor's house from the road, and the dented, rusty mailbox still attached to its broken post lay in a clump of weeds beside the road.

The run-down wooden house sat forty yards back from the road. A brick chimney protruded from the top of the rusted metal roof. A screen door stood propped beside the front door; the upper part of the screen hung loosely from the frame. None of the three wooden front steps had treads across the top, and the front porch was missing several planks.

Chance exited the car and surveyed the yard with his hands on his hips. It was huge and filled with large old-growth trees and an array of withered shrubs; the grass was almost up to his calves. Then he heard cursing in Spanish. At the end of a haphazardly mown swath of grass, a woman angrily jerked on the starter cord of an old push lawn mower.

She had dark olive skin and thick, unruly black hair twisted into a knot on her head. A dirty Virginia Tech T-shirt clung to her voluptuous breasts; smudged, faded jeans hugged the graceful curves of her hips and butt, and grimy white Nike sneakers completed her outfit.

Chance called out, "Excuse me; I'm looking for Dr. Hernandez."

She turned to him. "I'm Conswaylo Hernandez. Please tell me you're Chance Moore," she said with a relieved smile.

A timid smile crossed his lips as he shoved his hands into his jean pockets. "Yep, that's me."

Beaming, Conswaylo removed her work gloves, wiped the sweat from her brow with the back of her arm, and hurried to shake Chance's hand. "How about I show you around, and then you can tell me if you want the job?" she chirped.

Instantly hypnotized by the sparkling black eyes, full succulent lips, and welcoming smile, Chance followed her as if in a trance, his eyes glued to the back of her jeans.

In the backyard, they examined the contents of an old, dilapidated tool shed.

"Wow, it looks like you have enough tools to open a hardware store," he said, picking up a rake and leaning it against the wall.

"I know," Conswaylo said, laughing, "the previous tenants were university students, and their frat parties practically destroyed the place. So, the landlord and I agreed that he would cut the rent in half if I made the repairs. The tools belong to him."

Chance's mind raced as they walked back to the house. He could finish the initial yard work in a day or two but wanted more time with her. So, he lied.

"I... I was thinking, I'm struggling in my Spanish class. Maybe after I finish the yard work, you could tutor me in exchange for helping you around here. What do you think?"

Conswaylo stopped and looked at him in surprise. "Well, I don't know. I could certainly use the help. There's a lot to do, and I can't do it all myself. But you said you were pursuing a double major in computer engineering and computer science. That's a heavy course load. When would you have time?"

Chance could feel his excitement growing. "Oh, I'm good. I only have three classes this summer, and they're easy. I'll have plenty of time."

They fell into an easy routine. Conswaylo was like a magnet, and Chance welcomed any opportunity to be near her. The scent of her hair and sweat intoxicated him as they worked together in the summer heat. The way she moved, laughed out loud, and mumbled Spanish curses all fanned the flames of his desire. If they touched, the sensation lingered on his skin.

He was in love.

The Spanish lessons always began the moment he arrived at the house. She explained, described, and mercilessly drilled him until he left at the end of the day. They watched Telemundo and Univision, and she made him read Mexican newspapers online. Words, cloaked in her Mexican accent, flowed like honey from her lips, and he was hungry, an awaiting bee.

* * *

On a Saturday afternoon in late July, Conswaylo stood at the living room window, sipping iced tea and watching Chance push the lawnmower across the sprawling front lawn. It was ninety-six degrees, and the sky had turned overcast. Towering storm clouds moved swiftly in their direction. Chance wore a baseball cap, sunglasses, faded jeans, work boots, and no shirt. His brown skin glistened with sweat, and the muscles in his back and arms flexed as he pushed and pulled the mower.

Typically, whenever Chance was around, Conswaylo was in a good mood. But today, she was troubled about the budget cuts in the Foreign Languages Department. As a result, her professorship at Virginia Tech would end in ten months. Luckily, she had found another job, but it was on the other side of the Atlantic Ocean.

The dark, ominous storm clouds now hung directly over the house. The storm was moving fast because the wind was blowing. She walked out onto the front porch. "Chance, it's going to rain any minute; you can finish tomorrow. Come on in," she yelled.

Chance was too far away, and the lawnmower was too loud for him to hear her. He was tearing through the grass as if on a mission. So, she returned to the house, removed chicken cutlets from the freezer, and tossed them in the sink. Thunder rumbled. She returned to the window and smiled as she watched him so determined to cut the last blade of grass before the first raindrop fell.

She knew Chance was attracted to her but didn't think he had any idea of his effect on her. He had walked into her life and turned it upside down. At first, she only allowed him to work weekends, but as her infatuation grew, she created small chores for him during the week. Then, knowing he was always hungry, she insisted they cook together whenever he came, using it as an excuse to further his Spanish lessons.

Within the close quarters of the tiny kitchen, they moved as if in a dance. Their bodies lightly brushed as they reached over and around one another. The chopping and mixing, the sound of the hot sizzle of frying meat and vegetables, and the fragrance of the Mexican spices filled the kitchen. Chance's lips on a spoon sampled a dish, then hers.

Each time she stood on the porch, waving goodbye as his little car turned onto the highway, a lonely wave of sadness filled her heart. She didn't want him to go.

Constantly suppressing her emotions whenever he was near had become exhausting. The previous week, when they were painting outside the house, and Conswaylo was standing on a ladder, painting around a window, she stretched too far; the ladder shifted, and Chance grabbed her just in time to break her fall. They both ended up on the ground with her in his arms, laughing. But he didn't release her. Then his facial expression changed. Their faces were close, and the look in his eyes spoke volumes. He would have kissed her if she hadn't immediately broken the embrace and stood.

The awkward moment passed, but that's when she knew they wouldn't be able to avoid the inevitable much longer. Since then, the sexual tension between them had become palpable. The two of them were bashfully dancing around their longing.

Conswaylo loosened her ponytail, fluffed her hair, and walked down the hall toward the bathroom, thinking to herself.

*Your time here is running out. You only have ten months, and they're going to fly by. So, if you want him, have him. And when you leave, leave him with good memories.*

* * *

Chance was unable to finish mowing the lawn before the rain started. Heavy droplets streamed down his torso as he hurried toward the house. A loud thunderclap sounded like a bomb exploded, and a bolt of lightning streaked across the sky as he secured the lawnmower in the tool shed. In the downpour, he sprinted to the back door and removed his wet work boots and socks. Then, laughing, he walked through the kitchen barefoot, using his T-shirt as a towel.

"I almost had it. All I needed was a few more minutes," he yelled.

Assuming she was in her home office, he walked down the hall and stopped at the bathroom. The shower curtain was pulled back. Conswaylo was in the shower, massaging shampoo into her long, thick hair. Chance was speechless as he stared. The foamy lather slid down the curve of her back, butt, and muscular thighs. Foam dripped from the nipples of her breasts; white suds hung from her pubic hair.

Confused, unsure what to do or say, the T-shirt dropped from his hand. He knew he should move, look away, and close the door, but his feet stayed glued to the floor; he felt he couldn't breathe.

Conswaylo looked at him. There was no expression of shock or embarrassment at seeing him standing in the hallway, stunned. Instead, she smiled. "Come in; you need a shower."

Chance swallowed hard, and his hands trembled as he struggled to unbutton his jeans.

"It's okay, don't be ashamed," she said, looking at his swollen crotch with a knowing smile.

The jeans finally came off, and in three strides, he was facing her in the shower.

Conswaylo gently turned him around to face the shower stream. Then, she squirted shampoo in his hair and began massaging his scalp. Chance closed his eyes and tried to control his breathing as soapy hands firmly kneaded his shoulders and back. It felt glorious, but his entire body tensed when she touched him.

"Relax," she whispered. "We both want this." Then she squeezed shower gel into her palms and closed the gap between them.

Thunder rumbled, lightning flashed, and the rain pounded loudly on the metal roof as she massaged and manipulated his body until he could no longer restrain himself and exploded.

The water cascaded over them as Conswaylo planted soft kisses on his shoulders and back. Then, he slowly turned around, wrapped his arms around her, and kissed her as if it was his last day on earth.

Finally, she carefully stepped out of the shower, grabbed a towel, and wrapped it around her head. "You still have soap in your hair, rinse it out, and come to my bedroom."

Two weeks later, Chance moved in. They were discreet. Virginia Tech's campus was so large that they never saw each other during the day, but they did everything people in love do at night.

As the fall semester progressed, the temperature outdoors dropped. Then, as if they were in a time warp, time sped up. Winter came, the snow fell, and the calendar became their nemesis. Their time together was quickly running out.

One cold, snowy Saturday night, as soulful Latin jazz drifted through the air and an empty bottle of wine sat on the coffee table, they lay naked under a blanket. With Conswaylo's head on his chest and their bodies intertwined, they lounged on the sofa before the fireplace. The living room was dark except for the warm, yellow firelight.

Staring into the fire, Chance gingerly stroked Conswaylo's arm. "Conswaylo, I've been researching, and most of my academic credits can transfer to the University of Madrid. So, I can go to Spain with you when you leave Virginia in May. I've been working with a counselor at the School of Technology, and he will walk me through the entire process. All I need is a passport. Please let me go with you," he said, pleading. "Don't leave me behind."

A long minute passed before Conswaylo slowly sat up and looked at Chance. Her skin and black hair glowed in the firelight as the blanket slipped off her shoulder.

"Chance, I love you, but we both know that your moving to Spain isn't practical right now. You'll lose credits, a scholarship, and a stipend. I can't say yes to you throwing all that away when you have only a year left to graduate. It hurts me to say no, but you can't go because it's not what's best for you, trust me in this."

Chance had known what she would say but he had to try. Tears glistened in his eyes as his heart broke. He tossed the blanket onto the floor and pulled her to him.

Winter passed quickly, and the spring semester was in its final stages. It was the last Sunday in April; they lazily lay in bed spooning, his body curved around hers. Propped up on his elbow, Chance nuzzled Conswaylo's hair and lightly kissed her shoulder. "When do you leave?"

"The week after graduation. Graduation is in two weeks; I fly out the following Wednesday."

On the appointed Wednesday, Chance loaded Conswaylo's bags into a waiting taxi in the driveway. They had agreed that he wouldn't go to the airport. Instead, they wanted to say goodbye where they had first said hello. She came down the steps, hair in a ponytail, sunglasses perched on top of her head, in a loose-fitting tunic, jeans, and flats. A large tote bag hung from her shoulder. She walked into his arms and kissed him.

Chance's entire body was limp with dread, and his voice cracked. "I'll always love you, Conswaylo; I'll never forget you."

Conswaylo looked into Chance's tear-filled eyes, touched his cheek, and tenderly smiled. "Chance, there is a place in my heart reserved only for you. No other man will ever fill that space. I'll miss you every day."

Chance stood with his hands pressed deep into the pockets of his jeans, watching as the taxi drove down the dirt driveway. Conswaylo turned and blew a kiss through the rear window. He waited until the car turned onto the highway, then sat on the porch's top step and let the tears flow.

* * *

In the corner of the one-room shack, the two Mexican guards had finished their meal and stood looking down at Chance, curled in the fetal position on the dirt floor, shoulders shaking, silent tears streaming down his cheeks.

Curious, the first guard asked, "What's going on? Is he awake?"

The second guard stooped and closely examined Chance. "Naw, he's crying in his sleep; he must be having a bad dream."

The first guard smirked. "Well, considering who's waiting for him, he should have nightmares. Let's get him loaded up. We need to deliver him on time."

# 6

# VONNIE

Three weeks after visiting the National Bank of Belize to review the plantation's finances, the midmorning sun blazed in the sky as Vonnie trekked toward the plantation's clinic. Beads of sweat dotted her forehead. She wore a loose-fitting T-shirt, beige cargo shorts, and a colorful headscarf from which crinkled tendrils of gray hair protruded. Her Birkenstock sandals flopped as she walked across the uneven ground beside the service road. Then, without warning, her knee buckled, and she fell hard to the ground.

A large white box truck emblazoned with Castillo's Delivery Services was one of the vehicles on the service road. Dominic Castillo, the driver, saw her fall. He quickly pulled off the road, jumped from the truck, and ran to assist her.

Vonnie struggled to stand. She rolled onto her side and pushed with her hands but to no avail. Finally, Dominic stooped beside her and gently touched her shoulder.

"Take it easy. Are you hurt?" he asked.

Flustered and sweating, Vonnie looked at her rescuer. He was striking—salt-and-pepper dreadlocks hung loosely past his shoulders, long black lashes encircled his eyes, his lips full and luscious, and his satin brown skin glistened in the sunlight.

"I'm okay, just clumsy and embarrassed. I don't know wh-what ha-happened," she stammered. "One minute, I'm walking, and the next, I'm on my butt in the dirt."

He smiled. "Where were you headed? Let me help you up. Do you think you can stand, or should I carry you?"

The thought of this man carrying her anywhere left her mouth dry.

"I... I was going to the clinic," Vonnie stuttered, brushing dirt from her hands. "I feel foolish for not being able to get up."

Instantly, Dominic put one arm around her waist and the other under her knees, lifting her to a standing position. His arm remained around her waist.

"Put your arm across my shoulders," he instructed.

Unnerved by his swift action, she wobbled, unsure of her footing. The relentless sun bore down on them. Sweat trickled down his face. Leaning on him, she caught a whiff of his masculine scent.

"It's my knee; I'm afraid to put weight on it," Vonnie said, concerned.

Dominic maintained a firm hold on her waist and supported her weight. She could feel the muscles in his arms and shoulders as they slowly moved toward the clinic.

"What's your name? Or should I call you my knight in shining armor?"

"Dominic Castillo at your service," he replied, flashing a dazzling smile. "And I'm always available to assist a beautiful damsel in distress."

Vonnie was surprised; he was flirting with her. It had been years since a man had shown even the slightest interest.

"Well, Mr. Castillo, I'm Yvonne Hollister, and your timing was perfect. Thank you."

As they were about to enter the clinic, Hadwin Lopez, the plantation's operations manager, appeared out of nowhere, sweating, huffing, and puffing as if he'd run for miles.

Hadwin, his wife Ana, and Vonnie had been inseparable growing up on the plantation. Ana was her best friend, and Hadwin was like a big brother to her. Even Vonnie's father, Pearl Hollister, had treated Hadwin like the son he never had. Now Hadwin was the plantation's principal operations manager, and Ana not only managed the plantation's medical clinic but was also one of the government's primary healthcare providers for the region. Together, they were the plantation's version of a power couple.

"What's going on here?" Hadwin barked, his eyes flashing with anger.

Vonnie was startled by his tone. "What?" she said, frowning. "What's wrong with you?"

"I want to know what you're doing," Hadwin growled, glaring at Dominic.

Dominic remained silent and returned Hadwin's gaze with a sly, amused smile.

"I fell and hurt my knee," Vonnie replied. "This gentleman was kind enough to help me. We're going to see Ana."

Dominic eased Vonnie's arm from his shoulder and handed her off to Hadwin.

"I think it's best if this gentleman assists you from here," he said. "I need to get back to work. But, Miss Hollister, it's been a pleasure."

Vonnie and Hadwin watched as Dominic swaggered back to his truck. A scowl marred Hadwin's face, and he breathed like a raging bull. Sensing Hadwin's hostility toward Dominic, Vonnie refrained from discussing the incident further when he helped her into the clinic. He quickly exited after leaving her in one of the clinic's examination rooms.

She was lying on the examination table when Ana entered the room wearing pink scrubs. Black and gray cornrows were in a bun on the back of her head. Small diamond earrings, an anniversary gift from Hadwin, sparkled in her ears. Vonnie immediately began describing her ordeal.

"I don't understand why Hadwin was so rude to the guy. It was uncalled for; he was only helping me."

Ana frowned as she lightly probed and manipulated Vonnie's legs.

"He was just being protective and probably overreacted when he realized it was Dominic," she said. Her fingertips explored Vonnie's kneecaps. "Dominic has a less-than-stellar reputation, especially with women. But frankly, I find it hard to believe he was making a delivery himself, especially in this part of the country."

"Why?" Vonnie asked.

Ana remained focused on her examination as she rotated Vonnie's ankles. "Castillo's Delivery Services is his company. He has fleets of trucks, vans, and cars, and dozens of drivers. He's the suit-and-tie guy; he doesn't make deliveries. It's just odd; that's all."

"Well, I can see why women are attracted to him—he's gorgeous. So, what's his story?"

Ana released a long, exasperated exhale and stepped back from the examination table. "I don't want to talk about Dominic Castillo. My breath is too valuable to waste talking about him. I'll give you something for pain and inflammation, but I want you back tomorrow for X-rays." She turned and began searching through a metal wall cabinet.

Vonnie was taken aback by Ana's comment.

"Wow, Ana, that's pretty harsh coming from you. What's the big deal? The man helped me out. That's all. It's not like we were wallowing around on the ground having sex. But between you and me, when that man put his arm around my waist and lifted me off the ground, my body lit up like a Christmas tree. One long, hot night of looking up into that handsome face might not be bad."

Ana whirled around, her dark eyes flashing. She leaned toward Vonnie and raised her voice. "Don't even think about it," she snapped. "Dominic Castillo isn't someone to play with. Keep as far away from him as possible. He's nothing but trouble!"

Frown lines creased Vonnie's forehead. She was startled again by Ana's response. "Whoa, Ana," she said, pushing herself onto her elbows. "Chill out! It was just a joke. I was only kidding."

"You might be kidding, but I'm not. I meant every word! Dominic runs in circles you don't want to know about or get mixed up in." Then, Ana released a long exhale. "Sorry for the attitude, but I have a lot on my mind. This COVID-19 virus has me worried."

"No problem. We're good," Vonnie said, still slightly annoyed. Finally, she sat up, dangled her legs off the side of the examination table, and changed the subject. "I'm glad you brought it up. I want you and Hadwin to create a COVID-19 Response Plan for the entire plantation. We need to get out in front of this thing."

Ana retrieved a small jar filled with brown stems and green leaves from the cabinet and handed it to Vonnie.

"Brew a cup of this, add a little honey, and drink four cups between now and when you go to bed. It will help with the pain and inflammation, and I must warn you—it will make you pee."

Vonnie held the jar up to the light and shook it.

"The mad scientist of the Hollister Plantation strikes again. Damn, Ana, I was hoping you'd give me some real pharmaceuticals. I want the good stuff. Where are the real drugs?"

Ana laughed. "You know me. I'll give you the hard stuff if I have to amputate." She crossed her arms and leaned back against the closed door. "Seriously, Vonnie, based on my research, COVID-19 is a monster. This virus can kill like nothing we've ever seen. Frankly, it scares the hell out of me. If the US and Europe, with all their medical resources and money, are having problems containing it, then poor little Belize doesn't have a chance."

* * *

That night, Vonnie decided to sleep in the downstairs guest bedroom. Climbing the stairs to her room on the third floor wasn't an option. Sheer mosquito nets were draped back and tied to the bed's four posts. The nets fluttered from the breeze of the ceiling fan. As with the rest of the house, the furnishings were antiques, and all the accessories were outdated. Pictures of her and her parents hung on the walls and sat on every flat surface of the room.

Yawning wide, she untied the headscarf, ruffled her hair, and tossed her clothes onto the upholstered bench at the foot of the bed. As she limped toward the hall bathroom, her mind returned to the man who had assisted her when she had fallen—the way his body felt and smelled, the twinkle in his eyes when he looked at her. It was clear he was flirting, and remembering the scene made her smile.

Her reflection disappointed her when she wiped the steam from the vanity mirror. She was no diva, nor had she ever been. But now, everything from her face to her ass sagged. The refusal to dye her gray hair compounded the issue even more. She wiped her face with the towel and leaned close to the mirror, turning her face from side to side.

*When was the last time I had a facial or had my hair or nails done? Hard to believe someone flirted with me looking like this.*

Back in the bedroom, she flopped heavily on the bed and examined her legs. Then she took two pills from an orange plastic bottle, washed them down with the remains of a glass of wine, and lay down. The cotton sheets felt good against her skin as she settled herself and turned off the bedside lamp.

As the ceiling fan whirled, images of Dominic floated through her mind until she drifted off to sleep.

Late the following afternoon, Vonnie was sitting in her father's old leather chair, her leg resting on the ottoman, an ice pack on her knee, flipping through a magazine, when the front doorbell chimed. A young man with a broad, toothy smile peeped around a colossal bouquet. In the driveway was a white Castillo's Delivery Services van. Surprised, Vonnie thanked him and set the flowers down on the accent table beside the door.

Her fingers feverishly tore open the envelope containing the card.

*I've been thinking about you, and I hope you're doing better. Call me the next time you're in the city; I'd love to take you to lunch or dinner.*

*Dominic.*

"YES!" she shouted, grinning from ear to ear. She placed the flowers in the center of the dining room table as a sly smile crossed her lips, and a devious thought crossed her mind.

*What Ana doesn't know can't hurt her.*

7

# DOMINIC

Castillo's Delivery Services was one of the largest trucking companies in Belize. The company's vehicles transported goods throughout the country's interior and to Belize's borders with Mexico and Guatemala. Usually, hidden among deliveries of produce, appliances, and other general items was a variety of illegal contraband.

Tall, fit, and handsome Dominic Castillo considered himself one of Belize's leading entrepreneurs. The salt-and-pepper dreadlocks, close-trimmed beard and mustache, and tailored suits gave him a sophisticated, distinguished look that exuded confidence, power, and money.

The power and money were dwindling fast because the illicit side of his business was spiraling out of control. In the past, there had been long-term partners, and the shipments had been uncomplicated. Castillo trucks secretly hauled hundreds of pounds of marijuana from one border to the next. The terms were reasonable, and everyone made money. Then everything changed. His old partners were forced out of business by cartels across the border, and the bloodsucking government officials he paid for protection were as bad as the criminals.

Three years ago David Mendez, deputy commissioner of the Belize Law Enforcement Bureau, summoned Dominic to the Christmas Mass at St. Matthew's Cathedral in the heart of Belize City. St. Matthew's was the largest and most prestigious church in Belize. Worshippers throughout the city and surrounding areas attended the annual Mass, and the cathedral overflowed; it was a standing-room-only event. So, no one noticed when Dominic entered the sanctuary and exited through a nondescript door that led to the church's offices.

The tiny office belonged to one of the priests. There was no air-conditioning, and the window was closed. An oscillating table fan sat on top of a filing cabinet beside the door, blowing hot air from one side of the room to the other. Floor-to-ceiling bookshelves filled with books, magazines, and papers occupied the back and left walls. Pictures of the pope and bishops within the Diocese of Belize hung on the right side of the room. In front of the bookshelf, on the back wall, sat an old wooden desk. In front of the desk were two wooden, straight-backed chairs.

Mendez was seated behind the desk when Dominic entered.

David Mendez was in his late sixties; tall, thin, and bald, with piercing green eyes. Dominic found him fanning himself with a magazine, a distasteful look on his face.

Regardless of the room's temperature, Dominic refused to sweat in front of Mendez. He sat in the uncomfortable wood chair with an air of superiority, released the buttons on his suit jacket, and leaned forward with folded elbows on the desk, closing the distance between himself and Mendez, who leaned back.

With eyes as piercing as daggers and a voice like ice, Dominic asked, "Why am I here?" He despised Mendez and his crooked law enforcement cronies. They were all a bunch of slimy, bloodsucking leeches.

Mendez retrieved a handkerchief from his coat pocket and wiped his face and head. Then he continued fanning himself with the magazine.

"You're here because, once again, you've broken our agreement. We've warned you several times not to transport certain commodities through Belize, and you've ignored us."

Dominic shook his head in frustration. "Look, why do you keep making a big deal about this? There haven't been that many shipments. Nothing bad has happened. And you and your compatriots are making double your annual salaries. You could make more if you stopped harassing me."

Mendez's face flushed red with anger. He stopped fanning. "We won't allow you to turn this country into a cartel pipeline. We all agreed you could move marijuana but nothing else. But our sources tell us you're now hauling hardcore drugs, guns, and explosives. Have you lost your mind?

"Compared to our neighbors, Belize is a highly respected country on the world stage. As a result, we are experiencing foreign investments unlike anything we've ever seen. Foreigners love it so much that they retire here and bring their euros, dollars, and francs. You're putting all that in jeopardy, and we won't have it. There's too much at stake!" he snarled, slamming his fist on the desk. "You don't run this country; we do. You operate because we allow it, and I'm under pressure to invalidate every license you own!"

Dominic leaned back. "Calm down, calm down. I hear you, but maybe it's time we renegotiate our agreement. The drug scene in the States has changed since they began legalizing marijuana; marijuana profits aren't there anymore. So to continue making money, we need to think differently. It's a new day."

"How about this? What if I increase the percentage allotted to you and your compatriots, and you allow me to move whatever I want? I promise to keep my head down and nose clean and not cause any problems." He could see dollar signs flashing in Mendez's shifty eyes.

Mendez stopped fanning. Suspicion covered his face. "How much of an increase?"

Confident that he was reeling Mendez in, Dominic said, "10 percent will be tough, but I think I can swing it."

"Twenty, and that's on top of what you currently pay," Mendez countered with a steely expression.

Dominic raised his eyebrows in shock. "What the fuck, Mendez? How about eleven or even twelve? All you do is sit on your ass and count your money; I'm the one taking all the risks. Twenty percent on top of what I'm already paying you? That's too high. Be reasonable."

Mendez smirked. "20 percent. Otherwise, our original agreement stands, and your trucks start receiving additional scrutiny," he responded, and resumed fanning. "And one more thing. If there is even a hint of a problem related to those shipments, we'll put you in a shithole under the prison, and you'll never see the light of day for the rest of your miserable life."

Dominic stood, rebuttoned his jacket, and leered down at Mendez. "Leave me alone. Let me do my thing, and you'll get your money."

Mendez stood, wiped his face with his handkerchief, and begrudgingly shook hands with Dominic. Then he walked around the desk and slapped Dominic on the back.

"Now that our business is complete, let's go in and light a candle for our souls; after all, it's Christmas," he said with a broad smile.

"Don't waste the wax," Dominic said, scowling, and hurriedly left the room.

Dominic was livid as he sped away from the cathedral. Mendez had his balls in a vice and wouldn't hesitate to squeeze them if anything went wrong with the shipments to the borders. But eventually, something would go wrong because the men he conducted business with were insane, and their depravity had no limits.

Initially, the transfer operations went well; money flowed into his bank account, and there was no reason to complain. But now, the cartels paid him whatever they wanted, when they wanted. Currently, he was losing money on every shipment, and the last time he summoned the courage to complain, they resolved his complaints by sticking an automatic rifle in his face.

After that, there was no way to end the madness. The only way out was to flee the country. Otherwise, he would either end up in prison for the rest of his life or dead.

* * *

Vonnie Hollister didn't exist in Dominic's world until he saw her at the National Bank of Belize in Belize City three weeks before their encounter on the plantation. He was in the bank to see Franklin, a low-level customer service representative, and his partner in a lucrative credit card scam that used identification and credit cards stolen from tourists.

Glass-walled offices lined both sides of the bank's plush lobby. Royal blue upholstered chairs were grouped in the center of the room. Franklin's office was on the left side of the room. Diagonally across the lobby, the most ostentatious office was occupied by the bank's elderly long-term president, Mr. Benjamin C. Turay.

Impeccably dressed in a black suit, white shirt, gold tie, and sunglasses, Dominic flipped through a magazine, patiently waiting for Franklin to finish with a customer. Briefly glancing up, he noticed a woman sitting in the upholstered wingback chair in front of Turay's desk. The woman was well-dressed, mildly attractive, but otherwise unremarkable. When a secretary entered the office with a tea tray, Dominic slid his sunglasses down to the bridge of his nose and began paying closer attention.

From Dominic's viewpoint, Turay was a stingy, indignant snob and ancient relic who treated the small local business owners like trash stuck to the bottom of his shoe. Yet here he was, laughing and serving tea to this woman like she was the queen of England.

With the customer finally gone, Franklin waved to Dominic, who swiftly entered the office, closed the door, and took a seat across from Franklin's desk. Franklin was pudgy, bald, and dark brown. A green tie hung down the front of his rumpled green plaid shirt. He leaned back in his chair, laced his fingers across a bulging belly, and smiled.

Eager to satisfy his curiosity, Dominic asked, "Who's that woman in old man Turay's office?"

Franklin turned and leaned to get a better view. "Oh, that's Yvonne Hollister. She owns the Hollister Plantation. Her father and Turay were friends until he died two years ago."

"What makes her so special that old Turay is serving her tea? He's in there grinning at her like a mule chewing glue."

Franklin chuckled. "Man, considering the money her family has stashed in this bank, Turay's old ass would willingly mop her floors and grin while he's doing it. Rumor has it that the money she has here is only a drop in the bucket compared to what she has in the States."

Dominic's curiosity peaked, and he leaned in. "So, how much is she worth?"

"Millions, and I'm talking US millions not Belize millions. The Hollister's are members of this country's 1 percent."

Dominic's brows raised in surprise. "Can you access her accounts?"

"Nope, I'm too far down the food chain for that type of access."

Dominic leaned back in his chair and folded his arms. "Is she married?"

"Nope, she's single. She hasn't been in the country long. Based on what I've heard, she's only here to sell the plantation."

"I've heard of the Hollister Plantation but never paid much attention to it. So, how much is it worth?"

"A lot. Go online and check the real estate ad. It's huge and privately owned. They don't answer to anybody but themselves."

Dominic's gaze returned to Yvonne, who was smiling and sipping tea while engrossed in conversation with the bank's president.

"Are you getting ideas, my friend?" Franklin asked, a sly smile spreading across his lips.

Dominic reclined in his chair, grinning, and clasped his hands behind his head. "Is pig pussy pork?"

Both men erupted in laughter.

For days, Dominic had pondered how to meet Yvonne. A chance encounter would be simple if she lived in Belize City, but the plantation was in a remote southern area five hours away. A quick scan of his company's delivery schedule sparked an idea. A one-hour flight from Belize City to Punta Gorda would put him within twenty-five miles of her.

Two days later, a Castillo's Delivery Services truck filled with farm equipment and bound for the Hollister Plantation stopped at a roadside restaurant. Dressed down in an old T-shirt, faded jeans, and dusty, worn work boots, Dominic exchanged places with the driver.

He had never been to the plantation, and as he slowly drove down the service road, he marveled at the scale of the property. He was surprised and impressed by the size of the operation, the professional appearance of the buildings, and the level of activity. Far ahead, he spotted the grand house.

*So that's where the princess resides. Well, Miss. Hollister, I was born to play the role of Prince Charming,*

He mused, ignoring an impatient horn from behind. But then luck intervened—thirty yards away from him, Yvonne Hollister fell beside the service road.

# 8

# CHANCE

It was 1996. Chance was thirty-three, and eleven years had passed since he'd sat on the front porch of a wooden house in Shawsville, Virginia, brokenhearted, crying as Conswaylo's taxi disappeared onto the highway. After leaving Virginia Tech, Conswaylo moved to Spain to teach at the University of Madrid.

Chance relentlessly called, emailed, and sent cards. Finally, he proposed, and she tearfully declined. She loved him but wanted him to discover who he was and have the freedom to pursue his dreams. She refused to consider marriage because she didn't want to deprive him of the opportunity to be a father; she felt too old to have children. None of her reasons swayed him; he yearned for her but accepted her decision and sadly moved on with his life.

Chance left Virginia Tech three days after finishing graduate school, moved to Washington, DC, and started working for the Federal Bureau of Investigation's Cyber Crimes Division. The agency's goal was to seek out and prosecute those who compromised US networks, stole financial and intellectual assets, or endangered critical infrastructure.

Chance thrived as a cybercrime investigator. Patient and meticulous, he solved the puzzles and followed the breadcrumbs that ultimately led to the convictions of cyber criminals. Stalking hackers through the entangled threads of the dark web became an obsession that consumed almost every minute of his life. Days, nights, weekends, and most holidays typically passed unnoticed while he sat glued to his laptop.

At his eighth annual Bureau Christmas party, he leaned on the bar, took a long swallow of beer, and then looked at his watch. He was only there because it was mandatory. He intended to make the rounds, speak to the people that mattered to his career, and then sneak out and go home.

On the dance floor, his coworkers' drunken, frantic gyrations held his attention until he noticed one of the most beautiful women in the room striding toward him. Her long blond hair bounced as she walked. Her sapphire-blue eyes focused on him like laser beams. With the figure of a fashion model, she wore a sparkling red minidress, the neckline plunging almost to her waist, and matching sparkling red shoes. As she closed the distance between them, her red lips parted into an alluring smile.

"Somebody told me you were from New Orleans," she purred in a thick southern drawl. "And I told them that couldn't be true because I know everybody in New Orleans, and I've never seen you before." An empty martini glass dangled from one hand, and she extended the other hand to Chance. "I'm Charlotte LeBlanc, and I'm honored to make your acquaintance, Mr...."

The over-the-top, fake southern drawl was the sweetest sound Chance had ever heard, and he was pleased by the attention of such a captivating woman. "I'm Chance Moore, and yes, I'm from Ne-New Orleans," he stammered, standing a bit taller.

Charlotte coyly batted her lashes. "Well, my, my, I must be getting slack to have let a man as handsome as you escape my notice." She placed the empty martini glass on the bar, signaled to the bartender for a refill, and slid onto the barstool beside Chance the minidress riding up her thigh. Leaning in, elbow on the bar and hand cupping her face, she asked, "Well Mr. Chance Moore, why don't you tell me about yourself?"

They laughed and talked until a young man approached, shyly informing them it was time to leave. The party had ended. Chance was shocked as he scanned the room, which was empty except for catering staff who bustled about clearing tables, stacking chairs, and collecting party trash.

"Well, it's still early," Charlotte said, smiling. "Your place or mine?"

Caught off guard, Chance's mind reeled. His one-bedroom bachelor apartment was in no shape for guests. "Your place," he nervously responded. "Should we stop and pick up a bottle of wine?"

"No need. I've got plenty," Charlotte replied, already heading for the door.

He was overly impressed when they arrived at Charlotte's luxury apartment. A uniformed security guard stood stoic at the entrance doors, a parking valet quickly opened their car doors and drove the car away, and a doorman gave a cheerful holiday greeting to Charlotte.

The lobby resembled an expensive, upscale hotel—all glass, chrome, and marble. There were hundreds of string lights hanging from high ceilings, conversational groupings of low-profile chairs and tables, modern sculptures, and accents.

A security guard sitting behind a counter nodded to Charlotte and typed on a keyboard as they walked past. The elevator doors slid open as they approached. Chance noticed there were no exterior buttons beside the elevator door. Before the doors closed, he saw another security guard walking across the lobby. "I don't think I've ever seen this much security in an apartment building," Chance commented.

"Oh, that," Charlotte said with a smirk. "This place is home to several senators and House reps. I'll introduce you if we pass one in the hall."

The entrance of the apartment faced unadorned windows with floor-to-ceiling views of the US Capitol and other monuments. The windows extended across the spacious living room on the left to the dining and kitchen areas on the right.

The decor was minimalist and modern with white walls and tile floors. In the living area, was a modern-streamlined red suede couch, a large, shiny, black cube-shaped coffee table, cluttered with books, magazines, and a plant in an orange ceramic pot. Two high-backed yellow accent chairs with metal legs were on opposite sides of the cube. In front of the dining area window was a glass table with six red, suede, high-backed chairs. The adjacent kitchen boasted gray-and-white granite countertops, cabinetry with translucent glass fronts, and high-end stainless-steel appliances completed the look.

"Fix us a drink while I slip into something more comfortable," Charlotte said, kicking her sparkling red shoes across the room.

As he waited for Charlotte to return, Chance stood by the living room window, sipping his drink, gazing at the Capitol and Washington Monument in the distance. The view was magnificent—here was the epicenter of the most powerful country in the world, beautifully illuminated against the night sky.

Shy and socially awkward, Chance had managed a few short-term friends-with-benefits relationships during his eight years in Washington. Most of his close friends were already married with children, but there wasn't a woman on his phone's contact list with whom he wanted an exclusive relationship.

No one had ever filled the void left by Conswaylo. Online searches had allowed him to see her face whenever thoughts of her became too strong to resist. Then six years ago, while viewing her Facebook page, a wedding picture of her broke his heart for the second time, and the online stalking stopped.

A wave of melancholy swept over him as he stared through the floor-to-ceiling window at the picturesque nightscape. His reverie was broken when Charlotte returned, now in red plaid flannel pajamas and black fluffy slippers, her face bare, and her hair in a ponytail. Chance looked at her with surprise and confusion.

A coy smile crossed Charlotte's face. "Don't look so surprised, I'm still getting to know you."

They talked until dawn about their childhoods and growing up on opposite ends of Louisiana's social, economic, and political spectrum. He was the only child of an African American mother and a Coushatta Indian father. Chance told her about the death of his mother when he was ten years old and living with his grandparents on the Coushatta Indian Reservation because his father worked extended, rotating shifts on an oil rig on the Gulf Coast. Charlotte was also an only child but was hopelessly spoiled and entitled, the daughter of a wealthy, conservative Louisiana senator. Finally, neither of them could finish a sentence without yawning.

"Charlotte, this has been great. I've had a wonderful evening. When can I see you again?" Chance asked, standing, stretching, and yawning.

"Oh, I meant to ask you, do you snow ski?" she asked, following him to the door.

Chance's hand was on the doorknob. "I do, but I haven't skied since college. Why?"

"Oh, don't worry; it's like riding a bike. Once you learn, you never forget. I'm flying to Vail to spend Christmas and New Year's with friends. Would you like to be my escort?" she asked.

Chance's eyes lit up. "Sure, but an airline ticket might be hard to come by this close to Christmas."

"Oh, we won't be flying commercial; my friends own a plane."

* * *

They dated for a year, and from Chance's perspective, every day with Charlotte was like fireworks on the Fourth of July. She was beautiful, fun, and fully aware of her sexuality. It was as if the nerdy computer geek awoke each morning to find a supermodel in his bed.

Their wedding was an opulent affair on the sprawling lawn of the LeBlanc family estate in Baton Rouge. The backdrop was as picturesque as *Gone with the Wind*; a large, two-story white antebellum plantation house with six columns, centuries-old oak trees with Spanish moss fluttering lazily in the hot summer breeze, and five hundred guests.

In addition to Louisiana's business, social, and political elite, the Coushatta Indian chief and members of the tribal council were in full ceremonial regalia alongside members of Chance's extended African American family from New Orleans. The event received comprehensive coverage in the state's top newspapers, accompanied by pictures of the senator and the Coushatta Indian chief shaking hands. The same images later appeared in the senator's reelection campaign brochures.

After a whirlwind five-country honeymoon in Europe, the house-hunting began. They were inspecting the upstairs rooms in a luxurious waterfront home on the Potomac River in Virginia, just outside Washington, DC.

Chance opened a closet and peered inside. "Wow, this house definitely has enough space for two or three kids, but I didn't check where the nearest elementary school is. I didn't see one on the drive here, did you?"

Charlotte was in the bedroom's en suite, where Chance couldn't see her exasperated expression as she rolled her eyes. "Chance, stop sliding kids into every conversation about our future. We've discussed this a dozen times: no kids for now. But maybe in a few years, we'll see. I'll let you know when the time is right." She left the room and walked down the stairs.

Chance caught up with her in the living room. "Charlotte, this house is awesome, but we've just married. Don't you think it's too big? And the price tag..." he said, looking up at the twenty-foot ceiling.

Charlotte released an irritated exhale. "Daddy's wedding gift puts us ahead of the game; don't worry so much. This type of house is what we need; it's perfect. I'll call the realtor and tell her we'll take it. I already have a decorator on standby."

Charlotte had the most assertive personality in the relationship. A charming, modern-day southern belle and politician's daughter, she navigated Washington's political and social scenes like a pro, dressed in the latest fashion, ready for the publicity photo shoot that appeared in newspapers, magazines, or social media. Chance had married a peacock instead of a hen and became content basking in her shadow.

Their life was good, and the years quickly passed. They were married for twenty-one years before the relationship plummeted into a death spiral. It was late on a Sunday morning, and Chance was downstairs with a trash bag, tossing in the debris from the previous night's cookout. The clang of one beer bottle hitting another triggered a recurring thought: excessive amounts of alcohol seemed to flow through their house.

He hauled two large bags of trash out of the house to put them in the garbage containers, but they were already full. Finally, upon reentering the kitchen, he called out to Charlotte. "We need to open a bar and start charging for drinks."

Charlotte's laugh echoed down the hall. "We can't entertain without liquor, Chance. It's no big deal, stop worrying about it."

She walked into the kitchen with messy hair piled on her head and a white T-shirt that stopped above her navel. A personal trainer, yoga, and Pilates made her body look ten years younger. She was sexy and never missed an opportunity to flaunt it. Her nipples protruded through the shirt fabric; there was no bra. The black yoga tights hugged her hips and ass like a second skin. She was barefoot.

Putting her arms around his neck, she kissed him on each cheek. "This week, we've hosted three fundraisers: a luncheon for twelve, a dinner party for eight, and a cookout for ten, and they've all been for worthy causes. I'm just trying to save America," she said in a sultry voice as she kissed him on the nose.

Charlotte never ceased to arouse him. Chance wrapped her in his arms, and they kissed long and slowly. Her hands slid down the front of his gym shorts. He closed his eyes and moaned.

"Babe, I want you so bad, but I need to finish the cleanup and put in a few hours of work," he said, eyes closed, not wanting her to stop.

Charlotte stepped back, yanked off the T-shirt, seductively pulled off the tights, and kicked them to the side. Then, naked, she bent over the kitchen island, spread her legs, and looked back over her shoulder.

"Take a good long look at this, Chance Moore," she said, wiggling her ass. "And tell me which you'd prefer—this or stalking computer hackers?"

Chance brooded later that evening as he lounged in a deck chair overlooking the river. He knew Charlotte was right; they did entertain a lot. She knew everyone who was anyone in Washington, and she managed multiple large charities to which a lot of important people donated. However, her attitude about drinking alcohol was nonexistent. She flitted to and from brunches, dinner parties, and fundraisers with wealthy power brokers, where she drank practically every day. A martini, wine, or liquor glass was an accessory to her outfits, much like a necklace or purse. It had been a way of life for her since her teenage years. But now at fifty, her consistent drinking had become an issue.

The arguments about Charlotte's drinking became cyclical: Chance reluctantly pointed out the issues, she justified her behavior, and the topic wouldn't resurface until a new incident occurred.

He hovered over her at gatherings, covering for inappropriate remarks and monitoring the number of her drinks, one ear always listening for slurred speech; a discreet arm placed around her waist to steady the wavering or unsteady steps; feigning tiredness or the need to get up early as an excuse to get her to leave and go home.

They were attending one of Charlotte's fundraising galas, standing among a group of donors, engaging in small talk, when he noticed the familiar signs—it was time to leave. But before he could make the usual excuses and gracefully steer Charlotte toward the exit, she wobbled and fell, taking two other people down with her. She drunkenly blamed the slippery floors and the five-inch heels. She passed out in the car on the way home.

During the night, Chance awoke in a warm, wet bed. He forcefully shook her several times. "Charlotte, wake up, damn it. Wake the fuck up!" he shouted. Charlotte mumbled incoherently but didn't budge; she was out cold. Furious and disgusted, Chance hurled his wet pajamas across the room and grudgingly slept in a guest room.

It was midafternoon the next day when Charlotte finally shuffled into the kitchen wearing a white bathrobe. Wet from the shower, limp strands of hair hung past her shoulders. Dark rings encircled her puffy, bloodshot eyes. A guilty, embarrassed look crossed her face as she slowly filled a coffee mug.

Chance was sitting at the table in the breakfast nook, scanning emails on his laptop. His brow was furrowed with contempt and his voice was stern. "I think it's time for you to see someone about your drinking, Charlotte. There's no excuse for what happened last night" he said.

Charlotte stood at the counter, holding the mug with both hands, slowly sipping her coffee. "It was an accident, Chance. Nothing more. I'm throwing away those damn shoes. I shouldn't have worn them in the first place."

"You pissed in bed again last night. Are you going to blame that on the shoes as well?"

Charlotte let out an audible, exasperated exhale. "It was an accident, Chance. Let it go. I'm sorry. It won't happen again."

Chance walked over and gently placed a hand on her shoulder. "Charlotte, we've talked about this. You have a problem and it's getting worse. You know you have my support, but we can't continue like this. You need professional help."

"Get off my back, Chance," Charlotte snapped, shaking off his hand. "I'm not in the mood for one of your lectures. You have no clue what I'm going through. Do you think it's easy to organize and juggle these events, beg rich assholes for money, smile until my face hurts, and be charming to people I despise?"

Chance stepped back, upset by Charlotte's attitude. "Then give it up; it's not worth it. Last night was embarrassing, not to mention downright humiliating. And I refuse to go through that again. It's affecting our marriage."

Charlotte rolled her eyes. "Oh, stop being so dramatic. Last night was a fluke, one big accident. And there's nothing wrong with our marriage." Then she looked at him with contempt. "You make me sick with all the damn whining. Don't you ever stop?"

Agitated and defiant, Chance yelled, "There *is* something wrong with our marriage—my wife is a drunk."

Eyes wild with rage, Charlotte spun around and slapped Chance hard. "Fuck you, Chance!" she screamed and stormed out of the room.

Three months later, home alone in bed, Chance received a late-night call from a hospital in Alexandria, Virginia, forty minutes away. There had been a car accident. Charlotte had hit two cars before swerving off the road and crashing into a utility pole. Two people were dead, and three, including her, were severely injured. She was unconscious when the paramedics removed her from the wreckage.

Chance arrived at an emergency room in chaos. Flashing lights from multiple ambulances and police vehicles filled the area, and a horde of people and news reporters seeking information harassed the first responders and medical staff. The dismal emergency waiting room was packed with people from all walks of life. Chance was leaning against a wall, drinking terrible vending machine coffee when a haggard and tired Dr. Abdul Kumar called his name.

Charlotte was in a coma with severe internal injuries. Her blood alcohol concentration was 0.23; the legal limit in Virginia is 0.08. Nevertheless, she was barely clinging to life.

After three days of an around-the-clock vigil and no significant improvement in Charlotte's condition, he went home. Before entering the house, Chance sauntered to the mailbox he rarely touched. The morning sun shone brightly on his neighbors' expensive designer homes, professionally manicured lawns, and the quiet street. He extracted a handful of junk mail and other correspondence; a FedEx letter addressed to Charlotte waited on the front porch. He tossed the stack on the kitchen island to sort through after his shower.

Wearing gym shorts and a ragged, faded Virginia Tech T-shirt, and holding a half-eaten peanut butter and jelly sandwich, Chance sat at the kitchen island, eyeing three letters addressed to Charlotte from creditors unfamiliar to him. A rock settled in his stomach.

With the letters from the creditors in hand, he immediately went to Charlotte's home office and rifled through file drawers, shelves, and papers on her desk, and, finally, her laptop. Charlotte hated remembering passwords and rarely changed them, so Chance was able to access her files and documents within minutes.

Early the following morning, he slumped in Charlotte's office chair, eyes red from lack of sleep, tired and crestfallen. Papers, notes, folders, and binders littered every surface; printouts and other documents covered the floor.

The overnight investigation revealed a level of debt that made him sick to his stomach. Charlotte's scheme was too complex for Chance to fully understand, but it was apparent that she had used the money from the various charities as if it were her own. An elaborate shell game shifted funds between organizations to cover deficits and show profits. Worst of all, she had mixed their finances with everything else—the house, cars, savings, and numerous maxed-out personal credit cards.

Chance remembered when he had first met Charlotte; she was a young Washington socialite living a lavish, fun-filled existence funded by a hefty allowance from her father, the senator. But the seventy-eight-year-old senator died unexpectedly two years after their wedding.

As the senator's only child, Charlotte assumed she'd inherit millions from his estate. However, the senator's fourth wife tearfully revealed his gambling addiction during the funeral. He had died broke and in debt; Charlotte had nothing of value to inherit. Born into wealth, the lifestyle of the rich was the only life she knew how to live.

Yet after her father's death, without any investments, property, or capital of her own, she elevated herself to a status in Washington society that would make even the most senior congressman's wife envious. And it was all accomplished using other people's money; the deceit had gone on for decades.

Exhausted, Chance flopped into a lounge chair on the deck, dropped his head, covered his face with both hands and slowly shook his head. Without Charlotte, the house of cards would soon fall, and he could do nothing to stop it. Some of Washington's most powerful politicians, movers, and shakers had donated to or were board members of Charlotte's charities. No one would believe that he wasn't involved or at least knew what was going on. Accusations, lawsuits, bankruptcy, a police investigation, and a horrendous scandal that would consume the media loomed on the horizon.

The early morning sky and draining fatigue reminded him that he hadn't slept in over twenty-four hours. As he reentered the kitchen, his cell phone vibrated on the kitchen island; the number displayed belonged to the hospital.

The sky began to fall a month after Charlotte's funeral. There were phone calls, voicemails, and emails from charity board members, lawyers, and a police detective. Images of reporters holding cameras ringing the doorbell appeared on the home's security system's display, and letters from debt collection agencies were strewn across the kitchen countertop. He ignored them all. Any explanation or excuse he thought of made him look like a total and complete fool. No one would believe that he wasn't somehow involved or wasn't aware of Charlotte's schemes.

Finally, depressed, grieving, and financially devastated, Chance hastily resigned from the FBI, tossed the keys to the house in the middle of the living room floor, and left Virginia without a destination in mind.

# 9

# AAPO

The Macy's Thanksgiving parade was over, and the Big Apple dropped to signify the start of the 2020 new year had been packed up and put away. It was February and freezing outside as Aapo Vasquez, the oldest son of Eloy Vasquez, stood straight with his head high, shoulders back, and stomach in. His perfectly coiffed chestnut-brown hair was combed back from his forehead. He wore a custom-made shirt and suit, along with imported leather shoes.

At forty-seven, everything about him exuded power, wealth, and prestige. He stood by the window of his thirty-eighth-floor office, taking in the Manhattan nightscape. Speckled lights glowed in neighboring skyscrapers, and the traffic below resembled a trail of dark ants. The white headlights and red taillights twinkled as they snaked through the cold, crowded Manhattan streets.

Located one block from Wall Street, Premier International Imports and Exports (PIIE) was surrounded by the world's largest banks and financial institutions. And it was from PIIE that Aapo sheltered, laundered, and funneled the Vasquez Cartel's money.

Aapo rubbed the raised scar on his left wrist—a subconscious action performed under stress. The circumstances under which he had received the scar were seared into his memory, serving as a constant reminder of his father's cruelty and the consequences of failure.

* * *

Eloy's grand plan to extend the Vasquez Cartel's reach beyond Central America included Aapo receiving an education from the best schools in the US. So, when Aapo turned twelve, Eloy sent him to a prestigious boarding school for boys in Massachusetts. There, Aapo was to live and learn among the privileged offspring of the wealthy.

Unfortunately, Aapo didn't fit in. He was a foreigner from a developing country, spoke with a heavy accent, and knew nothing about American culture. Severely bullied and ostracized, he became withdrawn, lost weight, and began failing his classes. Finally, the school's administrator called Eloy, who summoned him home.

Cartel soldiers were waiting at the airport when Aapo's plane touched down in Guatemala. In the back seat of the limousine, dressed in a black sweater bearing the school's coat of arms on the front, a white shirt, and black trousers, Aapo hung his head. His eyes were closed, and he sat on his hands to hide their shaking. Silently, he prayed.

The car finally stopped at a farm that the cartel had confiscated and converted into a regional outpost. Dented, outdated cars and pickup trucks littered the dusty, barren yard. A ragtag group of cartel soldiers loitered around, leaning on cars, standing under trees, or sitting on the porch. Behind the house stood an old barn.

The men fell silent as the limousine driver hastily escorted Aapo into what had once been the home's living room. In the center of the room, Eloy sat at a table, loudly berating three soldiers. The targets of Eloy's ire stepped aside, and Aapo cautiously moved to the front of the table, his head down and eyes on the floor. Terrified, he struggled to hide his nervousness.

Disgust marred Eloy's face. He leaned back in his chair and looked at his son. Then he turned to the men in the room. "Look, gentlemen... my firstborn son," he said, gesturing toward Aapo. "I sent him to the best school in the US so that one day he would help make us rich and more powerful. But what do I get?"

Aapo's chin trembled, and he began to cry.

Like lightning, Eloy sprang from his seat, leaned across the table inches from Aapo's face, and slammed his fist hard on the tabletop. His words dripped with contempt. "My son should be a leader, a fighter; instead, he snivels and cries like a little girl. How dare you disgrace me!"

Eloy roughly shoved the table aside, grabbed Aapo by his sweater, and forcefully pulled him out of the house toward the barn. Aapo stumbled and fell; the sweater came off, so Eloy snatched him by the shirt. Then he yelled over his shoulder at the soldiers, "Follow me, and let this be an example to you; disobedience and failure have consequences."

Inside the barn, he flung Aapo to the floor. Desperate, Aapo wrapped his arms around his father's legs and pleaded. "Papa, Papa, I'll do better; I promise. Give me another chance."

Eloy kicked him hard. Aapo screamed in pain, curled up into a ball, and sobbed. Eloy's eyes blazed; he clenched his jaw, yanked Aapo from the floor, and slammed him against a stall. "Bring me a rope," he bellowed.

Uncontrolled tears streamed down Aapo's panic-stricken face. "Papa, please, please, Papa, I'm sorry; I'll do better."

Eloy tied Aapo's hands together, looped the rope over the top of a post separating the stalls, and pulled the rope until Aapo's toes barely touched the floor. The screaming and pleading continued as a leather strap lashed Aapo repeatedly until the soft skin split and blood stained the white shirt. The friction from the rope cut deep into the skin on his wrists.

The soldiers witnessing the beating were hardened criminals, but they frowned, shuffled uneasily, and mumbled at what they saw; others looked away. All were afraid to intervene. If Eloy could do this to his son, what would he do to them? Eventually, Eloy's anger waned, and he stopped.

"Cut him down," he ordered, tossing the strap to the floor and leaving the barn. Aapo was unconscious, and his father left him lying on the barn floor until late that night.

Thirty days after the beating, Aapo returned to school, but the rope burns on his left wrist left a permanent scar—a daily reminder of his loathing for his father.

* * *

He was still hung over from a ruckus New Year's Eve party when he checked his online bank account and found a zero balance. After ranting and raving, and demanding an immediate face-to-face appointment, he stormed into the office of Gilbert Packard, special accounts representative for GRC Bank and Financial Services.

* * *

"Mr. Vasquez, please calm down and lower your voice," Packard said, moving quickly to close the office door and the horizontal mini blinds to block the view from anyone who might look inside the office.

Red-faced and agitated, Aapo glared at the man. "You must be out of your fucking mind if you expect me to calm down," he snapped. "Twenty million dollars is missing from my account, and all you can say is calm down?"

Gilbert Packard, a fifty-year-old man with slight balding and wire-rimmed glasses, wore a tailored black suit. He quickly returned to his position behind his desk, cleared his throat, and spoke in a low, measured tone. "Mr. Vasquez, based on the investigation by our IT team, your account was hacked. There's nothing we can do to restore the funds."

"WHAT! That's insane. You mean I can't get my money back?" Aapo asked in disbelief, wanting to leap across the desk and strangle the smug little prick.

Packard remained stoic. He lowered his voice almost to a whisper but didn't lean forward to ensure Aapo could hear him.

Instead, he eased his chair back a few inches to maintain as much distance as possible between himself and Aapo.

"Mr. Vasquez, remember that accounts like yours are unique and handled differently than, shall we say, normal or legitimate accounts. As a result, they don't appear in audits, and there's no insurance coverage. We informed you of the associated risks when you came to us. You insisted on being able to manipulate your funds without IRS or regulatory scrutiny, and that's the service we provided."

"Do you know who the fuck you're dealing with?" Aapo snarled. "I could have you killed for this."

The statement caused Packard to ease his chair back a few more inches. He despised dealing with men like Aapo Vasquez, who paraded around in designer suits and gold watches as if they owned the world when in reality, they were nothing but low-life scum. But the money such men paid him to hide their dirty cash was too good to pass up. One day soon, he would retire to his beach house in Tahiti. Until then, he had to deal with the super-rich, deplorable members of society who were no better than subway sewer rats.

"Mr. Vasquez, I'm fully aware of who you and your family are, and yes, I realize you could kill me. But my death won't restore the missing funds. If it's any consolation, your account wasn't the only one affected; several other customers also suffered the same fate."

"So, you're telling me the hackers got away with more than my twenty million?"

"Yes, a lot more," Packard responded. "Unfortunately, the level of internet security for these accounts is somewhat basic because we can't include them in our more sophisticated cybersecurity networks. As I said, we keep them separate from everything else we do."

Aapo became frantic. "So, how do I get my money back? What am I supposed to do? I need that money."

"I'm not an expert in internet theft, but there are people who can track and identify computer hackers; federal agencies do it all the time. If this had involved our legitimate accounts, we would have notified the FBI immediately, and they would have been all over it."

"I can give you the technical information uncovered by our IT team, and perhaps you can find someone with the right technical expertise to assist you. But I'm afraid that's all the assistance I can provide. I'm incredibly sorry for your loss."

* * *

Aapo checked the Rolex on his wrist. It was 8:00 p.m., and he needed to prepare for the dreaded meeting in Brooklyn. He sighed heavily, turned away from the window, and reached for his overcoat and scarf. He was meeting with Sergey Petrov, a high-ranking Russian crime boss who controlled a criminal network that included professional computer hackers. No one within PIIE or the larger Vasquez Cartel knew about this bank account except Aapo, and it had to remain that way. Therefore, he had to go outside the Vasquez organization to acquire the technical resources to track the thieves on the dark web. For $20,000, Sergey agreed to provide an expert hacker capable of identifying who had stolen from Aapo's account.

Aapo entered a crowded, upscale restaurant with minimalist modern decor, low lighting, and white tablecloths. Diners in expensive attire sipped from oversized wine glasses; small, decorative food items rested on oddly shaped white plates; a jazz trio played in the corner of the room. He went to the bar, ordered a scotch on the rocks, and waited. Finally, a large man with a grim facial expression appeared beside him.

"Follow me." the man said in a thick Russian accent.

Maintaining an appearance of control and composure was paramount. Aapo took his time, slowly drained his glass, tossed a fifty-dollar bill onto the bar, and followed the man through an exit door.

They entered Sergey's office, where the large man stood with his back to the door, blocking it. His arms were folded across his chest, and his legs were spread apart. Sergey's office featured baroque decor that contrasted sharply with the restaurant's modern interior. The room was dimly lit, with overstuffed upholstered chairs, heavy red velvet drapes, and gold accents throughout.

Sergey leaned back in a chair behind an oversized wooden desk with ornamental carvings on the front. Gold-tipped alligator cowboy boots, crossed at the ankle, rested on the desk. He had white-blond hair pulled back into a ponytail, ice-blue eyes, a square chin, and a gold canine tooth that glistened when he smiled. A shiny black shirt opened midway down his chest to display multiple gold chains. He used a large knife with a seven-inch blade to peel an apple.

Two more men were in the room. One sat slumped in a chair, smoking a cigarette and squinting at Aapo. The other stood at the end of Sergey's desk, eyeing Aapo with contempt; his muscles strained against a black T-shirt; the brown straps of a shoulder holster spread across his chest. The handle of a handgun protruded from the holster.

Brushing apple peelings from his desk, Sergey smiled at Aapo. "Ah, my friend Aapo, come in. Have a seat. What are you drinking?"

Aapo sat in one of the armchairs facing the desk. "Scotch on the rocks; thanks for offering."

Sergey's smile widened. "I'm pleased to let you know I have the information you seek. There, on the end of the desk." He motioned with the knife to a folded paper lying at the edge of the desk. "My people are very good at computer hacking. I think you will be happy with what they found for you."

Aapo picked up the paper, glanced at it, and inserted it into the inner pocket of his jacket. "Thanks, Sergey; I appreciate the favor," he said.

"No problem. We're friends; we work together and help each other. Yes?" The gold tooth flashed with each word.

"Yes, we work together," Aapo responded as he sipped his drink.

Sergey inserted an apple slice into his mouth and chewed as he spoke. "Now tell me, how are things in Guatemala? I'm hearing rumors that things aren't going so well."

Aapo lightly swirled the liquor in his glass. "You shouldn't believe rumors, Sergey, but tell me, what are you hearing?"

Sergey inserted another slice of apple into his mouth. While chewing, he stared hard at Aapo. "They say your products aren't flowing and that the stuff that does arrive is of poor quality. No one wants it. I'm beginning to believe it's true because some of your customers have asked me to sell to them. But I tell them no; I must talk to you first. You and I have a relationship."

Aapo remained composed and relaxed. "Sergey, you know how it is in this business. The competition is always fierce, and they'll do or say anything to make a dollar. Our pipeline had some minor glitches, but that's over. We're doing business as usual. There are no issues."

Sergey finished the apple, wiped his mouth with the back of his hand, removed his feet from the desk, and sat up. "I'm glad to hear that, but in fairness, my friend, I want to let you know that leaving money on the table is unlike me. Especially when I have a product to sell, and someone is willing to pay my price. So, if you can't take care of your customers and they come to me, it's only fair that I sell to them. Understood?"

"Understood," Aapo responded, taking another sip of his drink. "It's fair. I appreciate your honesty."

"Good. Now that we have that out of the way, let's talk real business." Sergey leaned toward Aapo and narrowed his eyes. His gold chains swung a few inches above the desktop as he gestured with the knife. "How is my investment doing?"

The flashing blade was distracting, so Aapo focused his gaze on Sergey's eyes and feigned irritation. There could be no signs of intimidation or fear; Sergey was like a dangerous animal, always on the hunt for prey.

"Your investment is doing well," Aapo said, lying, maintaining an air of indifference. "There's a lot of activity: the facility walls are up, the roof is in place, and plumbing and electrical work are progressing. Everything is on schedule, and there are no unforeseen problems."

"So, when can I expect my return on that investment?"

There was a hint of impatience in Aapo's voice. "Look, Sergey, we have an agreement. You'll get your money when it's due. What's the problem? If you have a concern, tell me what it is; don't beat around the bush."

Sergey's smile turned menacing. "Don't be so sensitive. As I've said, rumors are circulating, and I've invested a considerable amount in your new enterprise. You can't blame me for asking questions; I have a right to know."

"As I said, don't listen to rumors. If you want to know something, ask me directly." Aapo stood, placed his glass on the desk, and buttoned his jacket. "I think we've concluded our meeting. Thank you for the hospitality and the information. I'll be in touch."

Aapo walked to the door. The barrel-chested guard sneered but didn't move. Aapo glanced over his shoulder at Sergey. Sergey nodded, and the guard begrudgingly stepped aside.

Aapo knew security cameras were watching his every move, so he walked casually through the busy restaurant. On the street, his chauffeur quickly opened the door to the town car, and Aapo slid into the back seat. Once the vehicle was moving, he opened the door of the built-in bar and took out a bottle of scotch. His hands were so sweaty that he struggled to break the seal and unscrew the cap. Then, slumping onto the seat, he drank straight from the bottle.

After several deep swallows, Aapo ran his fingers through his hair and stared numbly out the car window. Pedestrians hurried along the sidewalks, traffic crawled, and colorful neon lights from restaurants and stores flickered through the vehicle's dark interior.

For years, Aapo had secretly and intermittently siphoned money from the cartel's cash flow, cooking the books to cover his tracks. His goal was to create a drug empire independent of his father. Unlike his father's organization, there would be no growing of poppies, coca, or marijuana; no chemical processing to transform the plants into heroin or cocaine; no meth labs. Above all, no risks related to transporting or selling the products.

Instead, he had begun constructing a state-of-the-art facility for large-scale production of cheap, addictive, synthetic drugs. These synthetics mimicked the effects of fentanyl, oxycodone, meth, cocaine, and heroin, and the formulas could be endlessly revised. And it would all be bought and sold anonymously on the dark web using various cryptocurrencies.

It was an excellent plan, but Aapo had severely underestimated the costs. As a result, everything was behind schedule, and there was never enough money to cover the expenses. In addition to stealing from the cartel, he solicited funds from despicable men like Sergey, who belonged to other organized crime syndicates. The hacked account contained the borrowed funds, and he needed to recover them quickly. He was indebted to dangerous men who wouldn't tolerate excuses or delays, and he had no idea how long he could keep his father from discovering the missing money.

As the chauffeur navigated through New York City's hectic traffic, Aapo retrieved the paper Sergey had given him from his jacket pocket. He took out his cell phone, called the cartel's captain in charge of Southern California, and ordered soldiers to pick up Mack Owens, the man listed on the paper.

# 10

# HUMBERTO

It was nearly midnight, and twenty-seven-year-old Phillippe Manuel scrolled through social media on his phone while sprawled across the rumpled black satin sheets of his king-size bed. For the past three days, he'd partied hard leading up to, during, and after the February 2020 annual Guatemalan carnival in Guatemala City, and now all he wanted to do was rest and relax. Long, wavy blond hair draped over his bare muscular chest and back, while a snug pair of light-blue Calvin Klein underwear encased his well-formed butt and toned thighs.

His home was in a rural wooded area forty miles east of Guatemala City along a dirt road devoid of streetlights. Other houses, barely visible and surrounded by trees and dense vegetation, were spaced intermittently along the road. Unlike Phillippe's, these homes were humble abodes, belonging to the oppressed and the impoverished. Most were little more than huts or dilapidated shacks.

Nestled among thick tropical foliage, Phillippe's house sat farther from the road than the others. It was a square structure covered in dark gray stucco and elevated twelve feet off the forest floor by cement pillars. The house featured all the latest modern amenities.

Beneath the elevated structure, a covered cement parking space accommodated his two-year-old Ford Mustang convertible and a shiny, neon-blue Ducati motorcycle. Concrete steps with black wrought iron railings led up to a small porch and a heavily carved black front door. Floor-to-ceiling windows adorned the front exterior. Inside, an open floor plan encompassed the living, dining, and kitchen areas.

The local residents, devout Catholics, shunned Phillippe. It was an open secret that he was homosexual; however, they primarily avoided him because his lover was Humberto Vasquez, the youngest son of Eloy Vasquez, the godfather of the Vasquez Cartel. And their fear of the cartel ensured that all eyes, ears, and mouths were sealed regarding Phillippe.

Phillippe's wall-mounted flat-screen TV and cell phone were the only sources of light as he relaxed in his bedroom. Startled by the sound of a car stopping near the house, Phillippe silently retrieved a gun from his bedside table, crawled to the window, and cautiously peeked out from the lower corner of the blinds. The car door opened, and the interior light revealed Humberto. He quickly scrambled to his feet, turned on a table lamp as he dashed through the living room, and flicked on the porch light.

Excitedly, he flung open the door. "Humberto, what are you—" His words choked off when he noticed the blood on Humberto's clothes. Humberto leaned against the doorframe, and Phillippe reached out to support him. "You're bleeding. What happened?" he asked, helping Humberto to the sofa before rushing to the kitchen to grab a small towel.

Humberto slumped on the sofa and raised a hand to ward off Phillippe's frantic attempts to clean the blood. Finally, he grabbed Phillippe's wrist. "I'm okay. I'll be all right."

"But what happened? You look terrible. Let me get you a drink." Phillippe hurried to the kitchen and returned with a bottle of whiskey and a shot glass. Humberto downed the liquor and extended the glass for a refill.

"The operation to transfer a load of ammunition was a disaster—an ambush. Our men were loading the truck when assault rifles began firing. We tried to protect ourselves and the cargo, but the thieves overwhelmed us within minutes. They took everything: the ammo and the trucks."

Confusion clouded Phillippe's face. "But I don't understand. Where were the captain, the lieutenants, the soldiers? Why were you there?"

"Someone set me up," Humberto said, sinking deeper into the sofa. "First, I received a text from the captain saying there was a problem with the shipment and that he needed to see me immediately. We've been waiting for this delivery for months, and everything needed to go as planned. Despite numerous attempts, I couldn't reach him or his lieutenants. Finally, my bodyguards and I jumped in the car and drove to the site as quickly as we could. I didn't know what else to do."

"The exchange point was in the middle of the forest. I kept calling people on the way, trying to sort out what was happening, but then my phone died, and I couldn't get a signal. When we arrived, the captain was upset and confused by my presence. We argued, and he swore he never sent me a text. Then all hell broke loose."

As Humberto narrated his story, Phillippe refilled the shot glass and began arranging lines of cocaine on a small hand mirror. He passed the mirror and a short plastic straw to Humberto, who leaned forward, snorted two lines, and then reclined on the sofa, letting the drug surge through his sinuses and flood his brain.

"How did you escape? What happened to the rest of your men?" Phillippe asked, continuing to separate lines of coke.

Humberto sat up, downed a third shot of whiskey, and lowered his head. The drugs and alcohol were taking effect.

"They're all dead," he said, his tone heavy with exhaustion as he looked up at the ceiling. "I managed to escape with one bodyguard but, he was shot in the chest and stomach. I tried to carry him, but I had to save myself."

Eyes closed; Humberto pinched the bridge of his nose; his voice quivered. "He was my friend. We had been together for eight years, but I had no choice. I did what I had to do. I put him out of his misery. I couldn't risk having any of my men captured alive. After that, I hid until I was certain I was alone, and then I came straight here."

Phillippe looked skeptical. "So, who sent the text?"

"I don't know; the number doesn't work anymore," Humberto said, leaning back on the sofa with his eyes closed.

Phillippe moved closer, gently pushing strands of Humberto's hair away from his forehead. "I'm worried about you. Too many things are going wrong. I think someone is trying to kill you."

"My family has enemies, and they aren't going away," Humberto said, his eyes still closed, the empty shot glass resting in his hand.

Phillippe set the mirror with the cocaine on the coffee table. "But this situation was different. It's as if someone manipulated the situation to draw you in. Otherwise, you wouldn't have been there."

"I know, I know. Don't you think I've thought about that?" Humberto shot back, glaring at Phillippe. "Someone within the organization is leaking information. I've turned everything upside down searching for spies, but I have nothing to show for it—not a single suspect."

"I know you don't want to, but when will you tell your family?" Phillippe inquired softly.

Humberto snorted. "Family? What family? Do you mean Aapo and my father? They aren't family. They're my overlords, my masters." He picked up the mirror, snorted another line of coke, and settled back on the sofa.

"Aapo will be furious because it means he'll have to send more money for ammo. It's humiliating to go to him, begging like a homeless person. He'll either ignore or insult me. He never transfers the amount I ask for anymore. And if he sends anything, it's less than what I have requested, and it always arrives late." He grimaced as his nostrils burst into flames from the cocaine.

"Aapo thinks he's better than me. He thinks I'm stupid because I didn't attend fancy schools or work out of a skyscraper in a big city like he does. But I'm smart enough to know he's playing games with the cartel's money. He's up to something. I can feel it."

Phillippe moved the mirror out of Humberto's reach and tenderly placed a hand on his thigh. "And your father? You need to prepare yourself to face him."

Exhaling loudly, Humberto massaged the bridge of his nose. "The old man is unraveling and becoming more unpredictable. I'll tell him what happened, and he might rant and rave, but then he might forget everything I've said within minutes. But then again, he might remember something that happened last month and ask for an update. I never know; it's like walking on eggshells. The captains are beginning to lose faith in his leadership."

Finally, Phillippe wrapped an arm around Humberto's shoulders and planted a light kiss on his cheek. "My poor love. I'm so sorry for you. Let's get you cleaned up," he said, standing. "I'll start the shower. You can relax and let me take care of you."

* * *

Humberto stood under the shower, head bowed, watching as the water mixed blood swirled down the drain. The sight sickened him. His chin quivered as he tilted his face upward, letting the water mingle with his tears.

As the youngest son of Eloy Vasquez, he was tasked with managing the cartel's ground operations in Guatemala, and he was failing miserably. Frustrated, he gritted his teeth and struck the shower wall hard with the palm of his hand.

*God, I hate this fucking life!*

Phillippe gently knocked on the bathroom door. "Are you okay in there? I'm just checking on you."

"I'll be out in a minute," Humberto replied, turning the knob to increase the water temperature. The scalding water stung his skin as the bathroom filled with steam. He found himself reflecting on the dysfunctional childhood that had led him to the events of that fateful night.

* * *

Growing up beside his father while Aapo was away at school in the US, Humberto had been a firsthand witness to—and participant in—the inhumane activities that fueled the Vasquez empire. At fourteen, he was forced to kill his first victim. A sixteen-year-old boy from a small village had resisted becoming a drug mule and had fled. Cartel soldiers terrorized the villagers until the boy was found and brought, kicking and screaming, into the town square where Eloy awaited him.

Villagers, fearful of being seen, secretly peered around the corners of buildings or from behind window curtains or cracks in doorways. The boy's mother, distraught and desperate, groveled at Eloy's feet, begging and pleading as she was roughly pulled aside by two soldiers.

Unmoved by the mother's pleas or the boy's tears, Eloy handed Humberto a pistol. "Kill him," he commanded, loudly enough for the hidden villagers to hear. "No one disobeys Eloy Vasquez without suffering the consequences."

Terrified but unable to show weakness in front of his father and the soldiers, Humberto reluctantly did as he was told. One shot, one kill, all emotions suppressed.

"Well done," Eloy said, grinning proudly and slapping Humberto hard on the back. The soldiers encircled him, congratulating him with laughter, handshakes, and back pats.

For years afterward, the feel of the gun in his hand, the deafening sound of the gunshot, the sight of the boy's lifeless body in the dusty street, the mother's anguished screams, and the mocking faces of his father and the soldiers haunted his dreams.

* * *

Finally, Humberto stepped out of the shower and into the steamy bathroom. As he wiped away the condensation from the vanity mirror, his reflection came into focus. Water droplets clung to his curly black hair. His pupils were dilated from the cocaine. The shadow of a beard darkened his face; he needed a shave. His upper torso flushed red from the scorching shower, displayed a patchwork of bruises, cuts, and scratches—remnants of his earlier escape.

*Someone is out to kill me, our enemies know every move we make, and Aapo is fucking with the money. The almighty Vasquez Cartel is swirling like shit down a toliet, and I don't know what the fuck to do about any of it.*

Two quick knocks on the door interrupted his thoughts. Phillippe peered inside the bathroom. "Would you like something to eat? I can fix something if you're hungry." Noticing Humberto's injuries, he quickly moved closer. "Oh my God, you are hurt," he exclaimed, lightly touching the bruises on Humberto's shoulder.

A weary smile crossed Humberto's lips as he looked at their reflections in the mirror. The only word to describe Phillippe was 'beautiful.' His hair was long, shiny, and luxurious; his athletic body was complemented by smooth, flawless skin. He wore makeup—eyeliner, lashes, red lipstick—as well as a red satin robe and a matching red thong.

Slurring his words, Humberto said, "Thanks, my love, but I don't need food. I'm finishing up; give me a few minutes. I'll be in shortly."

In public Humberto put on an act of hypermasculine bravado, a facade he had carefully crafted and fiercely maintained. Being gay in Guatemala could be a death sentence; gay men were tortured and killed, and their mutilated bodies hung from trees like ghastly Christmas ornaments. He had to assume his secret was safe from his father because he and Phillippe were still alive.

He sighed wearily and looked back at his reflection. The man staring back at him was only forty, an age when he should have been vibrant and energetic. Instead, life in the cartel had left him a tired, worn down, depleted shell who looked a decade older than he was.

Wrapping a towel around his waist, Humberto walked into the bedroom, now lit by glowing scented candles. Soft romantic music flowed from hidden speakers. A refilled shot glass and the mirror with neat lines of cocaine sat on the bedside table.

He sank heavily onto the bed. Phillippe moved closer, planting a gentle kiss on his cheek before beginning to apply ointment

to his cuts and scratches. As Phillippe's hands worked their sooth-
ing magic, Humberto reclined on the black satin sheets, his mind
drifting on a blissful, drug-induced cloud.

# 11

# VONNIE

Hadwin Lopez was annoyed with Vonnie. She'd been back in Belize for almost three weeks, and this was the first time she had agreed to meet with him. It was 7:30 p.m. and he was ready to go home, eat dinner, and relax. Instead he found himself sitting at her kitchen table while she painted her nails, seemingly indifferent to the production spreadsheets and expense reports he displayed on his laptop.

As the principal operations manager for the Hollister Plantation, Hadwin now reluctantly reported to Vonnie rather than her father, Pearl Hollister. He had always anticipated the day she would take over the business but was both surprised and hurt when she listed it for sale without consulting him. And worst of all, there was no plan for the plantation's residents.

Although not related by blood, Pearl Hollister had been his mentor and surrogate father, and Vonnie was like a little sister to him. His wife Ana, was Vonnie's best friend, and Vonnie was the godmother of their children. Their relationship had always been deeply personal, but now it had taken on a new, uncomfortable professional dimension. Tonight, it quickly became apparent that she knew little about running the business, and had no interest in learning.

"Did you read the email I sent yesterday?" Hadwin asked, folding his arms across his chest and leaning back in his chair.

With a sheepish smile, Vonnie replied, "Sorry, Hadwin. I haven't checked my email in days. What was it about?"

"Vonnie, I wanted you to be prepared to discuss it tonight," he said, frustrated.

"Well, you're here now; just tell me what it says," Vonnie said, smiling and gently blowing on her freshly painted nails. "But first, I want to discuss fixing up the house."

"What's wrong with the house?"

"Nothing's wrong, except everything in it is older than I am. So, I want to spruce it up and modernize some things. I'll handle everything. I'm bored and I need a project."

Exasperated, Hadwin said, "Vonnie, it's your house and your money. Do whatever you want."

"Good, now tell me about the email."

"It was about the spread of Panama Disease," Hadwin said, frustrated by her attitude.

"What's Panama Disease? The only disease I've kept up with lately is COVID," she said, examining her nails.

"It's a fungus that kills Cavendish banana trees, and currently, there's no cure."

Vonnie looked alarmed. "Are you serious? The Cavendish is the only banana we grow. Isn't there anything you can do?"

Hadwin smirked. Finally, he had her attention. "Nope, not much. The Cavendish banana is a clone. That banana you put in your smoothie five years ago is the same as the one sitting in that fruit bowl on your kitchen counter. And it's the same one some kid in Canada is eating right now." He rubbed the back of his neck to ease the mounting tension. "The Cavendish isn't disease-resistant because of its genetic design."

Vonnie's eyebrows shot up. "But the Cavendish is the most popular banana in the world. It's practically the only banana anyone eats. And they're all clones? I didn't know that."

"There were web links in the email that would have explained the possibility of the Cavendish becoming extinct in the next several years unless scientists find another way to alter it genetically. Or someone creates a nontoxic fungicide that kills the fungus without poisoning the tree. But as I said, there are no answers yet."

"EXTINCT?" Vonnie gasped. "What do you mean by extinct? What exactly are you saying?"

"Extinct, Vonnie," Hadwin said in frustration. "Nonexistent, gone for good, like the dinosaurs."

Annoyed, Vonnie stood up and put her hands on her hips. "I can't believe you'd put this in an email instead of telling me before now. Do you know what this means?"

"Sit down, Vonnie," Hadwin said, snapping. "Of course, I know what it means. I run this operation." His eyes bore into her. "I've been trying to talk to you since you returned, but you keep avoiding me. The fungus is just one of several problems we would have discussed if you had come to me before listing the plantation on the market." He leaned back in his chair and crossed his arms.

"Look, this is your plantation, and I work for you, but you need to get your head out of the clouds and start paying attention."

Vonnie flopped down in her chair and glared at him. "Sorry I haven't been available, but I have a lot going on. Everything can't be a priority. But keep going. I'm listening."

"Vonnie, we have trees showing signs of the fungus. Thus far, two other growers have also reported findings, so it's spreading. I've cleared the affected area, but the soil will be contaminated for years. We won't be able to replant banana trees in that area.

"This disease is a lot like COVID-19: If one plant contracts it, the infection spreads like wildfire to the others. However, we have a slight advantage because you're the sole owner of this plantation, whereas most of the other growers are owned by multinational corporations. That frees us from red tape and boards of directors telling us what to do, allowing us to address the problem however we think is best. I've already implemented protocols and quarantine measures, but only time will tell if my actions save the uninfected trees."

"Are you saying this is a worldwide issue, not just local to Belize? Did my father know about this?" Vonnie asked.

Hadwin rolled his eyes. "If you'd read the emails, you would know that it's a global issue. Cavendish growers worldwide are facing the same problem; and of course, your father knew. Before he passed away, he and I were working on a plan to diversify our crops. We were exploring other profitable fruits and vegetables that could replace the Cavendish. But as of now, the Cavendish banana is our primary source of income. Without it, we're dead in the water."

He angrily slapped the top of his laptop closed and walked toward the back door. Turning to face Vonnie, he said, "Vonnie,

I've been patient with you. I understand you want to sell this place and get the hell out as soon as possible. We've all seen the printed and online real estate listings; everyone in Belize knows and is talking about it. So, what's the plan?"

Dejected, Vonnie looked at the floor, and in a small, weak voice said, "I don't know, I'm working on it."

Hadwin looked at his friend with disdain. "Well, you'd better come up with one. If you don't start engaging with what's happening and stop acting like you're eighteen and down here on spring break, you might not have anything to sell." With that, he walked out and slammed the door behind him.

* * *

After Hadwin stormed out, Vonnie sat at the kitchen table for several minutes, speechless, processing what she had just heard. Eventually, she found a wine glass among the dirty dishes in the sink, opened a bottle of wine, and retrieved her laptop to read Hadwin's email. Then two glasses of wine and an Ambien tablet later, she collapsed into bed and stared at the ceiling in the dark.

For five years, she had been in a state of continuous mourning over the deaths of the three people she loved most. Finally, after two years of debilitating depression, she was taking baby steps on the road to recovery. But there were still too many days when she felt like a rudderless ship, drifting in a fog, going nowhere.

After her father's death, she reviewed the will and estate papers with his lawyer and was astounded at the wealth he had amassed and left to her. But even though she was exceedingly grateful for her father's generosity, two years of intense therapy made her realize the plantation could have no place in her future.

A moist breeze wafted through the room, assisting the ceiling fan in moving the mosquito nets that enclosed the bed. Vonnie laced her fingers behind her head, kicked off the top sheet, and waited for the drug's relaxing effects.

She had known rumors would run wild on the plantation as soon as it was put up for sale. The prospect of a town hall meeting where residents could pepper her with a barrage of questions frightened her. So, she thought it best to avoid saying anything until she received a firm offer that hopefully included the residents remaining on the premises. The residents had known her all her life; surely, they knew she would look out for their interests. But since her return, there were only accusatory expressions, downcast eyes, perfunctory waves, and timid smiles.

Nothing in her past prepared her to be a powerful, aggressive businesswoman. Owning and running a coffee shop was no comparison to managing a business of this scale and magnitude. Her inheritance meant she was now responsible for every banana planted, picked, and shipped on 2,000 acres, hundreds of employees, infrastructure, equipment, and the well-being and livelihoods of people who lived within the confines of the plantation. It was not only overwhelming but terrifying.

And it all came at a time when she was hurting, both physically and emotionally, alone, and desperately lonely. There was no release from the pressure she felt, no one to comfort her. All she could think of was making it through the day without feeling downhearted and hopeless, keeping the physical pain under control, and trying to sleep through the night. And none of those could be accomplished without prescription meds.

* * *

Two days after meeting with Hadwin, Vonnie was back in Belize City. As her taxi wound its way through the city, the view from the back seat was disheartening. COVID-19 was wreaking havoc on the Belize economy. No vacationers streamed from cruise ships, and no young foreigners with backpacks gaily navigated the city's once-crowded narrow streets. Metal security shutters covered storefronts. The sidewalk vendors, artists, and hawkers who tempted tourists with tours of the Mayan ruins had disappeared. Even boat traffic on the Belize River had dwindled.

But being a Hollister came with privileges in Belize, and store owners were more than happy to grant her private showings.

Her trip to the city had less to do with shopping and more to do with Dominic Castillo. Vonnie had wrongly assumed that her romantic life had died with Russ, and after her parents' deaths, depression consumed her entire existence. But the spark, lit by the brief encounter with Dominic, had caught her off guard, and it both surprised and pleased her. Even though she was apprehensive about seeing Dominic again because of Hadwin's and Ana's attitudes toward him, she was eager to explore what she hoped would be a nice distraction from her problems.

The objective of meeting with Dominic was to determine whether he had a romantic interest in her or if the flowers and offer to take her out to eat were his way of obtaining more of the plantation business.

Vonnie checked her watch—it was 2:30 p.m. and her flight back to Punta Gorda left at four. She had intentionally planned a short meeting with Dominic that would give her enough time to thank him for the flowers, make some small talk, and then leave. If he had romantic intentions, he would ask her out again before she left.

* * *

Castillo's Delivery Services was in the warehouse district near the Port of Belize. Even though the city was quiet due to the pandemic, the docks were still busy. In the distance, large shipping containers dangled high over enormous cargo ships guided by tall skeletal moving cranes. The ships towered over the buildings and warehouses along the docks. Wooden pilings wrapped in rubber bumpers and dotted with barnacles stretched along the waterline. Men drove forklifts or pushed trolleys as they moved cargo. The hot air smelled of saltwater, fish, and diesel oil.

Arriving at a nondescript brick building, Vonnie stepped out of the taxi. Large earth-toned ceramic pots with cascading multi-colored blooms sat on each side of a wide mahogany door, above which a navy-blue canopy displayed Castillo's Delivery Services in white lettering.

Her hair was in a braided updo, and she wore makeup beneath her face mask, a silver rope chain necklace and matching bracelet, a green sundress with three inches of exposed cleavage and skinny shoulder straps, and green-and-white rhinestone wedge-heel sandals. When she entered the building a blast of cold air greeted her.

The reception area was a light-blue, midsize room decorated with glass and chrome office furniture. The walls were decorated with large framed colored photos of the birds of Belize.

A thirty-something, auburn-skinned woman looked up from her computer screen. She wore an extremely low-cut, skintight, neon-yellow dress with several gold chains that rested on top of large breasts that threatened to explode from the top of the dress. A long, curly black weave cascaded down to her waist.

"May I help you?" she asked, smiling brightly and fluttering her extra-long eyelashes.

Vonnie cleared her throat. "I'm Yvonne Hollister, and I have an appointment with Mr. Castillo."

"Welcome, Miss Hollister. Mr. Castillo is expecting you. Have a seat, and I'll see if he's ready to receive you."

Vonnie's eyes widened as the woman rose and walked out of the room, hips swaying. The snug yellow dress stopped mid-thigh, and at the end of the long, shapely legs were yellow six-inch heels. Ana's comments about Dominic being a womanizer flashed through her mind as she settled into one of the waiting room chairs.

* * *

Dominic's office featured a glass wall on the entire left side, offering an unobstructed view of vehicles, loading docks, and parking areas. His desk, a handcrafted showcase of various shades of wood from the rainforest, was positioned against a backdrop of photographs of him with various politicians and celebrities, framed magazine articles, and awards. Two tan leather armchairs faced the desk.

A credenza, matching the desk, occupied the right side of the room. Above the credenza, on the wall, were more photographs of Dominic with famous people. On top of the credenza, on a silver tray, was an ice bucket containing a bottle of wine nestled in ice and two crystal wine glasses.

Clad in an indigo-blue suit, crisp white shirt, and red paisley tie, Dominic stood at the window with his hands in his pockets, deep in thought as he looked at the loading docks. It had been two weeks since his encounter with Vonnie. After sending her flowers, he'd been confident she'd reach out. While he waited, he researched her, her family, and the plantation. Yvonne Hollister was a walking, talking gold mine.

He was now transporting all kinds of contraband to and from the borders of Mexico and Guatemala through Belize. The risks were horrendous and increasing daily. It was time for him to leave Belize.

Dominic checked the time on his Rolex.

*Let her wait. She's not going to catch that plane. She's on my time now. I'll let her go when I'm ready.*

His gaze returned to the flurry of activity outside his office window. His primary concern was the increase in maintenance costs, which had skyrocketed. Unfortunately, new automotive parts were hard to obtain due to the pandemic's effect on imports, and used parts were practically nonexistent. As a result, his vehicles were regularly breaking down on the road.

One miscalculation, one stupid mistake, or one overly suspicious police officer would mean a disaster. That's why he needed to leave Belize—everything had become too unpredictable. He had money but not enough to live his desired lifestyle in Europe or the US, especially considering currency rates.

But, if he could make it work, and he was confident that he could, the woman waiting in the reception area would be his ticket to a life of wealth and luxury in the US and beyond. Straightening his tie, he buzzed the receptionist to send Vonnie in.

Greeting her with a smile that could melt butter, he took her by the hand and led her to one of the tan leather chairs, while he perched on the desk facing her.

"I'm pleased to see you. You can remove your mask; there are only good germs here."

Smiling, Vonnie immediately did as he asked. "Thank you. I hate these things."

"I have to say you look more beautiful than the last time I saw you."

Vonnie blushed. "I should hope so. I'm not sprawled in the dirt, flat on my behind. But all is well—it was a minor sprain."

"And I don't see any scars on those beautiful legs," he said, leaning down for a closer look. "I'm honored by your presence but slightly disappointed that you declined my offer to take you to dinner."

"I apologize," she said. "My errands took longer than I anticipated, and I only have a few minutes. But I wanted to thank you in person for the beautiful bouquet. It was very thoughtful."

"It was nothing. Beautiful women deserve beautiful things," Dominic said as he moved toward the credenza. "I was saving this just for you. Will you join me in a glass?" He poured the wine into two glasses without waiting for her response.

Vonnie hesitated and looked at her watch. "I only have a few minutes. As I said in my text, my plane leaves at four p.m., and I need time to get to the airport."

Dominic handed her a glass and sat beside her in the second chair. Vonnie's eyes went to the window. Two large eighteen-wheelers slowly passed one another, moving in opposite directions. "You have quite an operation here," she said, sipping the wine.

"Thank you; it's quite a handful. The delivery business is booming, but sadly, due to the pandemic, people are too afraid to venture out and prefer things delivered. When I'm short on drivers, sometimes I roll up my sleeves and help the men out. But it's not all bad. That's how I met you," he lied, turning on the charm and skillfully keeping her engaged in conversation.

Finally, Vonnie glanced at her watch. "Oh my God, I'm going to miss my flight." She quickly stood and placed the wine glass on the desk. "I'll never make it to the airport in time, and this is the last flight out today."

Recognizing her distress, Dominic stood and touched her arm. "I apologize, I should have checked the time." Then, feigning concern, he furrowed his brow. "Let me make this up to you. Let me drive you home."

Flustered, Vonnie asked, "You... you can't be serious. You're willing to drive me all the way home? Today?"

"Sure, it's the least I can do since it was my fault you missed your flight. Give me a few minutes to wrap up," he said, smiling as he walked to the credenza and refilled her glass.

"Dominic, I sincerely appreciate your offer, but it's a five-hour drive, and unfortunately, I'm not in a position to host you overnight. I don't blame you for missing my flight. That was my responsibility. I'll get a hotel room and fly out in the morning."

"Don't worry about it. It will be my pleasure. I'll get a hotel room in Punta Gorda. So, relax and make yourself comfortable. I'll be right back."

"But what about your work? I don't want to be an imposition."

"Believe me, it's no imposition," he said with an alluring smile. "I'm the boss. I give the orders around here. And if there's something I want to do, there's no one to question it. And I want to spend the rest of the evening with you."

Vonnie took a gulp of the wine, inhaled, and tried to slow her pounding heart. Dominic's confident, take-charge attitude was overwhelming, and she was unsure how to handle it.

*Damn, I hate to have him drive five hours and then stay at a dingy little hotel in Punta Gorda. But I can't take the chance of Hadwin or Ana seeing him leave my house in the morning; they'd lose their minds.*

Her thoughts swirled. This turn of events wasn't part of her plan, but as she stood at the window, sipping wine, watching the parade of vehicles come and go, she found herself warming to the idea. It was exciting. His attraction to her was palpable, but she wasn't used to a man like him. The difference between him and Russ was like night and day.

Russ was laidback, creative, and intellectual—an artist. Dominic was a 100 percent alpha male, physically fit, and confident. He moved like a cat, fluid, agile, and self-assured. She looked down and noticed the wine glass quivering slightly in her hand. His ultra-masculine demeanor and sultry sexuality sent shivers down her spine.

* * *

After twenty minutes, Dominic finally returned. The suit jacket and tie were gone. The white shirt was open at the collar. They walked through the reception area to the street; the receptionist wasn't at her desk. Dominic noticed Vonnie's raised eyebrows and surprised expression when he escorted her to a white Mercedes Benz C-Class convertible parked at the entrance. "Did you think I would drive you home in a delivery truck?" He laughed, opening the passenger-side door.

The drive down the Hummingbird Highway toward the southern part of the country was magnificent. The sun was going down. The balmy evening weather was perfect. He joked, she laughed. Eventually, they stopped at a rustic, outdoor, oceanfront restaurant. The smoked fish was superb, and the rum punches were refreshing. The two glasses of wine earlier plus two rum punches caused Vonnie to become more relaxed as the evening progressed. Finally, the sun went down, and the string lights glowed around the deck where they sat. Tiki torches flickered, and the ocean waves became louder and more active.

Dominic suggested they take a short walk on the beach before continuing the drive south. After a few minutes of struggling to walk in the deep sand, Vonnie braced herself against a leaning palm tree to remove her sandals. When she stood up, he moved in close.

"I've wanted to kiss you from the moment I met you. Tell me I can." His voice was low and husky.

"Yes" floated like a whisper from her lips, and he kissed her. He pulled her closer with one arm around her waist and the other around her shoulder. Her body slowly unfolded as she responded to his kiss. She went limp, gave in, and surrendered to him.

With her leaning on a tree, he pushed himself against her. His kisses made their way down her neck, and his hands slipped the dress straps down her shoulders, exposing her breasts. Dominic buried his face in her neck, licking and sucking as he slowly slid one hand up her dress, between her legs, and began massaging her through her panties until they were soaking wet.

Vonnie opened her legs wider as Dominic's fingers probed and stroked deeper. Her hips automatically moved in rhythm with his hand. She shuddered. He could tell her body was on the verge of exploding, so he removed his hand and slowly put space between them. Vonnie was trembling, breathing hard. He kissed her cheeks and forehead as he returned the dress straps to her shoulders.

He stepped back, lifted her chin with his finger, and looked seductively into her eyes. "Vonnie, I want you, but not here and not like this. You're special. I want to take my time and relish every part of you. I want to do this the right way. "he whispered.

Vonnie was speechless and confused. Dominic took her by the hand, and they returned to the car. He held her hand for the remainder of the drive, often bringing it to his lips and kissing each finger. They didn't talk as much as before; the mood was quiet and mellow.

* * *

Vonnie's head rested on Dominic's shoulder as he drove with their fingers intertwined. It was as if rain was finally falling on a dry, arid desert. Dominic had brought her body back to life in a few short minutes. Her panties were wet, her thighs sticky, and her feet were bare; the sandals were still under the palm tree.

The warm ocean air washed over them as they sped down the highway. The halogen headlights of the Mercedes blazed a path through the darkness on the empty road. With little traffic, they moved deeper into the southern part of the country.

* * *

It was close to midnight, and Ana was leaving a patient's home on a rugged dirt road leading to the highway. The patient was eighty years old, in poor health and exhibiting symptoms of COVID-19. The family had insisted on taking him to the hospital, but Ana knew he would probably die while waiting for the hospital to find a bed. Unfortunately, all hospitals and clinics were ill-equipped, unprepared, and already feeling the strain of too many COVID patients.

She pulled onto the highway just as the white Mercedes passed. She was taken aback when her headlights caught the prominent Mercedes emblem on the trunk as she drove behind the car. No one in the area owned such a luxury vehicle, let alone could afford one. The landscape was marked by rocky, potholed, muddy dirt roads, except for the highway. The convertible's top was down, and two people were in the car, but Ana had no idea who they could be.

As they approached the plantation, the Mercedes's brake lights illuminated. The car slowed almost to a halt, then turned into the main entrance of The Big House.

Ana's heart sank. The woman's profile was unmistakable. A whispered "no, no" escaped her lips as she cautiously drove past the entrance, her eyes following the red taillights up the driveway. Distraught, she heaved a sigh, then began searching for the road sign that marked the plantation's service road entrance.

* * *

Strategically placed time-controlled landscape lighting illuminated the lawn and accentuated the beauty of the towering white house. Dominic was impressed with the view, and a sinister smile crossed his face. He parked, walked around the car, opened the passenger door, and escorted Vonnie up the steps to the door, where they kissed passionately.

"Today was one of the best days I've had in a long time," he said, his arms around her waist while he planted kisses on her neck.

"Yes, it was," Vonnie said, stifling a wide yawn. "I'm going to sleep like a log."

"Just dream of me," he said, kissing her one last time on the forehead, and returned to his car.

Ten minutes later, he turned off the highway onto a dirt road eight miles farther south. Driving slowly, trying to avoid the ruts, he pulled into the yard of a small cinderblock house.

A tall, physically striking, dark brown woman in her early thirties opened the door wide. Dressed in a sheer, white-laced nightie and wearing a seductive smile, she asked, "What took you so long?"

# 12

# CHANCE

Numb with grief over Charlotte's death and devastated by the financial scandal she'd caused, Chance left Virginia in March 2019. He had no concrete plans; his emotions were too raw to make any. But wanting to get as far away from DC as possible, he kept driving and eventually found himself in Los Angeles. After growing bored with Hollywood tours, he decided to call Mack Owens, a longtime friend and former FBI coworker, for a reunion.

Rather than meeting at a restaurant, Mack invited Chance to his home in the Hollywood Hills. The person who greeted Chance at the door bore little resemblance to the Mack he remembered. During his tenure at the FBI, Mack had been obese, weighing between 275 and 300 pounds, with long sandy-brown hair and emerald-green eyes framed by black glasses. His loose jowls merged with neck fat and bulged over his tight shirt collars. Now, Mack appeared lean, fit, tanned, coiffed, and stylishly yet casually dressed—more like a wealthy Bel-Air tycoon on vacation. His home, straight out of the pages of *Architectural Digest*, offered a panoramic view of the city below that could make anyone's jaw drop.

Chance and Mack had worked together in the FBI's Cyber Crimes Division. Awards, commendations, and other accolades had adorned Mack's office walls, while books, papers, trash, and empty food containers cluttered everything else.

For nearly two decades, Mack was hailed as a superstar in the division, until an internal investigation revealed he secretly circumvented several of the bureau's legal procedures in a hasty attempt to solve a case. Given the option to quietly resign or face federal prosecution, Mack left the bureau disgraced and disgruntled and moved to California.

The two men lounged on the patio, drinking whiskey and smoking cigars. Lights on the bottom of the infinity pool reflected on the aqua-blue water while the LA nightscape twinkled in the darkness. Chance blew a narrow stream of cigar smoke and looked at Mack.

"Man, you sure have come up in the world since our days at the bureau. Did you win the lottery or something?"

"No way. I don't play that shit," Mack said, laughing. "I'm into a lot of stuff, a little of this, a little of that—it all adds up." He glanced at Chance. "Since you're out here wandering around without a compass, why don't you check out of that cheap-ass hotel you're staying in and hang out with me until you decide what to do? As you can see, I have plenty of room."

Chance laughed as he puffed his cigar. "It's not a cheap hotel, Mack. Nothing in LA is cheap."

"You've got that right. So why pay to sleep down there with the roaches when you can live up here for free? Free food, free liquor, free pussy. I need a wingman, Chance, and it doesn't sound like you have anything else going on." He laughed with the cigar clenched between his teeth and then walked across the patio to the bar.

"The free food and liquor are tempting, but I have to think about the pussy. I'm a little rusty; it's been a while," Chance said in jest.

"Well, I know some girls who can grind that rust right off," Mack said. The two men howled with laughter.

One month with Mack gave Chance an insight into the world of the rich and famous. There were parties with music legends, movie stars, and TV personalities. The lavish extravagance and luxury were dizzying. Hours were spent around Mack's infinity pool with stunningly beautiful women or cruising the streets of LA in his Lamborghini.

They were on their way home following a Lakers game. The night air was warm, and the city's nightlife pulsed with energy. Beautiful people filled the streets, enjoying themselves. The Lamborghini's engine purred as it inched through thick traffic toward the expressway.

Mack glanced at his friend. "I'm planning a vacation in Dubai. Would you like to tag along?" he asked, smiling.

Chance smiled. "I would love to—in my dreams, but I'm looking for a job right now. I sent my resume to several cybersecurity companies in Silicon Valley and have received two interview requests."

Mack moaned. "Damn, Chance, are you sure you want to get back into that rat race at your age?"

"It's the only race I know how to run. I don't look forward to working with kids half my age, but the pension from the government is all I have left. Charlotte left me so deep in debt that I'm looking up at the bottom. I'll never pay it off in this lifetime. I'll never be able to retire."

Mack looked at his friend with concern. "Damn, Chance, is it that bad?"

"It's that bad… I'm just looking for a way to live out the rest of my life in quiet desperation."

"Hmm… I wish you'd mentioned this earlier. Maybe I can help you out," Mack said, steering the car effortlessly into the speeding traffic on the expressway as the Lamborghini's motor roared to life.

After being forced out of the FBI, Mack gave Washington, DC the middle finger, moved to California, and went rogue by designing a unique hacking scheme. He no longer tracked cyber-criminals to bring them to justice. Instead, he tracked perpetrators of financial schemes, followed their money trails, and once he found the bank where the trail ended, he hacked the bank account and stole the money. The luxurious lifestyle Chance had witnessed over the past month was funded solely by stolen money.

For two days after the Lakers game, Mack tried to convince Chance to become his partner. Late on the second evening, as the two men were on the patio watching the twinkling lights of LA, Mack stood and stretched. "Let's hit the sack and get up early. I want to show you my place in the mountains."

The next morning, they drove toward the Santa Monica Mountains in Mack's Land Rover. The scenic route offered breathtaking views of peaks and valleys. As the road snaked upward through the mountain passages, they passed a range of homes, from luxury estates on cliff edges to cozy wooden cabins.

Grinning, Mack shot Chance a quick glance. "Hold on; it's about to get bumpy." He steered the car off the road onto a steep, brush-covered trail. The Land Rover lurched and swayed as they navigated the forest. The incline increased, the engine whined, and the tires spun as they gripped the damp, uneven ground strewn with rocks and forest debris. Finally, they reached a clearing next to a single-story concrete structure.

"This is where the magic happens," Mack said proudly, pressing a button on a handheld remote control. A wall section slid back, revealing a spacious interior. He drove in, and the outer wall closed.

"I thought you had a cabin; this place is a bunker," Chance said, stepping out of the car.

"Go ahead, look around. I'll unload the car," Mack said, grabbing grocery bags from the back seat.

Narrow, rectangular windows lined the top of the walls. A single metal door without windows stood at the far end of the room. The vast interior was divided into what Chance considered functional zones rather than rooms. Unlike Mack's Hollywood Hills residence, there were no frills, high-end furniture, or breathtaking views.

The Land Rover sat in the zone dedicated to garage, maintenance, and hardware. Nearby, the lounge zone featured a flat-screen TV, sofa, recliner, and armchairs. The kitchen zone included a four-seater dining table, cabinets stocked with food, drinks, household cleaning supplies, a dishwasher, sink, fridge, stove, and a washer and dryer. A workout zone contained a treadmill, a Peloton bike, free weights, and weight machines, along with a blue yoga mat. Finally, the sleep zone consisted of a king-size bed flanked by nightstands.

The most impressive was the tech zone. It featured banks of computer monitors, three spacious worktables, two whiteboards with software schematics and engineering diagrams, a tripod with flip charts, and racks of computer servers.

After a dinner of spaghetti, the two sat at the kitchen table with beers. "Chance, you're looking at this all wrong," Mack said, leaning forward, his arms crossed and resting on the table. "The money I take doesn't come from hacking grandma's savings account or some poor guy's credit card; that's not what I do. I focus on the slimeballs who swindle grandmas out of their life savings and buy a new yacht. Or the guy who peddles fake investments in a Ponzi scheme, then flies off in his jet to Thailand, never to be heard from again. But regardless of the source, all this dirty money must be stashed on or offshore."

Mack slouched back in his chair with a sly smile on his face. "All I do is find out where the bad guys stash their cash and take what I want. I consider it my own form of justice."

Chance walked over to the kitchen zone and selected a bottle of whiskey and two glasses. "So, who are you supposed to be, an Avenger or some type of superhero?" He chuckled as he poured the drinks.

Mack laughed and swirled the liquor in his glass. "Call me whatever you like, but don't ask me to wear red tights. But seriously Chance, there's nothing wrong with what I'm doing. I'm stealing stolen money. Most of these assholes will never step foot into a courtroom or see the inside of a prison."

Chance leaned toward Mack, his brow furrowed with concern. "Mack, we both know anonymity on the internet and even the dark web is an illusion. A person can hack into a government facility, power grid, bank, or home computer. But if the right cybersecurity experts are persistent enough, they can identify the hacker. That's how we busted so many crooks. Your security protocols are some of the most sophisticated I've seen, but aren't you concerned someone will eventually find out who you are?"

Mack casually sipped his drink and shrugged. "Not really. I sweep up all my breadcrumbs and erase my tracks. You know me Chance, and how thorough I can be. Remember, I was once the FBI's cybersecurity golden child."

The more Chance heard the more appealing Mack's proposal seemed. They'd be taking from criminals, not innocent people. Their collective knowledge, technical skills, and cybersecurity expertise would make them a formidable team. And it was a far more attractive option than joining the millennial tech crowd in Silicon Valley.

The alcohol made both men relax. "Okay Mack, I'm in but it's only temporary. I want enough money to pay off my debts and stash a little cash for the future, so I won't have to work at Walmart when I'm seventy."

Mack looked elated. "I wondered how much more convincing it would take." He held out his glass, and they toasted.

"So, have you thought about how much money you would need to live your dream life? Do you have a figure in mind?" Mack asked, finishing off the whiskey in his glass.

Chance downed the last of his drink. "I know the amount of Charlotte's debt, but the rest needs some calculation."

"Well... I can't tell you how glad I am to have you on board. The moment you reach that magic number and want out, we part as friends. Agreed?" Mack held out his hand.

"Agreed," Chance said, firmly returning the handshake.

"This is going to be great, Chance," Mack said, his excitement peaking. "We need to start your education as soon as possible. Is your passport valid?"

Three days later Mack rented a private jet, and he and Chance flew to the Bahamas, the Cayman Islands, Panama, and Switzerland. I n each country, Chance opened a bank account to store the money he would eventually steal. Three weeks later, in their first joint hack, Chance doubled his previous annual salary from the FBI.

However, after six months of raiding bank accounts, Chance began to question his actions. His original justification for partnering with Mack began to lose its sheen. The idea of falling from grace within one of the world's most esteemed law enforcement organizations only to become a thief gnawed at him.

A top-tier lawyer in DC had worked out a way to quietly repay the money stolen from Charlotte's charities without publicity or IRS queries. The entire scandal evaporated into thin air. His debts vanished, and his offshore accounts bulged with enough money to live comfortably for two lifetimes. He wanted out of the game.

It was October, and the men were lounging in the main salon of Mack's yacht, adrift off the Mexican coast while the turquoise-blue Pacific Ocean lapped at the boat's hull. The salon's black-and-yellow-striped throw pillows accented the soft, white leather sofa and chairs. It was tastefully decorated with abstract paintings, a flat-screen TV, a bar, and exotic flower arrangements. Two nude swimsuit models sunbathing on the deck were visible through the salon's large windows.

Mack puffed on a cigar, sipped whiskey, and looked through the salon window at the models as one applied lotion to the other's back.

"You've hit your magic number already?" Mack asked in surprise.

Chance relaxed on a white leather chaise. "Yep," he said, looking at the label on his beer bottle. "It's been a wild ride, Mack... but I'm getting off. I'm ready to move on."

Mack walked over and sat diagonally across from Chance. "Well, I can't say I didn't see it coming. You're not as greedy as I am," he said, smiling. "I hate to see you go, Chance; you've been a great partner. But as a favor to me, can you hang on for just one more heist? I could really use your help."

"Sure. You've been a good friend, Mack. You helped me when I was down. I would be working for the rest of my life if it weren't for you. I'll do one more, then I'll ride off into the sunset."

"Well, if this will be your last hoorah, let's go big."

"How big is big?"

"Thirty million, fifteen million each."

Chance frowned. "I don't need fifteen million dollars, Mack. And thirty million is a lot to take from a single account. There's a huge risk of exposure."

Mack laughed. "Chance, you're the only person in the world who would admit to not wanting fifteen million dollars. Yeah, it's risky, but we've come this far without any issues. I say, let's go for it."

"What exactly did you have in mind?"

Mack set his cigar in an ashtray and leaned in, quickly glancing around to ensure no crew members were within earshot.

"I've been tracking a group of sleazy gold brokers. You've seen the magazine ads and TV commercials saying the US dollar is going to hell in a handbasket, and the only way to ensure your future is to buy gold. Of course, it's a scam, but thousands of people believe it, send these guys money, and receive nothing in return. Well, I discovered their money trails, and they all led to this one bank in New York: GRC Bank and Financial Services.

"Based on public records, GRC appears squeaky clean. So, I used some social engineering tricks to find a bank employee to whom I sent an official-looking email with a contaminated PDF file. When the poor guy opened the attachment, it released a bug into the bank's network. The bug's been crawling around for three months, so the IT security guys have no idea it's there and sending me information.

"GRC is running an illegal undercover banking operation. The bank has two systems: one is a pristine, cloud-based system with all the latest bells, whistles, and security protocols, and the other is a basic, low-level in-house system with minimum security that doesn't appear to get much attention because no one has updated the security software in over two years. The cloud-based system is for legal accounts and financial transactions, and the in-house system is for crooks and criminals."

"How do you know there aren't legitimate accounts on the in-house system?" Chance asked.

Mack drained his glass and inched closer to Chance. "Because, unlike the legal accounts, the accounts that belong to the gold brokers have the same four digits, 2506, in the account number string, so they're easily identifiable. And get this: there are hundreds—yes, Hundreds with a capital 'H'—of accounts with the same four digits, and they're worth millions.

"None of these accounts appear in the cloud-based system or in any of the bank's official records or audit reports. This means FDIC regulations don't cover them, and the IRS doesn't have a clue. From the intel I've gathered, GRC holds the dirty money until the clients either request a withdrawal or have it electronically transferred to another on or offshore bank."

Mack leaned back in his chair with a smug smile. "It's dirty money, Chance. And it's only right that we rob these motherfuckers. GRC has no recourse. If these were legitimate accounts, they could call the FBI to investigate the hack, but they can't, and they won't. We can take as much as we want."

Chance swallowed the last of his beer. "Are you sure? I don't want to touch accounts belonging to innocent people."

Mack's eyes sparkled. "I'm sure, and I have the data to prove it." He walked to the bar and refreshed his drink. "Chance, you can throw away your keyboard forever after this heist. You might not want the money, but I do. I refuse to let these low-life bastards get away unscathed. Donate your share to charity or something."

"Okay, Mack, I'm in. But after this, I'm done." He placed his beer bottle on the coffee table, walked toward the stairs that led to the deck and the naked women basking in the sun.

The following week, sequestered in the bunker with their heads down, Chance and Mack focused on writing code. The new program would stealthily breach the GRC bank's firewalls and snake through hundreds of illegal bank accounts until it accumulated thirty million dollars. Then it would kick off another routine that electronically transferred the funds into their offshore bank accounts. When the offshore deposits were complete, the program would initiate its final routine, erasing all evidence of its existence.

They launched the program at 11:30 p.m. on Christmas Eve, but error messages began scrolling on the screen, indicating problems. Mack quickly identified the issues in the code and immediately started making the corrections.

Chance rose from his computer console, stretched, and yawned. "How long do you think it will be before you complete the changes? I'm tired."

Mack rolled his neck and shoulders to alleviate the tension, but his fingers never stopped moving across the keyboard. He sighed heavily, staring at the algorithm on the monitor screen. "Not sure. Maybe an hour or two. Take a nap, and I'll call you when it's ready to relaunch."

Since the middle of October, the duo had been working ten to twelve hour days, including weekends. Exhausted from the long hours, Chance dropped heavily on a sofa and fell asleep in minutes. When he awoke two hours later, he found the bunker eerily quiet. Mack wasn't at the console, and all the terminal screens were black. He quickly glanced at the garage zone. His Jeep sat alone in the space; Mack's Range Rover was gone. Alarmed, Chance jumped up and rushed to the terminals.

On the terminal screen was a yellow Post-it note: "Merry Christmas, Buddy. Enjoy your new life, Mack."

Grabbing the note, Chance tried to access the program, but it was all gone—every trace of the code. Then, he anxiously pulled up the website for his offshore account, and the balance displayed on the screen made his jaw drop.

While Chance slept, Mack had changed the code, and fifty million instead of fifteen million had been deposited to Chance's bank account, which meant the program extracted 100 million from the illegal GRC accounts. Mack's greed had gotten the best of him.

It was 2:00 a.m. on Christmas morning, and they had become the Grinches who had stolen Christmas from some very wicked people. Chance exhaled loudly, slumped in the office chair, and stared at the screen. Even though the hack was successful, and the money was safely tucked away in his offshore account, a sense of foreboding slowly descended upon him like a dark cloud.

# 13

# VONNIE

In white capital letters on a red background "Breaking News" twirled on the TV screen. A serious-looking reporter stood before a screen displaying airplanes parked on the tarmac at the Belize International Airport. The chyron scrolling across the bottom of the screen read "International flights canceled due to worldwide COVID-19 pandemic." The reporter urgently explained the details. "... The government is monitoring the situation but doesn't know when flights will resume..."

Vonnie switched off the TV, tossed the remote aside, and went out to the back porch. In the distance, large trucks with clouds of dust billowing in their wake moved along the service road. Several women lined up to board a Hollister Plantation van that would take them shopping in Punta Gorda, and two pregnant women stood talking outside the medical clinic.

Vonnie ignored the sprawl of dirty dishes on the countertops, the stack of pots in the sink, the overflowing trash can, and the stained and sticky kitchen floor. She'd been online reading international news networks for information for days, so the local news was unsurprising. It was inevitable that Belize would eventually close its borders to protect its citizens from the spread of the virus. And even when local TV broadcasts showed the Belize airport overrun with tourists fleeing the country, she still couldn't decide if it was safer to return to the States or stay in Belize.

She sank into the sofa in the family room and surveyed the peeling layers of torn wallpaper, each with a unique pattern hanging listlessly from the wall. She had planned to strip the wallpaper and repaint it but had discovered layer upon layer of older wallpaper beneath the surface sheets. And behind all that paper was a cement wall.

Vonnie angrily threw the wallpaper scraper against the wall and slumped back onto the sofa. "This is just not going to work. There must be over one hundred years of wallpaper on these damn walls."

The room was a mess: furniture covered with sheets was huddled in the center, and drop cloths lay spread out on the floor. A stepladder stood against the wall. A garbage bag filled with torn sheets of wallpaper, tools, paint, paint thinner, and other chemical solvents lay scattered across the floor.

Her DIY decorating efforts had all been flops. Either she hadn't purchased the correct materials or didn't have enough of something, or the project was more complicated than she had imagined. Finally she removed the goggles, tossed them onto the sofa, and headed to the kitchen to prepare lunch.

She could have asked Hadwin to assign a crew for the redecorating tasks, but after their last conversation, he had stormed out upset because he didn't think she cared about what was happening on the plantation, and she hadn't told him she intended to sell the property before placing it on the market. So now she was avoiding him.

While eating a vegetable omelet at the kitchen counter, her thoughts wandered to Dominic. It had been two weeks since their erotic encounter on the trip from Belize City. He had promised to call and schedule an actual date, but she was still waiting.

Her initial calls to his cell phone went straight to voicemail. So finally, she called his office. His secretary was polite and professional, and she left a message. But after the third time, she was too embarrassed to call the office again.

The night on the beach kept cycling through her mind. Sexual intimacy with a man like Dominic was a new, exhilarating experience. Not since the early days of her relationship with Russ had she experienced such intense sexual desire.

* * *

Russell McCormick, a musician and singer, had entered Vonnie's life during her thirtieth birthday party. The party was at a local club, and she and her girlfriends had a reserved table in front of the stage. Russ's band was the featured entertainment, and all the women in the club screamed and swooned with delight at the handsome face, golden-brown skin, silky voice, and sexy moves.

The earth stood still when he came to her table, kissed her hand, went down on one knee, and sang a love song. After the party he asked her out, and three months later, they moved in together into an old, three-story building that housed Vonnie's Books, Coffee, and Wine. The bookstore, the coffee shop, and the wine store occupied the first floor, while the upper floors were her living spaces.

As Russ's career soared in the music industry, requests poured in from top jazz, rock, and soul performers for him to sing and play on their albums and accompany them on tours. He was living his dream. He was addicted to the adoring crowds and the fame and money. Even though he constantly expressed his love for her, music was his first love; everything and everyone else would always be secondary. And it wasn't long before Vonnie realized that the rumors about rock stars and groupies and their antics on the road were true.

Though they infrequently discussed marriage, it never became a priority. Russ didn't see the need to follow tradition. A marriage license was just a piece of paper; their commitment and love for one another were all that mattered. Vonnie, however, saw marriage as an official and legal representation of a couple's commitment to each other, but she also considered herself a realist.

Russ was rarely home for weekends or on holidays. And she realized if she had children, he wouldn't be there for soccer games, dance recitals, or school plays. So why get married only to assume the responsibilities of a single parent? She had two options: Option One meant selecting a man from the endless parade of eligible bachelors her mother invited to dinner. She could marry one of them, drive a Volvo station wagon, have two kids, a dog, and a second home on a lake. Or, if she selected Option Two, she could follow her heart and accept Russ for who he was, which would mean foregoing a traditional marriage and a family. Vonnie never gave Option One serious consideration. She wanted Russ, flaws and all.

She continued running her business in Raleigh, while Russ came home between gigs and for vacations. There were long, expensive phone calls and gifts from faraway places when he was away for extended periods. And when he was home, what happened on the road stayed on the road; he never allowed it to infiltrate their personal lives. Their relationship was respectful, loving, and passionate.

Vonnie traveled with him for many of his most significant events. She was there in Modena, Italy, when Barry White and Luciano Pavarotti took the stage; in Japan, with Michael Jackson when he crushed Tokyo; in Hong Kong with Sting; and in Rio de Janeiro with the Rolling Stones. The years passed, and her T-shirts, scrapbooks, and mementos piled up.

A reunion tour with great jazz performers from the '80s and '90s started with a concert in LA. The itinerary included eight US cities and three foreign countries. En route to Zurich, tragedy struck: a blood clot traveled from Russ's leg to his lung. He was pronounced dead upon the plane landing. He was fifty-five, and they had lived together for twenty-five years.

* * *

Vonnie sighed heavily as she squeezed the dirty dishes into the already overstuffed sink. She retrieved a Prozac pill from her T-shirt pocket and swallowed it without water. Then she located the TV remote in the family room, curled up on the sofa, and started a Netflix series. Six hours later, as the plantation wound down from the day's activities, it was still ninety degrees outside—even at 7:00 p.m. Then she opened a bottle of wine, settled into a rocking chair on the back porch, and brooded until the sun went down.

Finally, with less than a glass of wine in the bottle, she retired for the night. Another long, lonely day had come to an end without a call from her real estate broker.

Determined not to spend another day in the house, the following afternoon, Vonnie found herself unpacking her swimsuit at an all-inclusive resort on Ambergris Caye, a small island northeast of mainland Belize. Tourism was down due to the pandemic, but many retired expats had made the Caye their home. Front Street's bars, restaurants, and shops were only a short distance away from the resort and easily accessible by a golf cart.

Vonnie quickly fell in with a spirited group of retirees. Their days were spent snorkeling in the pristine blue ocean, playing cards, or lounging by their private pools drinking cocktails. At night, they met for barhopping and dancing. Alcohol had become her new painkiller, and her hips and knees didn't complain.

On the third night, the group picked a small bar with pulsating Caribbean music and strong drinks, and she rarely left the dance floor. Everything was fine until she rose from the table to visit the ladies' room and staggered. The day's alcohol intake had clearly caught up with her; she was more than a little tipsy. A glance in the restroom mirror confirmed it was time to say goodnight to her new friends.

Reentering the barroom, she caught sight of Dominic leaning casually against the bar and looking straight at her with a sly, knowing smile. Dumbfounded, Vonnie struggled to gather her thoughts. But she smiled, straightened her posture, raised her chin, and walked toward him, determined not to sway.

Dominic reached for her arm, pulled her to him, and gently kissed her cheek.

"My, my, my, aren't you the life of the party?" he said, his wicked smile never leaving his face as he squeezed her hand.

Vonnie blushed. "I have my moments. I didn't see you come in. How long have you been here?"

"Long enough," he said with a laugh.

"So, how have you been?" She propped her right elbow on the bar for balance.

Still holding her hand, Dominic responded. "I apologize for not being in touch. This COVID thing is great for business, but it's ruining my personal life. I've had to step in and help make deliveries and am here to oversee a shipment." He put her hand to his lips and kissed it. "I haven't forgotten you. I received all your messages but didn't want to schedule a date and cancel because of work."

"Oh, don't worry about that. I understand you have a business to run," Vonnie said, "I'm just surprised to see you here." Her legs were wobbling.

"Let's get out of here. Where are you staying?" he asked, pulling her toward the door.

The raw sexuality emanating from him was palpable, and Vonnie absorbed it like a sponge. She had come to the Caye to forget him, but instead, the universe had delivered him to her in the most perfect of settings.

Dominic's arm slid around her waist as they walked to the golf cart, and she leaned her head on his shoulder. His body felt warm and strong, and she wanted to melt into it. A pleasant breeze blew across the water, and a crescent moon hung over the ocean. She couldn't believe her luck. Was this happening? It was all too perfect.

Not trusting she could keep her balance, Vonnie asked Dominic to drive the golf cart back to the resort. Every word and every move were an attempt to conceal her intoxication, but the jostling of the golf cart made it impossible to show any semblance of sobriety.

The door to the suite had barely shut before Dominic kissed her and she hungrily reciprocated. A bulging erection pressed hard against her flimsy shorts. This moment was all she had thought and dreamed about for the past two weeks. The room began to spin as he laid her on the bed, hastily pulled the T-shirt and bra over her head, and threw them across the room. He moved so fast that Vonnie felt like he was eating her alive. Then, as a swirling vortex engulfed her brain, Dominic roughly pulled down her shorts and panties. She tried to push him away, but her brain kept sloshing around in her skull.

The shorts were down to her ankles, and he wasn't stopping, thinking she was lost in the throes of passion. Vonnie tried to sit up and turn to the side, but before she could manage, her body convulsed, and she vomited. She frantically gasped for air as vomit spewed from her mouth like a volcano. Eventually, she managed to hang off the side of the bed and puked on the carpet.

In shock, Dominic jumped from the bed, ran to the bathroom, and returned with a wet towel. By then, Vonnie was on all fours on the floor in a pool of vomit, retching as drool ran down her chin. Eventually, she dropped to the floor and blacked out. Dominic stood for a long moment staring down at her, then he left the room.

* * *

"Silly, stupid bitch," Dominic snarled as he walked through the resort's manicured grounds to the service entrance. He had known she was drunk when he saw her on the dance floor and thought it would make it easier for him to do what he wanted with her, but the stupid bitch couldn't hold her liquor and now he had a mess to clean up.

He'd been on the Caye for three days, enjoying the insatiable sexual appetite of a widowed, forty-year-old, cocaine-addicted expat from Germany named Olivia. Bored and restless while Olivia was in an alcohol- and drug-induced stupor, he decided to walk to Front Street for some fresh air.

It was during his impromptu stop at the bar that he saw Vonnie on the dance floor.

During their trip from Belize City to her plantation, she had unknowingly confirmed everything he needed to know. She was naive, lonely, and hadn't been fucked in years. Just feeling her up made her so wet that she'd left a stain on the seat of his Mercedes.

He hadn't called her because he wanted her to stew, let her anticipation build. Vonnie was a big game fish, and she would be his trophy catch. The key to catching a trophy fish was to use strategy to reel them in.

Two sixteen- or seventeen-year-old boys, dressed in white shirts and black pants, were hanging out on the loading dock beside the resort's service entrance. One boy stood while the other sat on an overturned crate and talked while smoking cigarettes. Dominic approached them, reached into his pocket, and peeled off two bills. He wanted them to see the money. "Would you gentlemen like to make a quick hundred dollars?" he asked as he got closer.

Their eyes brightened at the sight of the money, but suspicion quickly crossed their faces. "To do what?" the one standing asked.

"Nothing illegal," Dominic said with a snicker. "I need someone to clean a room."

"Why don't you call the front desk?" the boy sitting on the crate asked, blowing smoke and flicking the ashes.

Dominic leveled a cold gaze at the boy. "It's confidential. I don't want any publicity. But as I said, it's nothing illegal."

When Dominic and the boys entered Vonnie's room, their eyes bulged, and disbelief showed on their faces. The first boy gripped his head with both hands, and the second boy's mouth dropped open.

"Don't worry; she's just drunk. "Dominic said, standing over Vonnie, who was still unconscious, unclothed, and sprawled on the floor in the puddle of puke.

Terrified, the first boy eased back toward the door.

"Who is she?" the second boy asked, staring at Vonnie.

"That's none of your business," Dominic growled. "And I'd better not hear a single peep about this. AM I CLEAR?"

"We... we only have a fifteen-minute break. If we aren't back on time, we might get fired," the first boy said in a shaky voice, reaching for the door handle.

Dominic reached into his pocket, peeled off more bills, and tossed them on the bed. "Okay, I'll make it worth your while, but remember what I said. You," he barked at the boy by the door, "go get clean linen and something to clean up this mess."

The second boy was transfixed. Dominic pushed him roughly on the shoulder. "Go start the shower," he commanded.

* * *

The following morning, Vonnie awoke with a hangover and humiliation so severe she never wanted to get out of bed or show her face again. On the nightstand was a bottle of Tylenol, a tall bottle of water, and a note that said, "I'll be in touch... D." There was a smiley face on the bottom. Slowly she raised herself on her elbows, gulped down four Tylenol and most of the water, then lay back and covered her face with her arm. She moaned, recalling the previous night.

The rancid odor of her breath made her reluctantly pull herself out of bed and sluggishly walk to the bathroom to brush her teeth. The room was neat; a plastic laundry bag with her soiled clothes lay on the credenza. Even the carpet was clean; there were no traces of the previous night's horror.

The bright lights in the bathroom were unforgiving, and the vanity mirror revealed red-rimmed, bloodshot eyes framed by dark circles and puffy bags. Her dry, matted gray hair looked as if she'd stuck her finger in an electrical socket.

The lingering scent of perfumed body wash on her skin and hair filled her nostrils, and she shuddered at the thought of Dominic struggling to clean her up while she was passed out dead drunk.

After brushing her teeth, Vonnie sank heavily onto the bed and called the front desk to extend her stay. She was too sick to catch the ferry back to the mainland; the thought of the rolling waves and the rocking boat made her nauseous.

The perfect opportunity had slipped through her fingers. Dominic was gone again, and she had no idea when she'd see him. Ashamed, sad, and physically spent, she curled up and cried.

# 14

# CHANCE

Chance was conscious but disoriented, unsure how long he'd been in captivity. On the day of his abduction, his assailants had overpowered him in his own driveway and injected him with a sedative. Since then, he'd received two more injections. The drugs left him lethargic and confused, with no concept of time or what was happening to or around him.

The hood over his head had been removed, but he was still restrained; handcuffs connected to a waist belt, linked by a chain to ankle cuffs. He'd been transferred three times, each time to different handlers in different vehicles.

It was midmorning, and two Mexican men occupied the driver and passenger seats. Like all his previous handlers, they spoke to him in English but conversed freely among themselves in Spanish, mistakenly assuming he did not understand the language. He eavesdropped, learning that another transfer was imminent and that the men were uneasy.

Chance lay on a grimy mattress in the back of yet another cargo van; he was dirty and sweaty. His rank body odor penetrated his nose, and every part of his body itched. A metal grate separated him from the guards. The van's floor was dusty and cluttered with discarded food containers, empty beer and water bottles, and soda cans. The air conditioner didn't work, so the interior of the cargo hold was sweltering hot. Air flowing through the windows did little to decrease the temperature.

For the past two days, they had been driving through a barren desert. It was a desolate landscape punctuated with cacti, tumbleweeds, and dusty hills. The driver occasionally stopped at small, ramshackle stores for gas and food supplies. During these stops, Chance was allowed out for brief stretches. And then he read everything within his line of sight; he concluded they were somewhere in Mexico. At some point, amid bouts of unconsciousness, they had smuggled him across the US—Mexico border.

The ride suddenly became bumpy; trash and bottles slid across the floor, hitting the sides. Finally, the van stopped. The guards let him out and made him sit on the ground. The glaring sun made the air outside just as hot as the air inside the van.

At first, Chance thought they had parked beside a deserted road in the middle of nowhere. Nothing but more sand, cacti, and tumbleweeds surrounded them in every direction. Then he heard one of the guards say something about a plane. He instantly knew that what he was looking at wasn't a road but a makeshift landing strip in the middle of the desert.

Both guards shaded their eyes with their hands and turned in circles, searching the sky. Then suddenly, the van driver pointed to a dot in the clear sky. The men hurriedly reached behind their seats in the van and pulled out automatic rifles. It was time for the transfer.

As the plane approached the landing strip, Chance scrambled to stand. He watched in awe as the plane glided down, as light as a feather, and taxied to a stop. It was a sleek, gleaming Gulfstream G550 jet and a sight to behold. He and his captors stood captivated while, as if in slow motion, the plane's door gently touched down on the desert floor. Even in his deplorable situation, it was one of the sexiest sights he'd ever seen.

His escorts, each flanking him with automatic rifles slung over their shoulders, quickly snapped out of their trance and began pulling him toward the plane. A poised female flight attendant stood at the entryway and requested in Spanish that the men remove Chance's restraints. Once the guards removed the cuffs, she stepped aside, allowed Chance to board, and escorted him through the luxurious cabin area to a seat in the club section. After days in the hot, suffocating van, the air-conditioned interior caught him off guard. It felt like he had walked into a freezer; his skin tingled as he fumbled with his seat belt.

The club section featured two seats facing each other with a wide, polished table between them. On the left side of the aisle was a long sofa separated by an arm rest. Already seated were two men: one, who sat on the sofa across the aisle from Chance, looked like a bodybuilder with biceps the size of bowling balls. He was dressed in black; sunglasses perched on top of his head. He gazed suspiciously at Chance. Across the table, a distinguished-looking gentleman typed on a laptop. Once Chance was seated, he addressed Chance with a stoic expression.

"Mr. Moore, I am Aapo Vasquez," the unsmiling man explained in a businesslike tone. "Once the plane hits cruising altitude, you may shower. You'll also find a change of clothing. Once refreshed, we'll have lunch and talk."

Chance looked out of the window. His two Mexican guards stood beside the van, watching the plane take off. The plush leather seat engulfed his tired, aching body as the jet rocketed toward the clouds.

The bathroom was roomy with ultramodern fixtures. Recessed lighting shone on sleek white walls and floors. A granite-topped vanity with a stainless-steel sink sat under vertical light panels that framed the mirror. Drawers beneath held an assortment of designer toiletries and grooming items.

The bathroom also featured a linen closet stocked with plush white towels and a wardrobe with a white terry cloth robe with matching slippers, a pair of beige slacks and light-blue golf shirt covered with dry-cleaning plastic, a set of underwear, and a pair of leather loafers.

The shower's hot water felt like a gift from God. As he bathed, his thoughts returned to Aapo's brief introduction. Aapo's visual profile was of a rich hedge-fund manager or Wall Street banker. But Chance's instinct told him that regardless of his appearance, a dangerous man lurked beneath the controlled demeanor. He and Mack had hacked accounts and stolen millions from some of the most unscrupulous and corrupt people imaginable, so it was easy to assume this Aapo person was one of them. Finally feeling clean, Chance reluctantly stepped out of the shower onto a spongy shower mat and began to towel off.

*So, this is the man responsible for kidnapping and smuggling me across the US border into Mexico. And now I'm on a jet headed to*

*God knows where. Why the intrigue? If this were about him wanting his money back, why take me out of the country? He could have taken it in California. And what about Mack? Where is he?*

Chance's mind drifted to his childhood, growing up in Louisiana and hunting in the murky, decaying swamps with his grandfather. At all times, a person had to be aware of his surroundings—what was over his head, where he put his hands, and where he placed each foot—because nature had perfectly camouflaged the most venomous animals. Aapo might appear calm and sophisticated, but his eyes were cold and lifeless. The pupils weren't vertical, but there could be no doubt he was as deadly as any snake in the swamp.

Disheartened, Chance stood in front of the vanity mirror, a towel wrapped around his waist and white terry cloth slippers on his feet. The shaving foam's woody aroma filled the air as the razor glided effortlessly through the itchy stubble on his face. It had been a little over two months since their final hack on Christmas Day, and he hadn't seen nor heard from Mack since.

Chance rinsed the razor's blade and began shaving under his chin.

*Mack secretly changed the code because he knew I would disagree with the changes. And in his haste to finish before I awoke, he did a sloppy job sweeping up the breadcrumbs. The multiple layers of encryption and security failed to protect us from detection. And, somehow, this man was able to track us down.*

Wiping his face with a plush towel, he caught his reflection in the mirror and sighed deeply as he reached for the clothes hanging in the closet. The silky fabric of the blue golf shirt felt good against his skin as he tucked it into the slacks. He tossed the towels, robe, and slippers in a laundry hamper attached to the wall and the old, filthy clothes in the trash can.

Once back in his seat, the flight attendant served a lunch of Porterhouse steak, grilled asparagus, mashed potatoes with mushroom gravy, salad, and a chocolate mousse. The sight and aroma of the food made his mouth water. Across the aisle, the bodyguard silently scrolled through his phone.

Aapo cut into his steak without delay. "Mr. Moore, I have conclusive evidence that you've hacked my bank account and stolen money from me, and I want it returned. We've already spoken to your accomplice, Mr. Mack Owens, who confessed to the theft. But unfortunately, he was unable to repay the debt before succumbing to his injuries and dying from, how shall I say it, overzealous interrogation techniques."

Chance blinked multiple times, unable to conceal his shock. "What did you say? Mack is dead?"

"Yes. It was an unfortunate accident," Aapo replied, spearing a forkful of salad. "Sometimes, my men get overly excited and become too forceful. It wasn't supposed to happen. I wanted him alive for obvious reasons. They weren't supposed to kill him."

The knife and fork fell from Chance's grasp, clattering onto his plate. He slumped in his seat, gazing out the window, struggling to conceal his rising emotions. Below the plane, an endless carpet of clouds met his eyes; his mind raced.

Aapo dabbed his mouth with a napkin. "Fortunately for me, Mr. Owens told us about you before he died, so it's your responsibility to settle the debt. Of course, I've included interest and other related costs."

Despondent, Chance continued staring out of the window while he thought about Mack. The food on his plate remained untouched.

Aapo looked slightly amused. "I must say, Mr. Moore, I'm impressed by your sense of control. The average person in your situation would have panicked by now. Don't you have comments or questions?" he asked.

Chance fixed a glacial stare at Aapo. "It's obvious that if I don't give you what you want, you'll kill me too. But I don't understand why you smuggled me out of the US. You could have arranged for me to return the money in California. Where are you taking me?"

Aapo leaned forward, resting his elbows on the tray table and interlocking his fingers. "You see, Mr. Moore, your actions with Mr. Owens have given me an idea. I've been seeking new income streams, and your hacking skills can benefit me. The US has too many regulations and law enforcement agencies. So, I'm relocating you to a place where none of that will be an issue."

"Are you saying you want me to hack bank accounts and steal money for you?" Chance asked in disbelief.

"Yes, that's exactly what I want you to do after you repay what you stole from me. You're going to work exclusively for me. "Aapo responded, looking pleased with himself.

"You said you want me to WORK for you?" Chance asked. "For how long, and what do I get out of the deal?"

Aapo's demeanor instantly changed. His eyes became like daggers and his nostrils flared. His voice turned low and threatening as he leaned in closer. "You stole from me. No one, and I mean no one, steals from the Vasquez family and lives. You should be dead, but I need that money. Consider yourself fortunate even to be breathing. I'll tell you what you get you get to live, Mr. Moore. You get to live."

Sensing the rising tension, the bodyguard set his phone aside and sat up straighter.

Suppressing his urge to lunge across the aisle and grab Aapo by the throat, Chance turned and looked out the window.

The flight attendant quickly cleared the lunch trays as the plane began its descent. Beneath them, as the clouds dissipated, a canopy of green appeared. The jet was touching down on another remote, rural airstrip. But instead of being surrounded by a desolate desert, there were palm trees and dense, green vegetation. A black Mercedes S-Class sedan and a gray Toyota double-cab pickup were waiting beside the airstrip.

"Welcome to Guatemala, Mr. Moore," Aapo exclaimed, standing and collecting his belongings. "The men in the pickup will take you to your temporary accommodations. You'll receive further instructions soon." As he headed for the exit door, he abruptly tossed a brown manilla envelope in Chance's lap. "I have no patience for fools, Mr. Moore, and I expect nothing less than your full compliance. If for any reason you become uncooperative, I promise you there will be dire consequences."

Chance was in no hurry to move. He watched through the window as Aapo and his bodyguard strode toward the waiting

Mercedes. He slowly tore open the envelope, and his eyes went wide with shock as he saw the contents. Inside, there were four color photos of Mack's mutilated body. He flung the envelope and pictures to the floor and sat shaking with fear.

Finally, with no other option, on wobbly legs, he exited the plane.

When Chance stepped outside of the jet, an unexpected wave of hot air and humidity engulfed him; beads of sweat immediately formed on his brow. Two men with unsympathetic expressions waited beside the pickup truck. Surprisingly, neither of them tried to handcuff him. He was seated beside the driver, and the other man sat behind him in the back seat. Both men wore sidearms, and an automatic rifle rested on the back seat.

The pickup driver left the landing strip and drove down what appeared to be a hidden trail. The ground was soggy, and the truck bumped along, rocking and swaying as the driver navigated through and around deep mudholes. Tree limbs and foliage slapped against the front windshield.

After about five miles, the trail ended, and the driver turned onto a dry dirt road behind a large truck filled with avocados. The pickup crawled along, surrounded by a crowd of slow-moving vehicles, donkey carts loaded with fruits and vegetables, and people walking with large baskets of produce and other goods balanced on their heads or strapped to their backs.

Shanty houses, both multi-level and single level, clung haphazardly to the hillsides and along the sides of the road. Open-air markets with vendors selling household items, street food, and animals were scattered throughout. Salsa and mariachi music blared from unseen speakers as the truck moved through the street.

The pickup driver cursed, shouted, and motioned furiously with his left arm out of the driver's side window while honking the horn at anyone impeding his progress. Eventually, the truck turned down a side road, and the driver stopped at a ten-foot chain-link fence topped with razor wire. A man emerged from a tiny guardhouse and waved to the driver, and an automated gate slid back, allowing the truck to enter a run-down, multi-use warehouse complex.

Rusted metal barrels, discarded automotive and manufacturing equipment, and trash were everywhere. As they moved through the complex, Chance counted five buildings of various sizes. The most prominent building had noticeable plumes of white smoke emanating from small metal chimneys. He assumed it was the source of the chemical stench in the air.

Men unloaded large plastic barrels from a truck onto a loading dock, and a group of men and women exited another building and entered a van. Then there was a decrepit motor pool, with men in dirty, oily clothes, an assortment of damaged vehicles, car lifts, and stacks of old tires.

The driver stopped in front of an old single-story cinder block building. The interior was stiflingly hot, and the room smelled of greasy food, cigarette smoke, and sweat from unwashed bodies. Multiple ceiling fans lazily circulated the fetid air around the room, doing little to cool the space.

On the right side was a small, glass-enclosed room that appeared to be an office. In the center of the room, several men sat at three rectangular tables, engaged in conversation. Two men lounged on a dirty sofa watching a soccer game on a flat-screen TV positioned high on the left wall. At the back of the room were three closed doors. On the first door was the word ' toilet' and on the second was a sign for ' storage.' There was no sign on the third door.

All conversation abruptly ceased, and heads turned toward the three men standing in the doorway. A short, overweight man hurriedly left the office smiling while nervously wiping his sweaty face with a large green bandanna, which he quickly stuffed in his pocket. A holstered pistol hung low under a protruding belly.

The driver assumed a commanding stance and slowly surveyed the room with a menacing scowl. Immediately, the men at the tables and those watching TV stopped what they were doing and hurried outside.

"Senor Manuel," the sweating man said, grinning broadly while nervously folding and unfolding his hands. "I have been waiting for you; all arrangements are in place," he conveyed in Spanish. The bandanna reappeared, and he vigorously wiped his face and neck.

As with the Mexican guards, Chance's Guatemalan guards spoke to him in English but spoke to each other in a Spanish dialect slightly different from the one used by the Mexicans. It was challenging to understand everything, but he managed to piece together most of the discussion.

The driver cast a threatening glance at the sweating man. Chance was to remain under surveillance 24/7 and was not to leave the compound except under strict orders from the captain.

If he became unruly, he could be restrained but not harmed; some-one would come for him in a few days.

"Yes, senor, I understand," the man replied, now sweating even more profusely; he gave up on returning the bandanna to his pocket. "I will oversee it myself. I will guard him well. Please do not worry; you can count on me."

The pickup driver addressed Chance in English. "This is Jorge; he's your caretaker. If you need anything, talk to him. Someone will contact you with further instructions." Then, he and the second guard turned and left the building.

As soon as the guards departed, Jorge nervously exhaled as if the air were slowly escaping from a balloon. A hateful scowl covered his face as he watched the pickup truck drive away. "Fuckers," he snarled, spitting on the floor. Then he motioned with his head for Chance to follow him.

Jorge led Chance to the room without a sign on the door. The space measured about ten feet by fifteen feet and had peeling gray paint. A single light bulb with a dangling string hung from the ceiling. Against the wall stood a twin-size bed, and an oscillating table fan sat on a three-legged wooden stool at the foot of the bed.

Daylight struggled to filter through a dirty window covered by a series of rectangular panes; at the base of the window was a small hand crank to open and close the panes. A threadbare towel hung on a nail on the back of the door. The little room was like an oven.

Chance reached over, turned on the fan, then cranked open the window. "So, what do I do about food and something to drink? I'm starving."

An expression of extreme irritation crossed Jorge's face. Finally, he responded in English, "I'll have someone bring it to you." He walked out of the room, and to Chance's surprise, left the door open.

Exhausted from the strain of the day's events, Chance undressed down to his underwear, lay on the bed, and stared at the ugly water spots on the ceiling.

* * *

Chance had been in Guatemala at the warehouse compound for almost two weeks, and there was still no word from Aapo about transferring him to a new location. There was little to do except eavesdrop on conversations, observe the activities around him, and watch TV.

Frustrated and bored, he spent the long, hot, dull days rotating between sitting on an old truck seat propped up against the outside wall of the office building beside discarded automotive parts and trash cans, sitting inside in the lounge area, or lying in his tiny room brooding over his predicament. The TV news reports about the increasing death toll from the spread of the COVID-19 virus were alarming, and he kept his distance from everyone; the last thing he needed was to get sick.

He estimated that at least a hundred people occupied the compound within a sixteen-hour day and were separated into two categories: In category one were the free workers who arrived at dawn, driving pickups and cars or riding motorcycles, and they all carried sidearms.

Then, approximately one hour later, ten- and twelve-passenger vans rolled in carrying members of the second category, the zombies. The zombies were the saddest and most unhealthy-looking people Chance had ever seen. They emerged from the vans with blank, lifeless faces, drooping heads and shoulders, wearing colorless, oversized clothes that hung from their thin, emaciated bodies. They filed into the buildings and worked all day until the vans finally took them away after dark. Throughout the day, zombies rolled blue barrels, metal drums, and pallets stacked with large sacks into the warehouse. Then, at the other end of the loading dock, another group brought out large boxes of neatly wrapped brown packages in cellophane and loaded them into trucks, and a free man drove the truck away. Chance assumed the chemical stench wafting from the metal chimneys was a byproduct of illegal drug production, and the zombies were the people forced to perform the work.

By eavesdropping on conversations, watching the local TV news, and secretly reading anything he could find, Chance surmised that the warehouse compound was near the city of Puerto Maria. But he didn't know the exact location of Puerto Maria in Guatemala.

He could see a large wall map taped to Jorge's office wall from the lounge area, but if Jorge wasn't in the office, free workers would be in the lounge area throughout the day, making it impossible to enter the office without being seen. Then finally one afternoon, the perfect opportunity presented itself.

Chance was sitting in the lounge area watching TV, and Jorge was in his office, with his feet propped up on his desk, talking on the phone. Two free workers sat on the dirty sofa, facing the TV. The first man, head down, scrolled through his phone while the second man angrily cursed at the soccer match on TV.

An excited and highly animated third man rushed into the room and ran to Jorge's office. There was an equipment failure in the large warehouse. Jorge immediately ended his call and yelled to the men on the sofa, and the four men rushed out of the door, leaving Chance alone in the room.

He quickly entered Jorge's office and went straight to the wall map. The map was old; circles and lines drawn in ink and different-colored highlighters covered pertinent details, but within a few minutes, he located Puerto Maria. And, to his surprise, to the right of Puerto Maria, a dotted vertical line indicated the Guatemala—Belize border. Chance used the map's scale and a finger to estimate the distance and was astonished to discover the city was less than one hundred miles from the Belize border. Intensely absorbed in the map's details, he failed to notice Jorge reenter the building.

"What are you doing in here?" Jorge shouted, wiping the sweat trickling down the sides of his temples with a blue bandanna.

Chance thought it essential to exude confidence and not display signs of fear or weakness. He instantly looked annoyed at being interrupted.

"Don't yell at me; I'm not one of your minions. I didn't touch anything; I was bored, that's all."

Blustering, Jorge puffed out his chest; the buttons on his shirt strained to stay closed over his large belly. He extended his arm with his finger pointed toward the door. "There's nothing on that map that concerns you. So, get out of my office, and don't let me catch you in here again."

Chance rolled his eyes toward the ceiling, then swaggered to the door. In his stifling little room, he removed his shirt and shoes, stretched out on the bed, and stared at the ceiling's dingy water spots. Thoughts of escape consumed him, and different scenarios frequently bounced around in his mind. But the twenty-four-hour guards, free workers with sidearms, and the ten-foot chain-link fence topped with razor wire would quickly turn any attempt at escape into a futile effort.

The map displayed a dense rainforest that stretched beyond Puerto Maria, across the border, and deep into Belizean territory. And there was also a paved road that extended all the way to the Guatemalan—Belize border crossing. Belize was an American and European retirement and vacation haven. If he could somehow escape and make it across the border into Belize, someone would help him.

# 15

# ANA

Ana was at the kitchen sink finishing the dinner dishes when she glanced over at Hadwin sitting at the kitchen table, hunched over his laptop. Each evening, he appeared even more exhausted and drained than the day before.

Three years ago, he began shaving his head, too vain for male-pattern baldness or gray hair. Nevertheless, she liked the look and thought it made him appear younger. He was six feet eight inches tall, big but not obese, and the color of brown sugar. Ana had known at ten years old that she wanted to marry him. Hadwin was everything she had ever wanted: lover, husband, and father of her children.

Hadwin yawned widely, rotated his neck and shoulders, and shut down the laptop. Ana moved behind him and began massaging his shoulders.

"Hmmm, that feels so good," he mumbled, leaning against the back of the chair, relaxing as Ana's strong fingers kneaded the tight muscles.

She made circles with her thumbs, pressing deep into the back of his neck along the base of his skull. "I'm ordering medical supplies I can't get through the government's medical system. They're short on everything, and there are limits on the amount of Personal Protective Equipment I can order. So, I want to let you know that I need some money."

"How much?" he asked, eyes closed, his upper body relaxing as Ana's hands returned to his shoulder blades.

"I don't know yet; I'm working on the list."

"God, don't stop; that feels so good. Is the plantation included in this order, or is it only to cover the people in your region?"

"I'm ordering for both groups. The government usually covers regional health expenses, but the red tape is bogging down the process, and my team needs supplies now. I'll figure out a way to get reimbursed."

Hadwin's head bowed, and his chin touched his chest. Ana's thumbs were working the back of his neck and the base of his skull again.

"Ana, I admire what you're trying to do, but based on what I've seen on the news, we need to prepare for the long haul with this COVID thing. I hate to say it, but eventually, we'll have to consider self-preservation. The folks on this plantation are our responsibility, and they come first. You know I'll give you whatever you want, but it's the government's responsibility to figure this out, not you."

She kissed the top of his bald head, patted his arm, and smiled. "Can you get off early tomorrow? I want some time with you; it's been a while, and my body needs attention."

"Sounds good to me; I could use the stress relief," he said, rotating his neck.

Ana slid into the chair opposite him. Her tone became more serious. "There's gossip circulating about Vonnie and Dominic. If the stories are even close to being true, and I think they are, then Vonnie is in trouble and too naive to realize it. Dominic doesn't want Vonnie; he wants her money. And anyone who can read knows she's selling the plantation. It's advertised online and in print, so Dominic knows the asking price. If he has his hooks in her when this place sells, he'll charm her out of everything she has." She leaned forward and crossed her arms on the table.

"I warned her about him the day she fell, and you brought her to the clinic. But I don't think she took me seriously. And you know how he works his magic on women," she said, looking down and shaking her head. "If Vonnie becomes entangled in a relationship with that man, it could affect us. He's a gangster, and we don't need someone like him hanging around. It's too dangerous."

"I've heard it too," Hadwin said, moving from the table to his well-worn recliner. "I thought it was odd then, but now I know why Dominic made that delivery to the plantation instead of sending one of his truck drivers. He was checking her out, and she was giggling like a schoolgirl. But Vonnie's a grown woman with a mind of her own. I don't think there's much we can do if she's intent on being with him." He picked up the TV remote and pushed the lever on the recliner to elevate his feet.

Ana became agitated. "We can't just stand by and do nothing; he'll ruin her. Vonnie's not used to men like him. Russ was the only man she ever loved, and they were together until five years ago, and then her parents died. She hasn't had time to recover fully; she's not thinking clearly."

Hadwin kept flipping through the channels. "Well, I don't think we'll have to worry about her selling anytime soon. The whole world shut down because of the pandemic. And I can't imagine any food conglomerate buying a two-thousand-acre Cavendish banana plantation with trees infected with Panama Disease. And she still hasn't scheduled a meeting to discuss the details of the sale or what she intends to do about the residents.

What's the latest on COVID in the surrounding area? What do you see in the villages?" he asked, staring at the TV.

Ana moved into the living room, plopped on the sofa, and kicked off her shoes. "Belize City is bad; the hospitals are overflowing. People who lived in the city and lost their jobs moved back to the villages to stay with relatives. And they're bringing the virus with them. I lost three elderly patients in Big Falls this week, and two in Barranco are showing symptoms."

Her brow furrowed. She leaned over, placed her elbows on her knees, and turned to her husband. "Have you seen Vonnie lately? I've been so busy that I haven't been able to spend time with her, but I caught a glimpse of her yesterday, and she looks like the Walking Dead."

"I know," Hadwin said, still focused on switching from one channel to another. "She's been like that since she returned from Ambergris Caye. She insisted on redecorating the house, but I don't know how it's going. It's her project, so I'm staying out of it. She hasn't asked for help, and I have enough to do. But one of the guys did tell me that someone saw Vonnie with Dominic while she was on the Caye. I think Vonnie has forgotten how small Belize is. Everybody knows who she is, and word spreads fast."

"Well, I'm going to talk to her," Ana said with conviction. "It's obvious that she's depressed. And Dominic probably has something to do with it. He has women in every corner of this country; why can't he leave her alone?"

Hadwin stopped switching channels and sternly looked at Ana. "He's not going to leave her alone," he responded. "Vonnie's an easy mark. She's wealthy, a lonely, older woman with no man. She owns one of the most profitable fruit plantations in the entire country, and she stands to make millions when she sells it.

We all know he's crooked, but if Vonnie doesn't listen to you, she won't listen to anybody. Dominic can wine, dine, and charm her for as long as necessary. And he has no competition for her affection." He pushed the lever to lower his feet.

"I've had enough for one night. I'm going to bed." He stood, turned off the TV, and tossed the remote onto the recliner. "I'll get off at three tomorrow; is that good for you?" he asked, yawning, with his hands on his hips and bending backward.

"I prefer noon. I don't want to rush. We have some catching up to do" Ana said with a racy smile.

Hadwin raised his eyebrows in surprise. "I get to eat you for lunch—how can I say no?" He winked at her and walked down the hall toward their bedroom.

Ana sighed heavily and slumped onto the sofa. The house was quiet except for the ticking of the large, ornamental wall clock hanging over the TV. Her eyes scanned the room and stopped on a picture taken in the sixties of her, Hadwin, and Vonnie. Big Afros framed their grinning faces; they were in swimsuits, knee-deep in the ocean, arms linked together. They were all young, skinny, and happy.

Another picture taken at her and Hadwin's wedding was on a side table. Hadwin was handsome in his tuxedo; she was in her wedding gown, holding a bouquet of yellow and white roses, and Vonnie, her maid of honor, was dressed in a yellow gown.

Since birth, their lives had been intertwined and woven into the quilt of the Hollister Plantation. But if Dominic got his clutches on Vonnie, that quilt would be ripped to shreds. She and Hadwin would never accept someone like Dominic as part of their lives.

The following morning, Ana placed several items in an attractive gift basket and walked up the hill to the back door of The Big House. She knocked and rang the bell several times and was about to leave when Vonnie appeared in an old, faded nightgown and tattered robe, groggy and unkempt, the gray hair stiff, dry, and matted to her head. From the odor that surrounded Vonnie like a cloud, Ana surmised she had been drinking heavily and hadn't bathed.

Smiling cheerfully, she lightly pushed past Vonnie and entered the kitchen; it was a mess. There were dirty dishes stacked haphazardly in the sink; half-empty food containers littered the countertop; the floor was dirty and sticky; and two overstuffed trash bags leaned against an overflowing trash can.

From the kitchen, she could see into the family room. There were clothes, papers, and household items strewn around the room. The furniture was huddled in the middle of the room and covered with sheets. Drop cloths, paint cans, tools, a ladder, and decorating materials were scattered on the floor.

*Now I see why Vonnie hasn't requested the usual household staff to clean or Hadwin to send someone to help with the redecorating. She doesn't want anyone to see how she's living up here. One maid or handyman with loose lips and the rumor would spread like wildfire.*

Vonnie looked embarrassed, sheepishly pulled her robe tight, and followed Ana into the kitchen. She sat at the counter, pushed dirty dishes to the side, and folded her arms across her chest.

"What's up? What's going on? What brings you up here this early in the morning?" she asked, covering a yawn with her hand.

"It's not early; it's ten thirty," Ana responded. "I thought I'd bring you some goodies and see what I could do to help you. I'm worried about you." She searched for the kettle amid the disarray, gave up, and put a small pot of water to boil. She rinsed out a dirty cup and began preparing one of the teas from her basket.

Vonnie placed an elbow on the counter and rested her chin on her palm. "I'm fine, just a little tired, but I'll be okay. I think I have a bug or something."

Ana sprinkled herbs in the cup, poured hot water over them, and placed a saucer on top. "I'm sure you'll be okay, but you look like hell right now, and it looks like somebody dropped a bomb in here."

"I know. I know. I haven't been feeling well," Vonnie whined. "The house isn't going anywhere, and neither am I. So, there's no rush; I'll get to it."

"Well, I've put together a few things to help you get back on your feet. Promise me you'll eat and drink everything in the basket. "Ana said, placing the cup of tea in front of Vonnie.

"Okay, Ana," Vonnie said, looking suspiciously at the teacup. "What did you mix up? I know your little tricks, and I'm in no mood to have one of your secret potions make me turn backflips across the lawn," she said in jest.

"I promise you, it's only good stuff, and you'll love every bit of it," Ana said, smiling. "I'll be back tonight to check on you. In the meantime, take a shower and wash your hair. You stink." She laughed as she navigated the room to the door.

Later that night, Ana selected a bottle of wine and walked back up the hill to The Big House. She entered through the back door and first noticed the clean kitchen. Vonnie was sitting at the kitchen counter, eating a cookie from the gift basket and flipping through a home decorating magazine. She looked much neater.

"Well, you're looking and smelling better. How do you feel?" Ana asked, smiling.

A shy smile crossed Vonnie's face. "Better. Your secret potions are working—thank you."

"Glad to hear it," Ana said. She retrieved two wine glasses from the cabinet, made herself comfortable at the counter, popped the cork, and poured for them. They chatted about current events until Vonnie was well into her second glass of wine.

Ana took a deep breath and spoke slowly. "Vonnie, I know you have a thing for Dominic. You're a grown woman who can do what she wants, but I want to warn you to be very careful in your dealings with him. I know you're still recovering from your family's deaths, but please don't try to use Dominic as an escape to alleviate your pain. I don't know what he's telling you, but whatever it is, he's lying. He isn't the man he pretends to be. He's trouble, Vonnie, and you need to protect your reputation. People are talking about the two of you, and what they are saying isn't good."

Vonnie's mood switched in a flash. She sat the wine glass down on the counter with so much force the stem shattered. Wine sloshed out of the goblet, and she laid it on the countertop. It rocked and rolled, and the remaining wine trickled across the countertop and spilled onto the floor. Then she locked eyes with Ana.

Ana could see the unmistakable traces of a volcano about to explode.

Finally, Vonnie stood up, placed both hands on her hips, and leaned toward Ana. Her eyes blazed. She said in a low, steely voice, "What gives you the right to come here and tell me who I should or shouldn't be with? You don't know what Dominic and I do or don't do or how he makes me feel. That man has shown me nothing but kindness, courtesy, and respect. So, if I want to be with him, I will. And as far as the gossip goes, I don't give a damn what people say; this is my life, and I'm going to live it as I please."

Ana stood up. "Vonnie, getting angry at me won't change reality. Don't be so defensive; I'm trying to help you. Dominic isn't one of the local teenage boys you used to have flings with when you were sixteen and down here for summer vacation. He can ruin your life. Ask anybody; they'll tell you he's no good.

"Look, this pandemic can't last forever; if you keep your cool and stay focused, in another year or so, you can be in Egypt, riding a camel around the pyramids and sending us pictures. Dominic is a dog; he's scum. A louse-infested, greedy sewer rat, and he'll drag you into the sewer with him. You deserve better."

Enraged, Vonnie glowered at Ana and stepped closer. "Who are you to tell me what I deserve? As I said, it's my life, and I intend to live the precious few years I have left my way, on my terms, doing as I please. I'll decide if I want to catch lice from Dominic or anyone else. I don't need your advice or permission." She shouted. "Thanks for checking on me, but I think you'd better go. I'm sure *your man* is waiting for you."

Ana sighed, walked to the door, and turned back to face Vonnie with teary eyes. "I apologize for upsetting you, Vonnie, but I'm not taking back anything I've said because it's the truth. You've known me all your life, and you know I love you like a sister. I don't want to see you hurt or humiliated." Her voice was shaky. Then she turned and softly closed the door behind her.

Tears streamed down Ana's face as she walked home broken-hearted. She and Vonnie had never fought; they had always been the voice of reason in each other's lives. But earlier that morning she had seen the signs, and it was apparent that Vonnie was suffering from severe depression. And tonight, Vonnie's behavior confirmed that she was already entangled in Dominic's web.

Hadwin was sitting on the front porch in the dark, drinking a beer and watching Ana slowly make her way to the house. When she stepped onto the porch, he asked, "What's wrong?"

Ana bowed her head, covered her face with both hands, and wept loudly. Hadwin immediately jumped up and pulled her into his arms.

"She's not going to give him up." Ana said, sniffling into his chest.

# 16

# ANTONY

Guatemala's National Institute for Seismology staff members studied and monitored volcanic eruptions, earthquakes, and other geophysical events. Unfortunately due to the pandemic, the institute's director closed the office and asked everyone to work from home until further notice.

Antony Hernandez, a senior-level seismologist, was frustrated with his work-from-home arrangement. The Hernandez two-bedroom house was too small for a family of five, but the size had become even more of an issue since his wife, Maria, and his three boys were home all day due to closed schools.

To make matters worse two weeks prior, his elderly father-in-law died from the virus, and Maria insisted on moving her seventy-five year old mother in to live with them. The oldest boy now slept on the living room sofa while Maria's mother shared the bedroom with the two younger boys.

The three boys were rambunctious and rowdy during the best times, but being sequestered in the little house, on a rainy day, with no outlet for their pent-up energy made them almost unmanageable. The two older boys were pestering one another even though they were supposed to be in their room studying. Maria was in the kitchen cooking, moving between the sink, stove, and refrigerator while overseeing the schoolwork of their youngest son stationed at the kitchen table.

Antony sat on the bed in his and Maria's bedroom with his laptop and papers on top of two tray tables. The boys' constant bickering, Maria's frequent yelling from the kitchen chastising them for their unruly behavior, and his mother-in-law's daytime game show blaring from the TV in the living room made it impossible to concentrate even with the door closed.

He was also irritated with himself for forgetting to charge his cell phone; it was dead. Finally, after several failed attempts to access the internet, Antony decided to disregard the work-from-home mandate and go to the office. He hastily packed his laptop, grabbed his raincoat and umbrella, then peered around the kitchen door. "I'm going to the office. I can't get any work done here." he told Maria.

When she turned to look at him, he could tell the stress of their living situation was taking a toll on her—she had dark circles under her eyes. She waved a long-handled spoon in her right hand while pointing to something in their son's workbook with the other.

"Can you do that? Don't you have to ask permission?" she asked, tossing her head back to keep a strand of hair from falling into her eye.

"If anyone says anything, I'll ask for forgiveness, but I'm not asking for permission. The internet is down again, and I have too much work." With that, he left the house and walked toward the bus stop. He was relieved to be outside.

Before the COVID-19 shutdown, the Guatemala City buses were reliable, but now due to the lack of workers in the city, the buses came less frequently. No one else was waiting at the bus stop, so after fifteen minutes of standing in the pouring rain, Antony began walking the eight blocks to his office. It felt good to get out of the stifling house, move and breathe fresh air, even if it meant getting drenched.

As he plodded through the city's streets, he became increasingly uncomfortable the closer he got to his office. It was almost 9:00 a.m, and the downtown area—usually bustling with activity, cars honking, and people walking briskly along the sidewalks—was practically a ghost town. There was no traffic, no people, and no open stores. Standing at an intersection that should have been teeming with pedestrians, he felt like he was in a scene from a science-fiction movie.

He quickened his pace.

Reaching the office and discovering he was the only one there was a relief. Stripping off his raincoat, he went straight to the breakroom to make a pot of coffee.

Antony strolled to his desk with the coffee in hand, docked his laptop, and plugged in his phone. He took the first sips of the warm coffee as a bank of four monitors came to life. Then he leaned in close, scanning the colorful displays as his brain began processing the data and indicators on the screens.

A few minutes later, his phone lit up and began vibrating on the desk. As he scrolled through the long list of dire text messages, he lowered the coffee mug and slowly sank into his chair. A worried expression appeared on his face as he leaned closer to the screens.

*Thank God my team had my back while I was off-line and sent warnings to the proper authorities; this is going to be big.*

At 11:30 the previous night, indicators that monitored the Caribbean and North American tectonic plates began displaying warning signs of movement in the fault lines that crisscrossed Guatemala.

The monitor on his left displayed four panels with individual feeds from the leading international seismology agencies. Three panels contained information from US organizations, and the fourth presented material from the UK. The data was consistent.

Next to his cubicle, on the wall, was a large, brightly colored poster of Cizin, the wicked Mayan god of earthquakes, volcanoes, and death. Mayan myth described Cizin as the essence of pure evil, a devourer of souls with an insatiable hatred of humanity. Based on the data flashing on Antony's computer screens, Cizin was ripping away at the earth's foundation as he clawed his way up from the bowels of hell. He would show no mercy when he tore through the surface; people were going to die.

# 17

# CHANCE

The late afternoon rain made the air inside the warehouse office building hot, humid, and fouler. As soon as the rain stopped, Chance went outside. The vibrations began while he was sitting on his designated roost beside the office building. Suddenly, multiple loud explosions shook the compound. He was thrown into the air and landed hard on his left side. Dizzy, ears ringing, it felt like he was rolling on the deck of a ship caught in a heavy storm. Everything shook, and in seconds, the compound became an inferno.

Flaming debris rained down from the sky. Chance struggled to stand but couldn't get his footing on the shifting ground. Pure panic and pandemonium surrounded him. Human torches ran screaming across the pavement or lay writhing, engulfed in flames on the swaying concrete, which roared, rose, and burst open. Then, frantically searching for a place away from the fires and mayhem, he spotted a truck container used for miscellaneous storage, crawled under it, and prayed it wouldn't shift and crush him as the ground continued to rock and roll.

After ten minutes the vibrations lessened, but the hysteria proceeded unabated. Fires, black smoke, and toxic fumes billowed from the buildings. From under the container, Chance saw people rushing to the entrance. Scrambling, he quickly joined the mob, pushing and elbowing his way through the gate, not caring whom he hurt or trampled on the way out.

The crowd surged into the street only to encounter more devastation. The sky was black with smoke. Electrical lines connected to broken and leaning utility poles danced like snakes, spewing sparks. People tried to extract themselves from upturned vehicles, security systems screeched, and remnants from destroyed buildings blocked the road.

The asphalt had huge cracks and gashes, water gushed from broken sewer lines. Amid the confusion, people ran amok screaming and crying in every direction. Shanty houses crumbled like broken toys and slowly tumbled down the melting hillside.

Chance searched for a safe hiding place, but chaos surrounded him. He carefully maneuvered through the devastated city, taking detours and changing direction to avoid obstacles and the prevailing mass confusion. It would be dark soon, and the power had gone out.

Finally, he stumbled upon an official-looking three-story brick building. A bent flagpole with a drooping Guatemalan flag stood in the middle of the ruptured cement courtyard. The building's front windows were either blown out or cracked. Block lettering above the entrance indicated it as the Puerto Maria administrative office building. Chance hoped the building was empty as he slipped through a broken window.

Daylight was fading rapidly, and the building's interior would soon be pitch-black. He hurried through the lobby, searching for the elevators, assuming there would be a directory of offices nearby. He needed to locate the maintenance department; inside he might find something to defend himself against looters taking advantage of the chaos, or worse, someone from the warehouse who might realize he was missing and start searching.

The maintenance department was located in the basement, and Chance frantically scoured the walls, cabinets, and drawers for useful items. The first items he collected were a flashlight, two knives, and a machete.

The room had a solid metal exit door leading to the rear parking lot. He tested and re-locked the door; anyone attempting to enter from outside would require a key. As an extra precaution, he secured a bungee cord around the doorknob and then looped it around the leg of a large metal worktable. This would make it difficult for anyone with a key to open the door.

Overexcited and breathing heavily, he strained to push a metal cabinet in front of the entry door. Then, exhausted, he slid down the cabinet to the floor to rest and think. Outside the building, turmoil raged incessantly, the noise resonating through the broken windows.

Using the flashlight, Chance meticulously searched every floor in the building. Four hours later he had raided the vending machines, helping himself to the contents, and taken what he needed from breakroom refrigerators, employees' desks, and closets.

Four laptop backpacks, fastened together with zip ties, contained the essential items needed for survival. Over his clothes, he donned a soiled one-piece set of workman's coveralls. Muddy work boots replaced Aapo's hand-me-down Italian leather loafers. A frayed, sweat-stained straw hat rested atop the laptop bags.

Chance propped himself up in a corner and began to nourish himself with the food he had discovered in the breakroom refrigerators. The vending machine snacks were stuffed in a backpack; the machete was unsheathed and within reach. Then he settled in to wait for the first glimmer of dawn.

# 18

# ALEX

Alex Martinez stood with his hands in his pockets, gazing through the expansive, floor-to-ceiling windows in the family room of the Vasquez family's lake house. Alex was now sixty-one, tall, lean, with gray streaks in his stylishly cut black hair. A slight crook in his nose had resulted from a punch he received from a cartel soldier when he was fifteen. His posture and mannerisms resembled those of a stately butler or manservant, and his attire was impeccable.

The 20,000-square-foot house was situated high above the largest lake in Guatemala, Lake Izabal, and was isolated from the surrounding homes and businesses. A rarely used luxury yacht bobbed in the water, moored to the private dock below the house.

To the right of the door was a fifteen-foot custom-made teakwood bar stocked with top-shelf liquors and vintage wines. On the left side of the room was a seldom-used stone fireplace. Over the mantel hung an enormous blue marlin. Other trophy fish taken from the Pacific Ocean were displayed on the walls around the room.

Table tennis, billiards, and poker tables occupied spaces throughout the room. Six recliners faced a fifteen-foot flat-screen TV on the left wall. Informal groupings of sofas, chairs, and accent tables were all scattered throughout the room.

It was a beautiful, cloudless day as Alex observed luxury boats, catamarans, jet skis, and children enjoying colorful inflatables in the water. Loneliness engulfed him like a shroud. It was heartbreaking to see all the seemingly happy people enjoying themselves. Theirs was a lifestyle his role in the Vasquez Cartel didn't permit.

He missed his family. It had been years since he had seen them. But they were safe, and that's what mattered. Through the years, there had been no close friends, wives, or children because he served the overlord and tyrant of the Vasquez Cartel, whom he consistently undermined and betrayed. Discovery of his treachery would result in torture and death, and anyone close to him would suffer the same fate. Revenge was his sole obsession and all he cared about.

* * *

In 1974, a regional cartel captain offered Alex to Eloy Vasquez as a gift, as one presents a new pony to a child. Eloy was functionally illiterate but intelligent enough to realize the world was rapidly changing due to technological innovations, and he wanted to surround himself with more educated people. At fifteen, because of his education and intellect, Alex was the perfect gift at the perfect time. By eighteen, he was indispensable to Eloy.

As the years passed, Eloy was rarely seen without Alex in his shadow. It was a slow, steady progression, but eventually, Alex became Eloy's personal assistant, gatekeeper, and the conduit through which information flowed to and from Eloy.

He was quiet, blended into the wallpaper, and never spoke without being spoken to. Because he was so unassuming, his presence was either taken for granted or ignored. But by the time he was forty, neither Eloy, his two sons, nor the cartel captains grasped the true extent of his power and authority.

The Vasquez Cartel relied heavily on a consistent manual labor force, annually wrenching hundreds of people from their homes and families to coerce them into servitude. Thus, Alex was not alone in his hatred for the organization and its ruling family. Within the Vasquez organization and in villages throughout the country was a small contingent of rebels whose lives had been devastated by the cartel, and they acted as his eyes, ears, and hands.

* * *

The vibration from the Apple watch on his wrist drew Alex's attention from the window. It was a text from Humberto, Eloy's youngest son, letting Alex know he would arrive later than planned. Eloy had summoned his sons home, and they had plans to have dinner and discuss the state of the cartel.

* * *

The responsibility for the cartel's ground operations rested squarely on Humberto's shoulders, but he proved incapable of managing the perpetual chaos. Anonymous tips were surreptitiously sent to the cartel's rivals and law enforcement agencies. Inaccurate communications, negative rumors, and whisper campaigns sowed confusion among the cartel's rank and file. Fields of poppies, marijuana, and coca plants were mysteriously burned. Disrupted supply chains, hijacked shipments, and communication blackouts occurred. The pressure and stress from the uncertainty had Humberto drowning in an ocean of alcohol and drug addiction.

* * *

Before Alex could return his hand to his pocket, another text informed him that Aapo, Eloy's oldest son, would arrive shortly. Aapo had been in Guatemala for two weeks without notifying anyone. But Alex knew his whereabouts because Alex knew everything about Aapo.

To Alex, Aapo was as transparent as glass. Bugs and hidden cameras were placed in Aapo's executive suite at PIIE and his Manhattan apartment in New York. Within PIIE, Aapo's personal secretary, a junior accountant, an IT technician, and Aapo's chauffeur were all exclusively Guatemalan and handpicked by Alex. Surveillance records, illicit financial transactions, emails, text messages, and other evidence depicting Aapo's deceit and transgressions against his father and the cartel were all stored in an encrypted file on Alex's laptop. Aapo's plan for a synthetic drug facility was only a pipe dream; it would never come to fruition.

* * *

Alex let out a heavy sigh as he reluctantly tore his gaze away from the joyful scene of people by the lake and made his way to Eloy's bedroom. Eloy had been in a drug-induced sleep for twelve hours. The heavy green drapes were closed. In the semi-darkness, he could see the outline of Eloy's resting form in the hospital bed. Beethoven's *Moonlight Sonata* played softly in the background.

* * *

Because Eloy was distrustful and paranoid that his enemies would take advantage of his weakening state, he refused to visit a medical clinic or hospital. So, the same physician performed all his medical examinations at whichever residence Eloy occupied. When the doctor informed Eloy of his intent to retire, Eloy threatened his life and refused to let him go. The doctor was now eighty years old and meekly accepted Eloy's verbal abuse and insults as if he were the cause of the mounting medical issues.

Too terrified to deliver a negative diagnosis, the doctor never performed diagnostic tests that might require a trip to a medical facility. Instead, he wrote one prescription after another, which he handed to Eloy, and which Eloy then passed to Alex. Unbeknownst to the doctor, a mixture of deadly toxins secretly administered by Alex, was slowly destroying Eloy's organs and poisoning his system.

*  *  *

Another vibration from his Apple watch drew Alex's attention back to the window in the family room, where he observed a black Mercedes Benz slowly make its way up the narrow slope toward the house. Aapo had arrived.

Alex felt a sense of contempt as he watched Aapo hurriedly exit the car, suit jacket over his arm, laptop bag on his shoulder, cell phone to his ear. "Always the important businessman," Alex whispered as he approached the entrance and opened the door. "Welcome home, Aapo. How was your flight?" he asked, smiling, extending his hand for Aapo to shake.

Aapo ignored the greeting and Alex's outstretched hand. Instead he kept his head down and scrolled through his phone. "Where's my father?" he asked, not looking up.

"He had a busy day, so he's resting," Alex responded, maintaining his composure as he stepped aside, allowing the chauffeur to pass with Aapo's luggage. "He'll be down at six p.m. for dinner, your brother is running late but should arrive around two- thirty."

"Okay, let me know when Humberto arrives. I'm going for a quick swim. Oh, and ask Stella to stop whatever she's doing, bring the massage table, and meet me in the cabana. I need a massage after that long flight from New York," Aapo said, hurriedly walking away while still looking at his phone.

"Fucking liar," Alex whispered as Aapo left the room.

He walked into the kitchen. It was lunchtime, and most of the house's staff were eating lunch. Stella was an attractive, twenty-one-year-old housekeeper, gaily chatting with the other staff at the kitchen counter. Everyone turned to look at Alex when he entered the room.

"Everyone, Aapo just arrived. He's going for a swim," Alex said, looking at the group. "Humberto is due at two-thirty, and I'd like dinner served promptly at six p.m." Heads nodded; the group knew what was expected of them.

"Stella, may I speak with you for a moment?" Alex asked as he turned and left the kitchen. Stella followed him into the hallway. There was a note of empathy in his voice. "Aapo wants you to give him a massage in the cabana."

The bright smile on Stella's face instantly disappeared. She dropped her head and placed both hands over her face. Seeing her dismay, Alex gently placed a hand on her shoulder. "Go, prepare yourself. He's expecting you."

Head down, shoulders drooping, Stella slowly walked away, knowing she would have to perform more than a simple massage.

Alex retreated to his suite, sat at his desk, opened his laptop, and immediately initiated the downloading of files from Aapo's computer by clicking an icon. Another click on a separate icon started the download of data from his cell phone.

Humberto arrived at the house and greeted Alex jovially, gripping his hand tightly and pulling him into a bear hug. "It's good to see you, my friend. You look well. How have you been since we last met?" Humberto asked, smiling broadly, slightly slurring his words.

Alex immediately noticed Humberto's enlarged pupils, the smell of alcohol on his breath, and his overly exuberant attitude. "Same to you, my friend," he said, returning the smile and gripping Humberto's shoulders. "I'm well for an old soldier. Your brother is here, and he wants to talk to you. Your father is resting but will see you at six for dinner."

"Sure thing. I'll be in the family room. Want to join me for a drink and catch up?" Humberto asked.

"My friend I wish I could, but unfortunately, there are things I need to do for your father. Maybe before you leave, we can find a few minutes." Alex placed his hand on Humberto's back and gently guided him toward the door leading to the hallway. "Go relax. I'll see you later."

He watched Humberto walk away with an unsteady gait, then returned to his suite. Using his laptop, he activated the hidden cameras and microphones in the family room while simultaneously downloading Humberto's phone data. Then he sat back in his chair to watch the interactions between the brothers.

Alex watched as Humberto walked behind the bar, quickly sniffed cocaine from the back of his hand, then poured himself a drink. Then Aapo walked into the room.

"While you're at it, fix me a scotch on the rocks," Aapo said to Humberto, settling in one of the leather club chairs.

"I don't work for you. Fix it yourself if you want one," Humberto said as he moved from behind the bar, flopped down in a chair facing his brother, and sipped his drink.

Aapo sneered and walked to the bar. "Nothing changes with you, does it, little brother? No wonder things down here are in such a mess. Maybe we could make some 'real' money if you spent less time sampling the product." He poured himself a two-fingered shot, dropped in two cubes of ice, and returned to his chair. He watched as Humberto drained his glass and returned to the bar for a refill.

"Humberto," Aapo barked, "slow down; you're already fucked up. I want to talk and ensure we're on the same page before dinner."

Humberto leaned back on the bar. "Which page? Do you want the page that tells Papa you're not sending the money I've been begging you for over the past two months? Or do you want the page about men deserting us because we haven't paid them? There are plenty of other pages. Which one do you want?"

Aapo slid to the edge of his seat, both hands around his glass, legs apart. "Look, this is a huge organization, and I'm responsible for ensuring that finances are stable. But this pandemic has caused the markets to go wild. It's complicated. A lot is going on that you wouldn't understand even if I had time to explain it to you."

"Stop lying, Aapo," Humberto said with a sneer. "I may not have graduated from a fancy college, but I'm not stupid. Oh, I understand, all right. I understand you're fucking with the money. You have been shortchanging me since before there was a pandemic. We have plenty of money, but for some reason, you're playing games with it while the operations here on the ground are going to shit."

Aapo rose from his chair and moved to stand in front of his brother. "Will you just calm down and listen to what I say before we meet with Papa?" he pleaded. "One of our New York bank accounts was hacked, and we lost over ten million dollars, but I'll have it all back in a few weeks, plus interest. Then I'll give you the full amount you've asked for."

Humberto could not believe what he had just heard. He leaned into his brother's face, eyes flashing. "What the fuck are you talking about?" he said. "Ten million is nothing to this organization. You're out of your fucking mind if you think I believe a word you're saying. We're one of the largest cartels in Central America, and suddenly, we're in a position where ten million will make or break us. That's bullshit, and you know it."

Aapo's demeanor changed. He spoke rapidly. "Listen to me. We've lost much more than ten million. That's only a part of it. International borders are closed, and we're having difficulty getting products to our customers. I'm cashing in on some of our investments but need more time. I have the guy who hacked our account, and in a few weeks, he will make it rain money; we'll be drowning in it."

"That's all well and good, but you still haven't explained why you're holding out on me. We're supposed to have money stashed in banks all over the Caribbean and Mexico. You must think I'm a fool, and this bullshit about a hacker is nothing but smoke and mirrors."

Aapo spoke faster. "During dinner, all I need from you is to be vague about what I owe you. Then let me talk when Papa asks about the finances. I know how to spin it. As soon as the hacker starts work, you'll have the money you've requested and more. Tell me you'll back me up on this," he pleaded. "I promise, you won't have to worry about money anymore."

Humberto looked at his brother with disdain. "Fuck you, Aapo," he said, slurring his words. He drained his drink and lightly placed the glass on the bar. "Every day, I put my life on the line while you sit in New York, wearing designer suits and tailor-made shirts. I've had good men slaughtered because they didn't have enough ammo to defend themselves. They didn't have enough ammo because you didn't send me the money to buy it. You're fucking with the cartel's money and trying to cover it up. Unless you transfer the money that I've been asking for within the next thirty minutes, I'll tell Papa whatever I want."

Aapo fumed, shoved both hands in his pockets, and walked to the windows facing the lake, his back to Humberto. "Go to your room and clean yourself up—your nose is bleeding," he said with disgust.

* * *

Alex yawned, stood up, and stretched while monitoring the family room's camera feed. Another camera recorded Humberto's drunken trek to his childhood room. The conversation between the brothers hadn't revealed anything he didn't know. Aapo was an arrogant liar and a thief, and Humberto was a pathetic, incompetent addict.

He powered down the laptop, buzzed for the nurse, and went to Eloy's room. "Patron, patron," he said, shaking Eloy's shoulder. "Your sons have arrived. We must get you dressed for dinner."

Eloy's eyes remained closed, and he mumbled incoherently.

Alex turned on the bedside table lamp, pressed the button to raise the head of the bed, and poured a glass of water from the metal pitcher on the nightstand. Then he retrieved a slim bottle with a medicine dropper from his pocket. Swiftly administering two doses from the bottle into Eloy's mouth, he lifted Eloy's head, forcing him to swallow the water, which dribbled down the sides of his mouth, wetting his pajama top. Finally, a male nurse entered the room and approached the bed.

"Get him up, showered, shaved, and dressed. Dinner is at six o'clock," he said to the nurse before leaving the room.

Alex returned to his suite and opened the encrypted folder that contained Aapo's information. In the folder were drone shots of the construction site for the synthetic drug facility, still shots of Aapo entering and leaving the Russian-owned restaurant in New York, boarding the G550 jet at LaGuardia for the flight to Guatemala, and disembarking the plane upon its arrival on the rainforest airstrip.

He reclined in his chair and zoomed in on a picture of the man who disembarked from the jet after Aapo and entered the pickup truck.

"So, this is Aapo's computer hacker," he said, musing. Then he dialed his contact at the warehouse compound in Puerto Maria.

# 19

# AAPO

Aapo stood by the window in the family room, brooding. Clouds lazily drifted across the darkening evening sky, palm trees fluttered in the breeze, and lights twinkled in houses and businesses that dotted the shores of the vast lake. It created a serene, peaceful scene that did nothing to uplift his dark mood. Humberto was more of an adversary than a brother; they would never be allies. He had gambled and lost by asking Humberto not to disclose the lack of money to their father, but it was a gamble he had to take.

Fuming over his dilemma, his hands in his pockets curled into fists. The dream of constructing a state-of-the-art facility to produce synthetic, addictive drugs was sinking like the Titanic. Aapo returned to the bar, poured another drink, and tossed it back.

The German engineers hired to build the facility were long gone. Frustrated with missed payrolls, consistent delays in acquiring building materials and equipment, and the anxiety of being stranded in a developing country during a global pandemic, they had packed up and left. Work had come to a halt; the entire construction site lay abandoned in the rainforest.

Aapo glanced at his cell phone on the bar and quickly scrolled through the screen, inspecting the missed calls, voicemails, and texts from people he wished to avoid. The phone had stopped working earlier in the day, so there were no new messages, but the existing ones haunted him.

Most of the money used to fund the enterprise had come from other criminal organizations. They had all been promised lucrative returns on their investments, and Aapo had agreed to repay the money with interest. The scheduled payments were overdue, and until money began to flow from the bank accounts Chance Moore would hack, there was no alternative but to continue embezzling from the cartel to repay the investors. Finally, everything was ready, and in two days, Chance would be moved from the warehouse in Puerto Maria to a safe house in Guatemala City.

Aapo recalled his encounter with Chance during the flight to Guatemala. There had been a glimmer of defiance in the man's eyes. But, hopefully, the photos of his dead friend, Mack Owens, would be sufficient incentive to deter any thoughts of non-cooperation.

A slight tremor shook the house as Aapo walked to the dining room. He halted midstride and waited a few seconds to see if the shaking would resume. When nothing happened, he entered the family's dining room. Humberto was seated at the table, head down, scrolling through his phone. He had showered and changed clothes; the heavy scent of expensive cologne lingered in the air.

"I can't get a signal on my phone. Can you?" Humberto asked, still scrolling.

Two male servants were busy circling the table, filling water and wine glasses.

Aapo sighed heavily and sat facing his brother on the opposite side of the table. "I can't get anything either," he replied, swiping the phone screen with his thumb. "The cell service out here sucks."

The brothers turned as their father entered the room shuffling and leaning on a cane, one arm looped through Alex's arm for support.

Aapo was shocked by his father's appearance but didn't say anything. The once erect posture was stooped and bent at the waist. A pink scalp showed through wispy, thin, white hair; wrinkled skin sagged on his sunken, gaunt face, and his eyes were dull and filmy. Dark burgundy silk pajamas and a robe hung loosely on the once robust frame.

Alex assisted in seating Eloy comfortably at the head of the table and then left the room.

Shaken by his father's appearance, Humberto's mouth hung open. He leaned closer and placed a hand on Eloy's shoulder. "Papa, you're ill. Why didn't you tell us?"

Eloy's hands trembled as he carefully sipped a glass of water. "I'll fill you in on the details later. But first, I'd like to hear from each of you," he said in a raspy voice. "I have concerns about how things are going." He coughed, cleared his throat, and took another sip of water.

Aapo scrutinized his father's every movement, suppressing a dark satisfaction in what he observed. It was evident that whatever was afflicting his father wouldn't improve.

Aapo and Humberto were served an herb-encrusted roasted lamb, sautéed spinach with tomatoes and garlic, seasoned purple potatoes, and fried plantains. In front of Eloy, the servant placed a bowl of brown broth. Aapo wasted no time cutting into the lamb.

Eloy lifted a shaky spoonful of broth to his lips.

Concern crossed Humberto's face as he watched his father. "Papa, is that all you're going to have?" he asked.

"My stomach can't handle rich food anymore. This is better for my digestion," Eloy responded while hunching over the bowl and slurping the broth.

Humberto glanced at Aapo with a questioning look, signaling him to join the conversation, but Aapo ignored him and focused on eating.

"Papa, is there anything in particular you'd like me to address now, or would you prefer to wait?" he asked, popping a potato into his mouth.

Eloy stopped eating and looked at Aapo with a steely expression. "You can start by explaining why we're losing so much money. It doesn't make sense, and it gets worse every month. It's as if we're pouring water into a bucket with a hole in it."

Pretending to be irritated, Aapo sighed heavily, wiped his mouth with his napkin, and tossed it on the table. Then he sat back and folded his arms across his chest. "Papa, we've been over and over this. I even sent you spreadsheets with all the figures. The world has shut down because of the pandemic; countries have closed their doors. It's hard to move products."

"Pandemics, depressions, wars," Eloy growled, his eyes boring into Aapo. "None of that stopped us in the past and shouldn't stop us now. It doesn't matter what's going on in the world or where it's happening. The demand for what we sell never stops, nor should the money."

Aapo feigned shock. "Papa, I'm doing everything possible to stabilize our finances. But as I see it, we have two major issues: cash and the banks. Cash transactions are a significant portion of our business and a big problem to track. The second issue is the banks aren't as safe as they used to be. For instance, several months ago, a computer hacker stole money from one of our special accounts, and nothing can stop it from happening again. The solution to both problems is to switch to cryptocurrency. If we change, we could decrease our losses. Let me explain my new plan..." he said, attempting to deflect any additional inquiries.

As if waving off a fly with the back of his hand, Eloy ignored Aapo and shifted his attention to Humberto.

"What's this I'm hearing about our men not getting paid, our shipments being hijacked, and us barely holding our territory at the El Salvadoran border?" he asked, tearing off a piece of bread and dipping it into the broth.

Humberto's body tensed. He finished chewing before speaking. His knife and fork were clenched tightly in his fists. "It's true, Papa, and unfortunately, a lot goes wrong. I'm still convinced there are traitors and spies among us. The captains are your hand-picked men, faithful only to you, and I trust them, but thus far, they've identified no one."

"There are no spies. You've been talking about spies for years," Aapo said, looking at his brother with contempt. "That's just an excuse to cover your incompetence. You don't know what you're doing and never have. Why don't you finally admit it?"

Humberto ignored Aapo's remarks. "Papa, I ask Aapo for money, but he never sends me what I need when I need it. Even with the supply chain slowdown caused by the pandemic, I'm shipping products. Aapo either ignores me, sends less than I request, or gives me excuses. I need money now, but he won't give it to me.

"Good men desert us because our rivals entice them with more money. So, we're now fighting against men who know our secrets and are better armed. All because I don't have the funds to purchase weapons."

Aapo clenched his jaw; hatred for Humberto blazed in his eyes. "That's a lie," he shouted, slamming his fist on the table so hard the dinnerware rattled. "I send you money. The problem is you're too dumb to manage it properly. You're the reason for the hole in the bucket. That group of misfits you call soldiers is a bunch of losers. Don't try to pin the blame on me."

Humberto returned his brother's hate-filled stare. "I need money now, not tomorrow, next week, or next month. So, tell Papa why you don't give it to me. Tell him the lies you tell me." The fingernails on his clenched fists dug into his palms.

Eloy sat back in his chair and folded his arms across his chest. Then, narrowing his eyes, he squinted at Aapo. "Is this true?"

Infuriated, Aapo glowered at Humberto. "I don't keep money in a shoebox under my bed. Sometimes it must be transferred between banks in different countries to stay under the radar. It takes time and is too complicated for this ignorant bastard to understand.

"But my new plan will free us from all of that. If we shift to cryptocurrency, we won't have to worry about the damn banks." He leaned in toward his father. "Papa, I have a man who will use the internet to bring in more money than we can count. And we won't have to worry about banks or law enforcement."

Afraid of losing the argument, Humberto interrupted Aapo and grabbed Eloy's arm. "Papa, don't listen to Aapo's schemes," he said, pleading. "Can't you see he's trying to distract you? What about him not sending me the money I need now?"

Eloy turned toward Aapo. "And where is this wizard who makes money magically appear out of a computer?" he snorted.

"Right now, he's at the compound in Puerto Maria. I'll move him to a better location in a few days," Aapo responded, feeling more confident. He shifted in his seat to fully face his father. "Papa, we can't lose with this plan. In the next few weeks, it will start raining money."

"Puerto Maria? That's my operation, and those are my men. You don't have the right to show up and order my men around. You should have come through me," Humberto said, arguing.

"Your men?" Aapo responded, with a sinister smile. "Those are cartel soldiers. I can give anybody any orders I choose. But he's been there for two weeks, so why didn't you know about it if it's your operation and your men?"

At that moment, Alex walked into the room. "Excuse me, gentlemen, I hate to interrupt your dinner, but there's been an earthquake in the Petén region. TV reports say it was a 7.9."

"So that must have been the aftershock I felt earlier; 7.9 is big." Aapo said as he and Humberto grabbed their phones and began scrolling. There was still no cell service.

"Any idea which areas were affected?" Humberto asked anxiously.

"I received a message from one of our lieutenants on the ground, and Puerto Maria was included in the list of towns. There were several explosions in the warehouse compound; it's currently on fire, and several people are dead or wounded. There's no hope of putting the fire out. They're just letting it burn."

"How did you receive a message?" Aapo asked Alex. "We don't have cell service."

"I have a satellite phone," Alex responded coolly. "I reported your phone issues. You should have service within the hour."

"Any word on my prisoner? Is he okay?" Aapo asked, a tone of apprehension creeping into his voice.

"He's missing," Alex said calmly.

"FUCK!" Aapo screamed, jumping from his chair and hurling his wine glass across the room. The glass shattered against one of Eloy's photos hanging on the wall; it shifted precariously on its side, and wine trickled down the wall to the floor. He ran his hand through his hair and began to pace the floor. "Your men are as incompetent as you are," he bellowed at Humberto.

"Oh, now they're my men? You're the one who fucked up. If you—" He didn't have the opportunity to finish his sentence.

"Shut up, both of you," Eloy thundered. Gripping the table's edge with both hands, he struggled to stand up. His dark eyes flashed with rage. Leaning on the table, between heavy breaths, he directed his comments to Humberto. "How much money will you need to fix this?"

A pained expression crossed Humberto's face. Glancing uneasily at his father, he slowly stood and tossed his napkin on the table. "I'll go to Puerto Maria, assess the damage, and decide if it's worth salvaging or if we need to relocate. But, Papa, what about the money for everything else I've been asking for?"

"Send me one figure that includes everything," Eloy said.

Humberto placed a hand on his father's shoulder, gave it a light squeeze, and then left the room.

Aapo slumped back in his chair, folded his arms across his chest, and watched Humberto leave.

Eloy gave Aapo an angry, piercing stare. "I may be old, but I'm nobody's fool, especially not yours. I built this organization, and I know what goes on. I piss on your reports; I wipe my ass with your spreadsheets," he yelled as he forcefully swept his entire place setting from the table with the back of his hand. The broth splashed onto the table as the dishes clattered loudly to the floor.

"I don't know where the money is going, but you'd better find out. I forbid you to return to New York until I'm satisfied that you've accounted for every cent. Whatever amount Humberto comes back with, you will produce. Do I make myself clear?" he shouted; his words accompanied by spittle spraying from his mouth.

The stooped posture had disappeared; he stood tall now, his face twisted into an ugly, menacing expression. Through narrowed, dangerous eyes, he glared down at Aapo. "NO ONE steals from me and gets away with it." Then, turning to Alex, he barked, "Get me out of here."

A chill ran down Aapo's spine, his stomach clenched, and his leg nervously bounced under the table as he watched Alex guide Eloy out of the dining room.

# 20

# CHANCE

At the first sign of dawn, Chance crept out of Puerto Maria's administration building, wearing the straw hat, workman's overalls, and backpacks. In the dim light, total disarray surrounded him. Sirens still blared, smoke lingered in the warm, moist morning air, and the power remained out.

The city's residents, along with medical and rescue personnel, were focused on search and rescue missions and salvaging their wrecked homes and businesses. It seemed as if emergency vehicles and police cars were parked on every inch of unbroken ground. So, no one paid attention to him as he hastily walked through the streets, searching for signs leading to the road that would take him east. The plan was to travel the road at night and to rest and sleep wherever he found a safe place during the day.

But first, he needed to get out of town.

Traffic congestion met him at the intersection of the road he'd been seeking. Broken, elevated sections of asphalt had toppled vehicles, some lying on their sides or upended, with the wheels in the air like dead bugs. A few moving vehicles carefully circumvented the carnage by driving on sidewalks or any undisturbed patches of ground available. Looking east, Chance wasn't very optimistic about how quickly he could walk, but he had to get as far away from the city as possible before nightfall.

Several miles east of the city, evidence of the earthquake was still visible but not as pervasive. Unlike Puerto Maria which was overcrowded, the landscape became more rural, with significant gaps between the small businesses and houses. As shown on the map, the rainforest and dense vegetation ran parallel to both sides of the road.

As he trudged along in the sweltering tropical heat, sweat trickled down his face, stinging his eyes, and dripped from the tip of his nose. Insects swarmed like a cloud around him, biting whatever flesh they could find. The weight of the multiple backpacks strained his shoulders, and the unfamiliar work boots chafed his heels.

Late in the afternoon, towering cumulus clouds formed in the distant sky. Rain was on the way. With no safe options for shelter, Chance reluctantly waded into the high, thick brush lining the road until he found a suitable spot in the trees.

Rushing to beat the rain, he hastily cut small, flexible trees and used plastic sheeting stolen from the maintenance room to construct a lean-to large enough for him to sit up and stretch out. Additional brush and vegetation were used as camouflage to conceal the structure.

The rain arrived just as he pushed the garbage bags, filled with leaves and brush, and the backpacks into the space. The contents of the garbage bags snapped and crackled under his weight, but at least he wouldn't be sleeping on wet ground.

Listening to the rain, hoping his makeshift structure wouldn't leak, Chance pulled off the work boots and massaged his sore feet. Next, he used a knife to cut small strips of cloth from rags taken from the maintenance room, then duct-taped them to his heels.

His mind drifted back to the hours spent wandering the aisles of upscale sporting goods stores examining the latest high-tech survival gear, hiking and camping equipment—vibrant colored clothes, expensive gadgets, rugged boots, and shoes. "Where's REI when you need them?" he said, snickering.

Physically drained and aching from the day's exertion, he rifled through the backpacks. Inside he found Tylenol, an employee's lunch taken from a breakroom refrigerator, and a bottle of water, which constituted his meal for the day. Three more disposable containers held his "real" food—chips, crackers, cookies, candy bars from the vending machine, along with seven bottles of water, completed his food stock.

Stretching out, trying to relax, he reflected on the day's progress. He was still too close to the city. Aapo's golden goose had flown the coop, and things were going to get very ugly, very fast. He was loose in cartel territory. It was their turf, and they knew every nook and cranny. Even if he reached the border crossing, officials would detain him without a passport or identification. Who would they call first, the US Embassy or the Vasquez Cartel?

The garbage bags were uncomfortable, and the thought of snakes crawling in the under-brush was enough to prevent Chance from falling into a deep sleep. Finally the rain stopped, he crawled out of the lean-to and looked up through the treetop canopy. It was almost dusk. He hustled to reassemble the backpacks, deconstruct the lean-to, and find his way back to the road. Secluded in the tall brush beside the road, he sat in the soggy grass and waited for nightfall.

The night was pitch-black; there was no ambient light and hardly any traffic. Except for the sounds of night critters hidden in the vegetation and a random dog barking somewhere in the distance, it was quiet, making it easier to hear an approaching vehicle before the headlights appeared. Each time a motor rumbled in the distance, he'd take to the brush beside the road and hunker down until it passed.

It was his fourth night on the road. A full moon illuminated the star-filled, cloudless sky. Chance was hiding in the brush as a pickup truck roared past, heading west. Peering through the grass, he waited for the truck's taillights to dim in the distance. Instead, the brake lights came on. The pickup made a U-turn and slowly crept back toward him, stopping thirty feet from where he crouched. Holding his breath, he slowly removed the straw hat and quietly slid the machete from its sheath.

The first man jumped from the truck's passenger side and hastily walked toward where Chance hid. Chance's grip tightened on the machete's handle. The man stopped and scanned the road. Then, speaking loudly in Spanish, he said excitedly, "I know; I saw somebody walking along the road."

"I didn't see anything. It's too dark to see your hand in front of your face," the second man replied, leaning out of the driver's side window.

The first man stepped closer. "He jumped off the road. I saw him. I swear I saw somebody," he said, scanning the brush from where he stood on the road.

The second man got out of the truck and slammed the door hard. "Look, even if you did see somebody, we can't search for him now. It's too fucking dark. And, when we get back, don't you dare say one word about it, or the captain will have us back out here roaming around with flashlights the rest of the night. It's late; I've had enough of this bullshit for one day. So, get your ass back in the truck. I don't want to hear it." he shouted in frustration, quickly walking back to the truck.

Like a disappointed child, the first man returned to the truck, saying, "But that could have been him. I swear I saw somebody."

"Shut the fuck up," the second man yelled as he wheeled the truck around and sped off.

After replacing the straw hat and sheathing the machete, Chance watched the truck's taillights until they disappeared. He doubted the men, or their compatriots would return that night, but they confirmed his biggest fear: cartel soldiers were looking for him. This would have to be his last night walking the road.

The following day, he was so weak and tired that he overslept. All the vending machine snacks were gone, and his remaining food stock consisted of only a half bottle of water. Now that he knew the cartel had night patrols on the road, the new plan was to walk through the rainforest during the day, using the sound of traffic as a guide to remain parallel to the road.

Staying within hearing range of the traffic was more of a challenge than he had anticipated. The forest terrain was wet and slippery, with dips and slopes, and impenetrable vegetation, trees, vines, and thick undergrowth sometimes made it impossible to move forward. He had been bushwhacking with the machete for hours without making much progress. His back, arms, and hands burned and ached from the fruitless effort.

Despair and hopelessness sapped the last of his strength. Chance flopped down at the base of a tree, leaned his head back, closed his eyes, and fought back the tears. He could smell his rank body odor; the skin was raw underneath the damp, dirty clothes from scratching bug bites. The insects never ceased swarming around him; he felt them crawling on his body underneath his clothes. There were blisters on his hands, and he was hungry and thirsty.

Finally, he couldn't believe what he saw when he opened his eyes. A small wooden house was just forty yards away through the trees. Using the brush and vegetation for cover, he silently crept closer. A man was working in a vegetable garden; a woman, presumably his wife, was hanging laundry on a clothesline. A few feet away, a baby was toddling around chasing chickens with a stick. Chance could see a well with a bucket perched on the edge, a pigpen, a donkey tied to a stake eating grass, and a wooden shed.

Approaching the house wasn't an option, especially in his condition. He'd scare the hell out of them. He had to be patient and wait until nightfall. Then, after the family went to bed, he would raid the garden. His stomach growled in anticipation of eating fresh vegetables. With a plan in place, he returned to the tree and watched the tranquil scene.

Late that afternoon, a pickup truck roared into the yard, dust billowing in its wake, and stopped in front of the house. Two men were in the truck's cab, and a third man was sitting in the bed. Immediately, the family members stopped what they were doing. Dropping his hoe, the farmer hurried to the front of the house while his wife lifted the baby, placed him on her hip, and hastily joined her husband. Keeping low, using the brush for cover, Chance quietly crept closer to watch.

The driver was a large, overweight man wearing a white cowboy hat. He got out of the truck, hiked up his pants, and yelled to the man in the truck bed, motioning in an overhead circle with his arm. The third man, holding an automatic rifle, jumped from the truck bed and began walking around the property. The second man walked into the house as if he lived there. The driver spoke to the couple. Chance couldn't hear the conversation, but they seemed afraid.

The driver spoke to the father, who nervously scanned the area, looking from side to side. Finally, he called out in Spanish, "Tomas, Tomas, where are you?"

The driver turned to the woman, speaking to her while tickling the baby under its chin. The woman looked fearful and consistently shook her head as if to say no.

The farmer fidgeted as he watched the driver's interaction with his wife and baby but continued scanning the yard. Then, finally, he hollered louder with more insistence in his voice. "Tomas, where are you? Come to me now," he demanded.

The second man came out of the house, eating something in his hand. He walked over and casually leaned on the front of the truck. The third man looked in the shed, walked past the pigpen, and headed toward the garden.

Hearing a noise behind him, Chance glanced over his right shoulder to see a little boy about five years old, eyes as wide as saucers, staring at him in horror. Then, as quick as a rabbit, the boy ran straight toward the house screaming in Spanish, "Papa, Papa, a man, a man." He went straight into his father's arms and pointed toward Chance.

Chance scrambled to his feet and began to run. He could hear the men yelling; they were coming after him. In minutes, bullet spray shredded the foliage around him. The forest made it impossible to gain much speed, but he hoped the thick vegetation would interfere with the shooter's line of sight.

He was tearing through the brush, trying to stay low, ducking and weaving, moving as fast as possible. Finally, searing pains in his left leg sent him crashing to the ground. He rolled over, clutching his leg. The shouting, irritated voices were gaining on him.

Chance crawled behind a large stand of bamboo trees mixed with thick plants and vegetation. He quickly stripped off the backpack and threw it a few feet across from where he hid, ensuring it was visible. Then, gripping a sturdy stalk of bamboo and using his right leg for leverage, he raised himself to a standing position and unsheathed the machete. His frantic escape had left a trail large enough for a blind man to see.

The gunman made no effort to silence his approach. Chance could hear footsteps and heavy breathing as the man got closer. Seeing the backpacks, the man stopped, shifted the rifle to his left hand, and bent to pick it up. Chance lunged forward and swung down hard with the machete on the back of the man's neck. The head rolled, and blood sprayed from the neck like water from a garden hose; the body convulsed and then lay still. Wasting no time, Chance grabbed the automatic rifle and quickly returned to the bamboo stand. The second man was approaching.

Seeing the headless body, the second man stopped, uncertain whether to continue the pursuit or turn back. Chance didn't give him time to decide. Instead, he sprung from behind the bamboo screen and opened fire with the automatic rifle. The man twitched and bucked as the bullets ripped through his body.

He assumed the overweight driver of the pickup wouldn't immediately come into the forest if his comrades didn't return. But another search party would, and the path of destruction would be easy to find.

Excruciating pain ran like electricity through his wounded leg; the pant leg was soaked with blood. Unfortunately, there was no time to examine the wound, so he rifled through his backpacks, located the duct tape, grit his teeth, and tightly wrapped it around his pant leg, hoping to control the bleeding until he could find a safe place to hide.

With adrenaline coursing through his veins, and his heart pounding, he finally looked around at the gruesome scene. Broken and blood-splattered foliage, the bleeding decapitated body slumped beside a tree, the head with open eyes several feet away. Only the boots of the second man were visible; the body had fallen into a clump of bushes. Then, the vomit erupted from the pit of his stomach. Since there was no food in his gut, the extreme retching left him even weaker and more exhausted. His hands shook as he nervously tossed a handful of Tylenol into his mouth and washed them down with the last of the water.

After quickly discharging the magazine from the rifle, Chance threw it into the brush and tossed the rifle in the opposite direction. He limped to the second man's body and retrieved the pistol.

During the chase, he lost his bearings and had no idea about where he was. In addition, there were no traffic sounds. Finally, he looked up through the treetop canopy at the sky; he had approximately three hours of daylight left.

Chance staggered aimlessly through the rainforest in agonizing pain, desperately searching for a place to hide before nightfall. The only viable option was an outcropping of boulders, partially hidden by foliage, with a small crawlspace between them. As the evening showers started, he did what he could to make himself comfortable before the rainforest went dark.

The next day, he awoke gasping for breath and disoriented. His clothes were soaking wet, he had a fever, he ached all over, and his leg throbbed mercilessly. Delirium set in; confused, unbridled thoughts zigzagged through his mind. Were there voices in the distance? Had the men found his trail? Were they coming for him? Was he hearing people or animals lurking among the trees? Summoning the strength to move, he stuck the pistol into his belt, grabbed his backpack, and painfully crawled from between the rocks.

A troop of howler monkeys began jumping through the tree branches, hooting and shrieking above him. Startled he looked up, lost his footing, and plummeted head over heels, crashing through the brush, down a hill. A tangle of trees and vines abruptly stopped his descent. Overwhelmed with pain, he blacked out.

# 21

# VONNIE

Vonnie sat on her bedroom balcony, sipping a glass of wine as the hustle and bustle of the plantation's daily activities wound down for the day. The fragrance from the flowers and ripened fruit hanging on the trees surrounding The Big House drifted through the night air.

Her morning was spent watching TV news reports of the Guatemalan earthquake. While reclining on the sofa, she opened her laptop, accessed Google Earth, and examined the area in Guatemala where the earthquake occurred. The quake happened less than 100 miles from the Guatemalan—Belize border. As she zoomed in for a better view, she saw the expansive rainforest that blanketed the distance between the two countries, and then east of the vertical dotted line that indicated the border, an aerial shot of the rows of banana trees, and every building on the plantation.

After tiring of the news, it had been another long, dull day of Netflix, social media, and flipping through magazines. Her energy and motivation had vanished under another dark cloud.

It was almost eleven o'clock, and several lights still glowed in some of the workers' houses. Watching the plantation tuck itself in had become a relaxing bedtime ritual as, one by one, lights went out, and the families settled down for the night. But tonight was different; her mind whirled with worry as she thought about the people in the colorful little houses.

She had known these people all her life, and she was responsible for their well-being and livelihood. Their futures were in her hands. Two hundred and sixty-three residents, in mostly multigenerational households, resided on the plantation. The older adults were the primary craftsmen and skilled labor force for the plantation. They were the mechanics, plumbers, electricians, carpenters, groundkeepers, IT techs, and office workers. But thus far, none of the companies that had shown an interest in purchasing the property wanted the responsibility for residents living within the confines of the business.

Vonnie sighed heavily as two more lights went out. She had heard her family's story a hundred times about why families lived on the plantation, but the burden of solving an issue created by her ancestors felt like a two-ton weight on her shoulders.

* * *

In 1870, when Grover Hollister, Vonnie's great-grandfather, purchased the plantation from the original English landowner, it was severely neglected and barely functional. The original plantation workers were day laborers who lived in shacks and huts inside the rainforest. They traveled to work in whatever way they could, worked twelve-hour days, and received a subsistence wage.

Grover ensured he had a dedicated workforce by offering rental housing and a stable salary. For the workers it was a gain too, since they received a steady wage and a safe place to live. Over time, as the plantation prospered and grew, so did the number of people who lived there. Multiple generations of families had lived on the property during the past 150 years.

* * *

A car moving down the service road turned onto one of the neighborhood side streets. Dogs barked, calling out to their peers, who responded in turn until they tired of the communication, then curled up to sleep on the porches or under the raised houses. Then in the quiet, moonlit night, nocturnal creatures, hidden in the lush vegetation of the rainforest, began their nightly songs and mating calls.

Vonnie left the balcony and pulled the screened door closed. The ceiling fan slowly spun as she untied the mosquito nets over the bed. While reaching to turn on the bedside table lamp, she accidentally knocked the orange prescription bottle of oxycodone to the floor. She didn't pick it up; three pills were enough for today.

Her bedroom resembled the aftermath of a hurricane, with dirty clothes strewn on the chairs and floor, dirty dishes scattered about, empty wine bottles cluttering the dresser and sticking out of the trash can, and books, magazines, and her laptop on the bed.

Removing her nightgown and propping up the pillows to support her back, she climbed into the cleared half of the bed naked. She picked up a half-finished novel and impatiently waited for Dominic's call. It had been a week since his last call, and her calls to him had gone straight to voicemail.

The intermittent late-night calls started the week after her shameful, drunken episode on Ambergris Caye, and they all ended in phone sex. Dominic's sultry voice told her what to do to herself and described what he wanted to do to her until she breathlessly climaxed. Then affectionately, he said goodnight. Sexually satiated with loving thoughts of him drifting through her mind, she fell asleep.

The time displayed on her cell phone was 11:30 p.m., so she folded the corner of the page and closed the book knowing there would be no call. Finally, they had been planning a romantic weekend getaway—two uninterrupted days in San Ignacio—and she wanted to finalize the details with him. Disappointed, she loudly exhaled, resituated the pillows, and turned off the bedside lamp.

The following day, as Vonnie settled onto the back porch, savoring her morning coffee, her eyes fell upon another of Ana's baskets, perched on the top step. Vonnie sighed, shaking her head. It had been almost two weeks since their fight over Dominic. She wasn't speaking to Ana, but Ana continued to leave the baskets. Knees creaking, she retrieved the basket and returned to the kitchen to refill her mug. Then, munching a cookie and with a second mug of coffee in hand, she returned to the porch.

"Good morning, Miss Vonnie," one of the workers shouted, waving to her as he joined the parade heading toward the banana groves.

"Have a nice day." she responded, returning his wave.

Unlike in the States, where she lived as an ordinary person, in Belize, people viewed her differently because of her family's history and the plantation. It wasn't until she met with her father's attorney, Mr. Rodney Schmick, to settle her father's estate that she became aware of her father's accumulated wealth. And it stunned her.

* * *

Vonnie and Mr. Schmick were in his office, seated at a conference table, reviewing the will, investment documents, insurance papers, bank statements, and other items. Mr. Schmick looked concerned as he watched her shuffle through the papers.

"Vonnie, are you all right? Can I get you some water or something to drink? You look a little overwhelmed by all of this. I gather from your expression that Pearl never discussed any of this with you before his death."

Vonnie glanced from one paper to the other, trying to comprehend the information on the Asset Summary pages.

"Oh, I'm okay," she responded in a listless voice. "No, my dad didn't discuss his finances with me, and yes, this is overwhelming. My parents and I were close, but we lived in different worlds. I never gave much thought to their money here in the States or in Belize. It never entered my mind.

"Since I was an only child, I knew I would inherit whatever my parents left behind one day, but never in my wildest dreams did I think it would be anything like this. My dad drove a ten-year-old Toyota Camry, for God's sake. I wrongly assumed that whatever he made working at Bayer Corporation was used to help support the plantation in Belize."

A sympathetic smile formed on Mr. Schmick's lips as he leaned back in his chair. "That wasn't it at all. The plantation is self-sustaining. It generates enough money to cover expenses and a lot more. It has no debt. Your father invested profits from the plantation, and he did well. He was a very astute businessman."

"Yes, he was," she said with a sigh as she lay the papers down and leaned back in her chair. The Cavendish banana was one of the most common and inexpensive fruits sold in the world. How the bananas grown on the plantation in Belize morphed into the millions of dollars documented in the papers on the conference table was mind-boggling."

Mr. Schmick continued. "I receive monthly statements from the Bank of Belize, and I've included those figures in the summary. So, when you go to Belize, I recommend you acquaint yourself with Mr. Benjamin Turay, the bank's president."

Vonnie shook herself out of her stupor. "Oh, I know Mr. Turay. He and my dad were friends. We spoke at the funeral."

"Excellent. It's important that he and the other business leaders in the area know there's been a smooth transition and that you're confident about assuming your role at the helm. The banana industry is integral to the Belize economy, and many local companies depend on your plantation for their businesses."

After leaving Mr. Schmick's office, during the drive home, Vonnie thought of the dichotomy in which her parents lived— conservative and conventional in North Carolina versus stately and noble in Belize. Now that she owned the plantation, she knew that people in Belize would have certain expectations, which she dreaded.

In North Carolina, the family led a middle-class lifestyle. Her father worked as a chemist for Bayer Crop Science in the Research Triangle Park, and her mother was a business professor at St. Augustine's College. But somewhere over the Gulf of Mexico, on the way to or from Belize, her parents assumed different personas.

For over 150 years, the patriarchs of the Hollister family had played active roles in shaping Belize's economic, political, and social landscapes, and the Hollister name had become synonymous with status, wealth, and prestige. On the plantation, her parents entertained the wealthy social elite, foreign dignitaries, and international businesspeople, adhering to the outdated attitudes, formality, and etiquette of the British monarchy, which had remained deeply rooted in Belize's elite circles for decades.

At fourteen, Vonnie's parents thrust her into a world of pomp, circumstance, and formality, expecting her to hold her own, and impress their guests at the dinner table.

But she was a child of the rebellious sixties—sporting a big Afro, embracing liberal and radical ideals. By the time she entered college, she had all but rejected what she had perceived was her parents' old-fashioned and imperialistic Belizean lifestyle. Immediately following her college graduation, Vonnie insisted on leading an independent life without their assistance. She started Vonnie's Books, Coffee, and Wine in an old, run-down three-story building, two blocks from NC State University's campus, and the store quickly became a haven for academics, artists, poets, musicians, and anyone advocating for women's rights, social justice, or the eradication of poverty.

Belize had changed significantly over the past two decades due to a wave of gentrification by foreign corporations and retired expats who had made it their home. As a result, many Indigenous people were desperately trying to preserve their heritage and traditions before bulldozers plowed them under.

These were the people who insisted on placing Vonnie on a pedestal she neither wanted nor deserved simply because she was the last remaining Hollister and the owner of the esteemed Hollister Plantation. It was why Ana was treating her like the teenage daughter whose parents didn't want her dating the tattooed biker dude. It was also why people she didn't even know were whispering and gossiping about her behind her back.

Pushing the negative thoughts from her mind, Vonnie left the porch and began the painful ascent up the stairs. Her back and hips burned, and she winced in pain as she delicately applied pressure on each step.

* * *

She planned to drive to Placencia to visit the post office, which also served as an Amazon drop-off point. A package containing lacey underwear, a nightgown, and a robe awaited her.

Three hours later, the package with the Amazon logo lay on the car's front seat, and she was parking in the sandy parking lot of the Salty Tide bar. The Salty Tide was considered a local hangout by Placencia residents, and expats and tourists rarely ventured across its threshold. If they did, by any chance, un-friendly looks from the locals quickly sent them on their way.

Vonnie stepped out of the car and stretched. The bar had ex-isted for as long as she could remember, and there had never been but one proprietor—Miss Anne. The Belizean national flag flapped in the wind above a shabby wooden structure constructed with a patchwork of faded, weather-beaten, multicolored boards haphazardly nailed into place. A thatched roof covered the entire 1,500-square-foot open-air bar and restaurant. Once the sun went down, locals filled empty spaces at the handmade, twenty-foot-long mahogany bar, reggae music blared, and the delicious scent of grilled fish and meat, along with the sound of laughter, wafted on the ocean breeze.

Vonnie walked in and sat at the bar, admiring the polished sheen of the wood. "Good morning, Miss Anne. Can a girl get a cup of coffee in this joint?" she called out to an older woman sit-ting at the far end of the bar on the opposite side, reading a newspaper. Miss Anne's wrinkled skin was the color of coffee beans. Two white-haired plaits hung down her shoulders. Multi-ple silver earrings dangled from her ears, and a multicolored beaded necklace with a bejeweled cross graced her neck. She wore a loose-fitting white cotton dress with orange flowers to complete her outfit.

She looked in Vonnie's direction, squinting over the reading glasses resting on the tip of her nose. Then she made her way down the bar. "Vonnie Hollister, is that you?" Miss Anne asked, ques-tioning her vision.

"It's me and then some," Vonnie responded, smiling brightly and noticing the shaky footsteps and cane.

Miss Anne clasped Vonnie's hands in hers and shook them vigorously. "I heard you were back. Welcome home. Welcome home. I'm so glad to see you. I haven't seen you since your father's funeral. How long has it been? I can't remember anything these days."

"Two years, Miss Anne. My dad died two years ago."

"He was such a good man. Not many people around like him anymore. All the Hollister men were good men. They did a lot for this country; folks looked up to them," she said, retrieving a cup and saucer with one hand and a coffee pot with the other. The cup and saucer rattled as she placed them on the bar.

"I also heard you were selling the plantation. Is that true?"

"Yep, it's true," Vonnie said, carefully sipping the coffee.

A mournful expression covered Miss Anne's face. "That plantation has been in your family all my life. It won't be the same if some big company buys it. Those companies don't care about people; they only care about the money." The wrinkled hands tightly clutched a bar towel. "Are you sure you want to sell it?"

Vonnie looked compassionately at Miss Anne and gently clasped the old lady's hands in hers. "It was a hard decision, Miss Anne. I love the plantation and the people on it. But I'm too old, and I don't have the strength, energy, or desire to take on something that big at this point in my life. I could never fill my daddy's shoes, they're too big."

The conversation continued until Miss Anne became distracted when a truck pulled into the parking lot. Vonnie looked over her shoulder and was surprised to see it was from Castillo's Delivery Services.

The driver unloaded boxes onto a hand cart, pushed them inside, and unstacked them at the end of the bar. Then he walked over to Miss Anne and presented a clipboard.

The old lady frowned at the papers. "Are you trying to rob me? Why is this bill so high? You've delivered more than this before, and the bill was never this much."

The driver rolled his eyes and sighed with irritation. "I deliver the goods, lady. If you have a complaint, call the office. Now sign the paper. I need to get out of here. I have other stops to make."

"I won't sign anything until you explain why this bill is so high," Miss Anne said, snapping.

Exasperated, the driver wiped the sweat from his forehead with his arm. "Look, lady, I don't have time for this. Those boxes go back if you don't sign the papers."

"If you touch those boxes, I'll beat you black and blue," Miss Anne snarled, standing and waving her cane. "You're nothing but a bunch of thieves, always trying to take advantage of people. I'm no fool. Your Big Man, Mr. Castillo, will hear about this."

Frustrated, the delivery man snatched the clipboard, returned to his truck, and sped out of the parking lot as the tires spewed sand and gravel.

Miss Anne fumed as she shuffled to a wall and turned on the ceiling fans. "Thieves and crooks, that's what they are; they're ruining this country. And Mr. Big Man Castillo thinks he can treat people any way he wants." she grumbled.

She came back to sit across from Vonnie, breathing heavily from the exertion and clutching the cane in a death grip. The scowl lingered on her face.

"Calm down, Miss Anne, calm down," Vonnie said, leaning across the bar stroking the older woman's shoulder. "Why don't you hire another delivery service?"

"If I could I would, but Mr. Big Man Castillo is the only one who delivers liquor out here. There used to be other people I could depend on, but he's driven everyone else out of business. Delivery companies need a special license from the government to deliver liquor, and Mr. Big Man Castillo is the only one with a license in this part of the country," she said.

Vonnie couldn't believe her luck, this was the perfect opportunity to learn more about Dominic from someone other than Ana. So, feigning surprise and ignorance, she asked, "Wow, who is this guy, Castillo? What's his story?"

Miss Anne looked at the stacked boxes and sighed as she turned and looked at Vonnie with a weary, defeated expression. Then, finally, she stood up, shaking her head, and removed Vonnie's coffee cup. "If he's who you want to talk about, you'll need something stronger than coffee. How about I fix you one of my special mojitos?"

* * *

Vonnie didn't remember the drive home from Placencia. She switched off the car's ignition and looked up at the house, waiting for her brain to register her location. Then she entered the house, tossed the Amazon package onto the sofa, and flopped into her father's old leather easy chair.

Miss Anne was extremely candid about divulging the saga of Dominic. There were rumors and allegations of shady business deals, transporting illegal goods, and criminal ties but no arrests due to payoffs and bribes made to high-ranking law enforcement officials and politicians. And a trail of local and foreign broken-hearted women wound its way through the country.

Vonnie kicked off her shoes, placed her feet on the ottoman, and wiggled her toes. There was a permanent dip in the cracked, worn leather where her heels rested. An image of her father lounging in the chair and sipping whiskey while reading the newspaper flashed through her mind.

The family room was still in disarray from her failed attempt at redecorating. She looked at the wallpaper, ripped in places and exposing multiple layers or, in some instances, the bare cement wall. The tables and chairs, covered with sheets, the drop cloths on the floor, the cans of paint, paint thinner, wallpaper, glue solvent, and other tools had been pushed aside to form a walking path.

She retrieved a plastic tub from the back porch, poured a small jar of scented Epsom salt from Ana's basket into the bottom, and filled it with hot water. She settled herself back in the chair, gently lowered her feet into the water, leaned back, and closed her eyes.

Vonnie had come to Belize to sell the plantation, thinking that without it and the memories it held, she could turn her baby steps toward recovery into strides and move forward with life. But since her arrival, nothing had gone as planned. There were no firm offers to buy the property, she wasn't speaking to her best friends, the recommended dosages of her prescribed meds were being ignored, and she was drinking more than ever. When Dominic entered her life, he opened a small window through which she could see the light of future possibilities. But after all she'd learned from Ana and today from Miss Anne, the window had to close. Which meant the light would disappear, and she'd end up in the dark again.

She awoke, not realizing that she had dozed off. The water in the foot tub was cold, but she didn't move to take them out. Instead, her gaze fell upon the Amazon package on the sofa. A cloud of sadness surrounded her heart as she sighed heavily, removed her feet from the tub, and began drying them with a towel.

# 22

# VONNIE

It was finally Friday, the beginning of the long-awaited weekend with Dominic, and Vonnie was an hour into the four-and-a-half-hour drive on the Hummingbird Highway headed to San Ignacio. She had her car windows down as she drove through the lush landscape. The warm tropical air, heavy with the fragrance of pineapple, wafted through the car as she cruised past fields of workers harvesting the fruit.

Her emotions ricocheted like a ball in a pinball machine, bouncing from excitement to apprehension to fear in no specific order as the car sped along. The visit to Placencia earlier in the week weighed on her mind. Miss Anne told her things about Dominic that left her feeling there was no alternative but to end the relationship. Frowning, she tightly gripped the steering wheel.

Until she met Dominic, she had thought the romantic and sexual parts of her life had died with Russ. But Dominic made her feel alive, attractive, and desired. So even though the plan was to give him up, she would meet him in San Ignacio and then decide how best to end the relationship.

The sun shone brightly on the rolling hills saturated in greenery as the road's incline increased. She shifted in the car seat, moved her shoulders, and rotated her neck to ease the tension, but her mind continued to whirl.

The San Ignacio Resort was situated high in the hills of the rainforest. The entrance had red tile floors and yellow walls adorned with original artwork by renowned Belizean artists. Colorful hanging baskets overflowed with tropical flowers. The reception area had retractable walls pushed back on three sides, and a balmy breeze wafted through the open space.

When she entered her suite, Vonnie was delighted with the trendy, urban-styled decor mixed with Mayan-themed paintings and accessories. In the lounge area, a lavender, triple-wide chaise leather sofa faced the patio. Directly in front of the sofa, on a low bamboo table, was a wrapped bottle of champagne in an ice bucket, two flutes, and a fruit basket. Two more bottles were chilling in the refrigerator. A large flat-screen TV hung over a credenza topped with hand-carved wooden figures of Mayan gods. A small dining table with two twisted bamboo chairs was in the corner.

A patio extended from the lounge area to the bedroom. There was a small swimming pool, wooden lounge chairs with thick white cushions under a blue umbrella, and large clay pots overflowing with multicolored flowers. Through the treetops, she could see the town's rooftops below.

In the bedroom, at the foot of the California king bed, mahogany-framed glass accordion doors opened onto the patio. The bedroom's en suite contained a floor-to-ceiling window that looked out onto a beautiful view of dense tropical foliage that provided complete privacy, a two-person Jacuzzi tub, a glass-enclosed shower stall, and his and hers marble vanities.

Vonnie began to unpack her suitcase. She held up the new robe, admired it, and laid it gently on the bed.

She looked at the time on her phone; Dominic wasn't due for two hours, giving her enough time to slip into the oversized Jacuzzi bathtub and prepare for his arrival. She turned on the water, poured in some of Ana's bath salts, and swallowed another oxycodone tablet. As she slid into the tub, her back, hips, and knees welcomed the pulsating jets of warm, silky water, and the pain and stiffness floated away.

Hair and makeup done, wearing her new lingerie, she was curled up on the chaise, sipping champagne and channel surfing, when he knocked on the door. Relaxed and mellow, she unfolded herself, took a deep breath, lifted her chin, and walked confidently to the door.

"Wow, you look beautiful," Dominic exclaimed with a big smile. He dropped his overnight bag, pulled her into his arms, and kissed her lightly. Then, loosening his embrace, he seductively smiled at her. "I finally have you all to myself for two days, and I intend to use every minute to savor you from head to toe."

While he showered, Vonnie quickly turned off the TV and synchronized the room's Bluetooth speakers to a romantic playlist on her cell phone. He walked back into the room with a white towel wrapped around his waist.

Vonnie swooned as her eyes took him in. He was undoubtedly the most handsome man she'd ever been with, and for the next two nights, he was all hers. Her eyes traveled downward from the salt-and-pepper dreadlocks moist from the shower steam; several strands hung across his left eye. Encircling his captivating smile was a perfectly trimmed, close-cropped beard and mustache. Then a smooth and flawless chest, flat stomach, firm hips, and muscled legs.

Dominic slid onto the chaise and lifted his glass. "A toast to us and a future filled with love and happiness."

Unsure of how to respond knowing this might be their last time together, Vonnie smiled and touched her glass to his.

Dominic drained the flute, and Vonnie quickly refilled it.

He took her hands in his and looked into her eyes. "Vonnie, you're the most amazing woman I've ever known. We haven't spent much time together, but I can't get you out of my mind. You've touched my heart in ways no other woman has, and I want more with you than random phone calls and sporadic weekends. And, this weekend, I intend to show you how much you mean to me."

Vonnie's heart swelled with emotion at the words. "Thank you, Dominic," she said.

Dominic produced a joint the size of a cigarette, lit it, took two deep drags, lifted his chin into the air, and exhaled the smoke. Then smiling wickedly, he offered it to her.

Vonnie leaned back and shook her head from side to side. "Oh no, I haven't smoked weed since college."

"Well, let's make up for all the years you've missed," he said, sliding closer to her. "Come on, this is a celebration. You can trust me to take care of you. Just take a couple of hits, it will relax you," he said, pleading, with a wolfish grin.

Vonnie thought about it, then relented. She acted more confident than she felt. Tentatively, she inhaled the smoke, counted to three, slowly exhaled, then tossed back a swallow of champagne.

Grinning, Dominic topped off her glass. "That was great. You only need two more just like that."

Vonnie repeated the action twice, then returned the joint to Dominic, who finished it. Her head was thrown back, eyes closed, and all inhibitions replaced by a beautiful, timeless bliss.

"Tell me, how do you feel?" Dominic asked in a sultry voice, one hand gently massaging her upper thigh.

Vonnie felt as if she was bathed in a golden light, floating free of all earthly negativity. Her voice was low and sensual. "I feel absolutely wonderful."

Dominic lay back on the chaise, opened the towel, put his knees up, spread his legs, and clasped his hands behind his head. Then, looking at Vonnie with a devilish smile, he said, "This is yours all weekend. What are you going to do with it?"

The move was unexpected, and it left Vonnie speechless and mesmerized.

Dominic laughed at her expression and rapidly closed and opened his knees twice. "You didn't answer the question."

Vonnie shifted her position to be on all fours and crawled to him. The remainder of the night was a realized fantasy. Dominic was her sexual master, and she was more than a willing participant. Finally, feeling as light as a feather, totally serene, and wrapped in his strong arms, she drifted off to sleep.

# 23

# HADWIN

On Friday afternoon, while Vonnie was at the San Ignacio Resort preparing for her date with Dominic, three ten-year-old boys, Antoine, Luca, and Marcos, raced a quarter of a mile from the edge of Hollister Plantation to their favorite swimming hole on the Howler River. Then, stripping off their T-shirts as they neared the launch point on the river's edge, they cannon-balled forty feet off the riverbank into the water without slowing down or breaking their stride.

It was almost an hour of rambunctious play before Luca surfaced from a dive and swam to the opposite bank to rest. He lay back, rested on his elbows, and watched his friends playing tag in the water. Twenty feet to his left, he saw something strange in the trees along the riverbank. Curious, he went to investigate.

"Ant, Marc," he yelled as he stared at the crumpled body. "Come here, hurry."

His friends splashed and frolicked in the water, focused on their game.

Luca quickly turned to face them and yelled louder. "Come over here. There's a man over here, and I think he's dead."

He had their attention. Antoine and Marcos swam to the bank and ran to Luca. The group moved closer and gawked at the man sprawled in the brush beside the riverbank.

Antoine bent over, placed both hands on his knees, and peered at the man. Then, whispering, he asked, "Is he really dead?"

"How would I know? He looks dead to me," Luca responded, quietly stepping closer to get a better view.

Marcos picked up a long, leafless tree branch. "Here, poke him with this and see if he wakes up."

"You do it," Luca responded, eyes wide with fear, shaking his head. "You've got the stick; I'm not getting close to him."

Marcos looked at Antoine.

"Nope, don't look at me. I'm not doing it either," he replied. "I don't want anything to do with a dead body. It's your idea, You do it."

Resigned, Marcos slowly and timidly eased forward with the tree branch. Then, when he was about six feet away, he leaned forward and jabbed the tree branch twice into the man's shoulder. There was no response.

"Get closer. Poke him harder." Luca demanded.

Marcos crept closer and struck the man hard on the chest. The man turned his head, eyes still closed, and moaned. "He's alive," Marcos yelped, horrified, and jumped backward.

Luca took a few steps forward, squatted, and scrutinized the man. The man was lying on his back, on top of a backpack; he was filthy. There was duct tape around his left leg, and a dark stain extended to the end of his pant leg. A pistol lay on the ground three feet above the man's right foot.

Squatting down beside Luca, Antoine whispered, "What do you think?"

Marcos was agitated and scared. "I think we should get out of here," he said, nervously scanning the area around them. "We don't know where he came from. Someone might be chasing him."

The three boys dashed toward the river, swam to the other side, and scampered up the riverbank. Men working in the plantation's banana groves looked up as the boys blazed past, running at full speed. Then breathless and excited, they burst into the plantation's administration office.

* * *

Hadwin was up to his elbows in spreadsheets when he heard the commotion in the front office. Pushing back from his desk, he stood up, walked to his office door, and peeped around the corner. Three boys were gesticulating wildly, all three talking loudly and simultaneously to Maria, the office manager.

"Hadwin, you'd better come in here," Maria yelled over her shoulder.

Hadwin entered the reception area, looking from Maria to the boys. "What's going on?" he asked.

Animated, interrupting one another, the boys retold the story of finding an unconscious man at the river.

Hadwin turned to Maria. "Call John and tell him to get over here immediately," he said. "Boys, have a seat, We'll need you to show us the location. And Maria, call their parents. Let them know what's happening and that the boys are with me."

He immediately returned to his office and called Ana, He wanted her to be ready when he returned.

Excited and glowing with their newfound importance, the boys plopped in three orange plastic chairs, grinning from ear to ear.

John Ramirez, chief of security for the Hollister Plantation, was a retired lieutenant colonel who'd previously served in the Belizean Defense Force. He was forty-five, six feet tall, with caramel-colored skin and two hundred pounds of pure muscle. Thirty minutes after the boys reported the sighting, Hadwin, John, two security guards, and the three boys loaded themselves into two pickup trucks and drove to the river. The situation was just as the boys had described—the unconscious stranger was still there.

The two security guards immediately began searching the surrounding area. John knelt, took the stranger's vital signs, and performed a body search. While he examined the stranger, Hadwin picked up the pistol and stuck it in his waistband. The boys huddled in a tight group, eyes wide, taking in the entire scene. Later, they would eagerly regurgitate the whole story to their families and friends.

Hadwin stood with his arms folded over his chest, watching John. "So, what do you think—refugee?" he asked.

John removed his cap and scratched his head. Then, still looking down at the stranger, he said, "Hard to say; he's in bad shape, and there's something nasty under that duct tape. Let's load him up and get him to Ana. We can talk on the way back."

John was quiet and in a reflective mood during the drive back.

"What's on your mind, John? I know you. I can see the wheels turning in your brain. Do you think this guy is a refugee or not?" Hadwin asked.

"I don't know yet, but some things struck me as odd."

"Well, what is it? Speak up."

"Well, it's hard to tell his age because of the insect bites and facial hair, but he's not a young man. I'd put him in his late forties, maybe fifties, which is old compared to most refugees around here. The refugees that pass through here are typically in their teens and twenties.

"Next, most refugees perform manual labor to earn their way north. Take, for instance, the migrants who work on the plantation. Their hands are rough and calloused, yet the blisters and callouses on this guy's hands are relatively new."

"So, what are you saying? This guy doesn't fit the profile of a refugee because he has soft hands?"

"I'm just telling you what I observed."

"Well, what else?" Hadwin asked, his impatience growing.

"When I opened those coveralls to search him, he was wearing a Castore brand golf shirt and slacks underneath. I don't know if you know much about designer clothing brands, but that's real high-dollar shit. I've only seen it on wealthy foreigners and expats. Now, mind you, the clothes may have been stolen; I don't want to jump to conclusions."

Hadwin became irritated, and his tone sarcastic. "So, let me summarize, we have an unconscious man with soft hands, designer clothes, and a gun, and you don't think he's a refugee? Is that it?"

John stopped the truck in front of Ana's clinic.

"Let's wait and see what happens after Ana finishes with this guy. Unfortunately, his vitals weren't that good. Looks like he's lost a lot of blood. But hopefully he'll survive, and we'll have an opportunity to interrogate him before turning him over to the authorities."

* * *

Ana was sitting in her tiny office in the plantation's clinic, with her head down on the desk, sobbing over the death of a family friend. Her cell phone vibrated with calls, emails, and texts from families of loved ones suffering or dying from COVID-19. Upon hearing a truck stop and Hadwin's voice outside the clinic's entrance, she snatched a tissue from the box on her desk, blew her nose, and wiped her eyes. She entered the waiting room just as two security guards came through the door, struggling to carry an unconscious man. One guard held the man under his shoulders; the other had his feet. Hadwin and John trailed the guards into the room.

"Where do you want us to put him?" the first guard asked, breathless, straining to carry the load.

"Put him in the examination room on the left." she said, scrutinizing the patient as the guards lumbered past. She, Hadwin, and John followed them into the examination room.

The guards placed the man on the examination table and stepped aside.

Ana quickly snatched open a drawer, retrieved a pair of medical shears, and handed them to John. "We need to get him out of those clothes. Remove the fabric around that duct tape but don't remove the tape; I'll handle that.

"I'll be right back. I need to get an IV and some drugs from the safe. Hadwin, call Alicia; tell her it's an emergency and ask her to come and assist me. John, I want you to stay, the rest of you OUT!" she barked.

* * *

It had been seven hours since Hadwin and John had delivered the unconscious stranger to Ana, and now it was almost midnight. Hadwin sat in the dark drinking a beer on his front porch. The lights showed through the clinic's windows, seventy yards away.

Most of the houses around him were dark; neighborhood dogs barked at one another, and insects chirped. The scent of the fruit trees and tropical flowers was heavy in the warm night air. It was a calm, star-filled night that did not compare in any way to the day's events.

In the illumination of the clinic's exterior light post, he saw John's figure emerge and begin the trek toward the house. Hadwin rose from his chair, entered the house, and grabbed three beers from the refrigerator: another for him and two for John.

By the time he settled back into his porch chair, John approached the steps. He handed John the beer and asked, "Well, what's the verdict?"

John leaned back on the porch post facing Hadwin and guzzled the whole bottle before speaking. "Damn, I needed that," he said, wiping his mouth with the back of his hand.

Hadwin handed him the second bottle. "That bad?"

John accepted the bottle, reached into his front pocket, and stretched his hand to Hadwin. "Here's a present for you," he said, dropping a 9mm bullet into Hadwin's outstretched palm. "Your wife removed that from his leg."

"Whoa, so that was the reason for the duct tape."

"That's not all. It looked like something with a larger caliber took out a nice slice of his thigh. I'm guessing an automatic rifle grazed him," John said, taking another swallow of beer.

"What else?"

"Ana tested him for COVID-19 and malaria; he's positive for malaria. She has all types of painkillers, antibiotics, and fluids going. He was filthy and infested with all kinds of bugs. Alicia was starting to shave him when I left," John said. "That guy has no idea how lucky he is to have ended up with Ana."

"Shaving him—why shave his beard off?"

"I'm not talking about his beard; they're shaving his whole damn body. That's the only way Ana could be sure she found every critter. That guy had bugs making a home in his ass," John said, laughing. "Those days in the forest had to be some of the most miserable days of his life. Ana will have to spend a week disinfecting and sanitizing that place; it's a mess."

"Spare me the gory details, please." Hadwin said, smiling.

"A few more things, and I need to get out of here; I'm tired. We might be dealing with a US citizen." John said, draining the beer bottle.

Hadwin immediately sat up straight. "A US citizen; what makes you think that?"

"Two tattoos; the first was from a Native American tribe called the Coushatta Tribe. I looked them up on Google, and their reservation is in Louisiana. The second was an African Zulu tribal symbol for strength. There's also a Zulu social group in Louisiana that participates in the annual Mardi Gras. I also found that on Google. I'd venture to say those two are linked somehow," John answered. "Last but not least, there was duct tape on his feet to relieve the friction from the boots. Those were not his boots. His feet were as soft as a baby's ass, the same as his hands."

Concern crept into Hadwin's voice. "So, some pretty bad people were obviously chasing this guy."

"Yep, but I don't think they wanted to kill him. They just wanted to wound him. Slow him down, perhaps. You'd have to be a pretty awful shot not to kill a man with an automatic rifle."

"So, you think they just wanted to capture him?"

"That's my assumption. He was running from someone when they shot him. Ana removed the bullet from the back of his thigh. But unfortunately, he couldn't travel very far on that leg, so whoever was chasing him may be too close for our comfort. I've already briefed my team, and they're on overlapping shifts. So, remember that when you see the timesheets," John said, covering a yawn. "Is Vonnie aware of what's going on?"

"No, not yet. I don't know where she is. I've called and sent her text messages, but she hasn't responded."

Yawning again, John said, "Go check on your wife. She should be able to talk to you by now. Don't try to call her; she turned off her phone." He walked down the steps and walked out of the yard.

Hadwin picked up the beer bottles, went into the house, and tossed them into the trash. Then he extracted bottled water, sandwiches, and salads from the refrigerator, put them in an awaiting picnic basket, and walked to his truck. Pillows and blankets were already on the seat.

He was worried about Ana; she was depressed and grieving heavily over her COVID-19 patients and her relationship with Vonnie. As it was, she was losing weight and not sleeping well—and now this.

"I brought food," he hollered as he walked into the clinic's reception area and set the picnic basket on the reception counter.

Ana stepped out of the examination room and stood in the hall dressed in full PPE. "Hey, baby, thank you so much," she said through her face mask. She didn't come closer.

"Hello, Mr. Perez," Alicia shouted from the examination room. "Thanks for the food; I'm starving."

"No problem, Alicia. Just let me know if you need anything else, and I'll make sure you get it," Hadwin shouted back.

"The only thing I need besides food is a long, hot shower. You wouldn't believe what we're going through in here," she said, laughing.

Turning his attention back to his wife, Hadwin said, "You look cute in your new outfit. Is that the latest in designer wear? I never realized how sexy blue booties could be."

"Yes, it's the latest from Paris; everyone's wearing it," Ana said with a giggle as she put her hands on her waist and stuck her hip out.

"Well, I spoke with John, and he told me about your heroic efforts and a few horror stories. So, I assumed you'd be spending the night down here."

"I can't leave him tonight. It's too serious right now, and none of the doctors I usually consult with are available; they're busy fighting COVID."

"I have pillows and blankets in the truck; I'll bring them in. Maybe you'll be able to take a nap."

"Thanks again, baby; I wish I could hug you." Ana waved goodbye.

"I do too, but I'm a patient man; I'll be back in the morning with breakfast and coffee."

He returned from the truck and placed the linens on the counter. "I'm gone. See you in the morning." he yelled out. On the way out, he locked the door and tested it to ensure it was secure.

He could tell Ana had been crying when they arrived with the stranger earlier that day. Her eyes were red and swollen, and she was holding a tissue. But, from the moment they laid the stranger on the examination table, she became laser focused, and began shouting orders like a general—she was in her zone.

An uneasiness descended upon him as he parked the truck and lumbered into the house. He sighed heavily, tossed his truck keys on the kitchen table, and walked down the hall toward his bedroom. The man in the clinic wasn't a lost tourist hiking the rainforest or a refugee seeking a better life. If John was right, some bad people were chasing this guy, and he had been running for his life. Whoever he was, they had to get him off the plantation as soon as possible.

# 24

# VONNIE

Vonnie awoke Saturday morning, swallowed in the luxurious white duvet without Dominic beside her. Sunlight flooded the room. The doors to the patio were open, and humid air wafted through the room. Groggily rising on her elbows, she glanced at the bedside clock—it was almost 10:30. There was no movement in the bathroom or the lounge area; the suite was quiet.

"Dominic, where are you?" she called out. There was no response.

She flopped back on the pillow and covered her head with the sheet. The bedding was saturated with the scent of sex. It aroused her, and she wanted more. Nestled deep under the duvet, she sighed.

*How can I ever give this up?*

After thirty minutes, Vonnie decided another pill and a soak in the Jacuzzi would help keep the aches and pains at bay. So by the time Dominic returned, she'd be fresh and ready. The medication and hot water jets relaxed her, and without intending to, she dozed off and awoke with a jolt in tepid water. The digital clock on the bathroom wall displayed 11:45.

"It's almost lunchtime; where did he go?" she asked aloud. "He could have left a note saying when he'd be back."

Pulling on her robe, she went to the bedside table, and then called him. The call went straight to voicemail. "Dominic, where are you? You left without saying anything." she said, trying not to sound too anxious or angry. Her stomach growled, reminding her that she hadn't eaten.

Room service promptly arrived with bacon, eggs, waffles, fruit, freshly squeezed orange juice, and coffee. She turned on the TV in the lounge area and began eating, but she focused solely on the delicious food and the impotent cell phone lying beside her plate. It wasn't until she heard the words 'Castillo's Delivery Services' that she stopped chewing and glanced at the TV.

It was breaking news. The chyron crawling across the bottom of the screen read: "Local Delivery Company Involved in Human Trafficking." Police cars, emergency aid vehicles, and a large Castillo's Delivery Services truck were the backdrop for a news reporter interviewing a police officer.

A Castillo's Delivery Services truck transporting forty-eight illegal Honduran refugees had broken down on its journey to smuggle the human cargo north to the Mexican border. The driver abandoned the vehicle on a rarely used dirt road, leaving the refugees locked inside the trailer in the sweltering tropical heat. Three people were dead; emergency response teams were transporting the others to the hospital. Authorities were seeking both the truck driver and the trucking company's owner.

Vonnie was dumbfounded. Her hands trembled as she fumbled with the remote, switched to another station, and heard a slightly different version of the same story. This reporter's back-drop was outside the Castillo's Delivery Services building in Belize City. Displayed prominently in the corner of the screen was Dominic's picture. Anyone with information about his whereabouts should contact the police immediately.

She was on the verge of hyperventilating as she staggered to the bedroom door, knowing what she'd find. Dominic's overnight bag was gone. Her legs were so weak that she couldn't stand. She slid down the doorframe to the floor, holding her hand to her chest, frantically gasping for air.

"You fool! You stupid, stupid fool!"

* * *

After discovering Dominic's involvement in trafficking Honduran refugees, Vonnie didn't leave the San Ignacio Resort on Sunday as initially planned. Instead, she stayed until late Monday afternoon, popping anti-depressants, finishing off the champagne, and scouring the news media, trying to reconcile the idea of the caring and passionate man with whom she had spent hours making love to the villain responsible for the horror playing out in the news media. The images of men loading body bags into emergency response vehicles made her physically ill.

Instead of telling Dominic the relationship was over before she left the plantation or the moment he walked through the door, she had willingly allowed herself to be swept away, not realizing her foolishness would drop her headfirst into the vortex of a hurricane.

The implications of being with Dominic when the police discovered the refugees were too disastrous to imagine. If the Hollister name came up during the police investigation, there would be a media frenzy. A scandal would taint her family's legacy in Belize and possibly destroy any hope of selling the plantation.

She hadn't told anyone about the weekend getaway, so no one knew about her liaison with Dominic unless, if caught, he used her as an alibi which could put her in jeopardy of being an accessory to murder. The thought made her furious. If the police came to question her, an army of lawyers would meet them; she wasn't going down with Dominic's ship.

Finally, at 10:30 p.m., humiliated and not wanting to alert anyone of her return, Vonnie slipped into the dark plantation house like a thief. Nightlights on the wall baseboards guided her through the unlit downstairs and upstairs to her bedroom. In the semi-darkness of the bedroom, she closed the drapes, turned on the bedside table lamp and fell back on the bed, covering her eyes with her forearms.

The bedroom was warm and stuffy, so she raised herself from the bed, started the ceiling fan, and checked the messages on her cell phone. She had silenced her cell phone to prevent interruptions while she was with Dominic, then forgot to turn the ringer back on. She was surprised to see four texts and two voicemails from Hadwin. She responded to his latest text and agreed to a meeting the following afternoon.

Stiff and sore from the drive, she popped two oxycodone pills, washed them down with the remnants of stale wine in a glass left on the nightstand, and then fell asleep lying across the bed, fully clothed.

The following day, childhood memories came rushing back to her while she walked across the grounds to Hadwin's office. Recollections of running between the houses playing, eating from fruit trees growing in the yards, hot days swimming in the Howler River or the ocean, birthday parties, weddings, and cookouts. Then there were the summers she spent working at various jobs; walking the rows cutting bananas from the trees, gossiping and joking with other women and teenage girls at the flowing water trough where they washed away the dirt and debris, wrapping and packing the bananas in boxes. And flirting with the handsome, brown teenage boys as they loaded the boxes onto the trucks that would take them to the wholesalers. The joyful memories were too numerous to count.

She expected to encounter older women sitting on porches or hanging laundry on clotheslines, but remembering it was ninety-eight degrees, she assumed they were performing chores inside. Then she was surprised to see air-conditioning units protruding from the windows; only The Big House had air-conditioning when she was a girl.

Vonnie abruptly stopped and shielded her eyes to block the glaring sun. Then slowly turning in a circle, she scanned the surrounding area. Other noticeable improvements revealed themselves. In the distance, in what had been an open, barren field, were four picnic shelters, a baseball diamond, soccer goals, and what appeared to be a community building. As far as the eye could see and beyond, was her land, but since returning to the plantation, she hadn't noticed any of it.

Finally, she arrived at the plantation's administration building, winded and sweaty from walking in the searing heat; the chill of the air-conditioned room felt refreshing. The receptionist, an attractive woman of about forty, with a broad smile covering her face, quickly jumped to her feet, and said, "Good afternoon, Miss Hollister."

The woman looked so pleased to be in Vonnie's presence that Vonnie thought she might bow or curtsy. "Good afternoon..." Vonnie noticed her name tag: Maria Mendez, Office Manager. "Good afternoon, Maria. I'm here to meet with Hadwin." she said, snatching two tissues from the box on the counter and patting the sweat on her face and neck.

"The first door on the right, they're waiting for you."

Hadwin's office was slightly larger than a closet. His desk sat between two tall filing cabinets. On top of the cabinets were boxes and stacks of papers. Behind him, over his head, were shelves filled with colored binders and books.

Three orange plastic chairs, confiscated from the reception area, were placed in the narrow gap between the front of the desk and the back wall. A vacant chair sat at the end, inside the doorway. John sat beside the empty chair; his knees almost touched the desk. Ana occupied the third seat next to John, her right shoulder only inches from a window. All heads turned as Vonnie entered the doorway.

Ana suppressed her shock at Vonnie's appearance. Her friend looked bedraggled and worn down. There were dark circles under her eyes, her hair was haphazardly clasped in a ponytail, and she was wearing wrinkled, oversized T-shirt and Bermuda shorts.

*Something's wrong with Vonnie; this isn't like her. She knew we had a meeting today, but it's as if she just crawled out of bed and came down without a second thought. I wonder if it has anything to do with Dominic and the police investigation.*

Vonnie greeted everyone with a smile, expecting small talk before discussing business, but the pensive facial expressions told her something was wrong. Hadwin wasted no time describing the events related to the discovery of the stranger, John's suspicions of the man being a US citizen, and Ana's efforts to save his life. When he finished his report, Vonnie turned to John. "Has any of this been reported to the police?" she asked.

John turned to face her. "I spoke with the local chief, and for now, he's leaving it to us to handle because the man's still unconscious and under Ana's care. And every hospital in the country is over capacity with COVID-19 patients, so there's nowhere else to take him. But I know the chief personally, and he trusts me, so we agreed I'll call him and discuss the next steps once this guy is conscious."

John's brow was furrowed, and he shifted in his chair. "My primary concern is that whoever shot his guy might not give up and come looking for him here. The security team is on double duty patrolling the grounds, but we have over two thousand acres with no physical border. So, if my men encounter anyone or anything suspicious, they know how to handle it."

Vonnie sat up straighter, her body stiffening. "And what does that mean?" she asked.

"Vonnie, you know what law enforcement is like in this district. They lack resources and training. It's my job to protect the plantation. My men are all ex-military professionals; they're trained to handle dangerous situations."

Vonnie's eyes widened, and her voice rose in astonishment. "Surely you aren't talking about shooting or killing people?"

"Hopefully it won't come to that, but we don't know the whole situation or with whom we're dealing. Someone shot this man twice, once with what I believe was an automatic weapon. He couldn't have traveled very far with his injuries, so until we know who and what we're dealing with, I'm going to be hyper-vigilant about security. My men have orders to neutralize any threat they encounter."

Vonnie let out a sigh, folded her arms across her chest, and leaned back in her seat. "I agree we need security, but I don't agree with shooting or killing people on this property. I won't have it. These situations are for the police to handle. If our security guards find anything, they should turn it over. I think we may be getting ahead of ourselves. I disapprove of guns."

John looked at Hadwin, his eyes signaling for him to step in and take control of the conversation.

With both elbows on his desk and hands clasped together, Hadwin leaned toward Vonnie. "Vonnie, I agree with John. Ensuring the security of the plantation was the reason your father and I hired John; to assemble a professional security team instead of a bunch of mall cops. Mr. Hollister realized the remote location of the plantation and its proximity to the western and southern borders make us vulnerable. He also used his political influence to obtain the government's permission for John's team to possess automatic rifles. Your father wasn't only thinking about protecting his investment; he was thinking about the security of the people living and working here. Let John handle this his way."

Vonnie's indignation waned as she listened to Hadwin. He was right; her father was fiercely protective of the plantation, it was his inheritance and his family's legacy. If he thought there was a need for this level of security years ago, it was highly likely that it was much needed now. Her shoulders slumped, and she took a deep breath.

"My dad never told me any of this. I had no way of knowing. He and I didn't have much time to discuss the workings of the plantation before he died. So, forgive me for going off like that. This is all new to me; I'm a little overwhelmed." She turned from Hadwin to John. "Has anything like this happened before?"

"We've had several serious altercations over the past five years. We haven't killed anybody and don't want to, but with the never-ending flow of refugees and cartels to our west, we're on alert 24/7. As I said, the local chief and I are close, but I have working relationships with every law enforcement agency in the country."

"So, what's this man's medical status?" Vonnie asked, looking past John at Ana.

Ana took a deep breath and turned to Vonnie. "I'm concerned; he lost a lot of blood and isn't responding well. Alicia and I are doing all we can, but it's touch and go. If he makes it, a full recovery from the leg wound and the malaria will probably take two or three months."

"He's still on the examination table in the clinic, and I need to move him to a better location to treat him properly. A hospital is out of the question. None of them have a bed or room. So, I want to move him into one of the downstairs bedrooms in The Big House." She held her breath, anticipating the imminent explosion she knew was coming.

Vonnie looked at Ana in disbelief. "What! Let me get this straight—you want to move a stranger, from who knows where, who was shot by God knows who, into my house? Are you out of your damn mind?!" she shouted.

John leaned back in his chair and sucked in his nonexistent belly. The women leaned toward one another like boxers squaring off in the ring, their faces were getting closer.

Ana's voice picked up speed. "Either Alicia or I will be there around the clock, and John says he'll post a guard in the house. There's no way this man is going anywhere or doing anything drastic because of his leg. He'll be on the first floor, and your bedroom is on the third. We don't have another option."

John tried to slide his chair back, only to discover it was already touching the wall.

"And you expect him to be in my house for two or three months?" Vonnie said, snapping.

"I can't be sure; as I said, it's touch and go," Ana said, pulling her head back and sitting up straighter. "Once he's cognizant and stable enough to transfer, it will be up to John and the police to determine where he goes."

Vonnie stood up suddenly and stepped into the doorway, struggling to maintain her composure. "Well, it appears the three of you have made all the decisions before I arrived, and you invited me to this meeting only as a courtesy. I'm surprised you didn't move him in while I was away." she sniped.

Hadwin sighed heavily, annoyed and insulted by Vonnie's remarks. "Now hold on, Vonnie. You left and didn't tell anyone where you were going or when you were coming back. I tried contacting you, but you didn't respond until late last night. So, we made a plan to do what we thought was best. That's what you pay us for—to make decisions. You have a five-bedroom house, and a man is clinging to life on an examination table in the clinic. Are you insinuating that we should leave him there?" he asked, glaring at Vonnie.

Vonnie was taken aback by the sharpness in Hadwin's voice. He had never verbally attacked her like that. She looked at the group, her face flushed with embarrassment. "I... I apologize for my comment; I shouldn't have said that. But of course, you made the right decision, given the circumstances. I'm having a hard time processing all of this."

John tried to mitigate the tension in the room. "Vonnie, we know it's a major encroachment on your privacy, but it's our best option if we don't want this guy to die on our watch. I promise to protect you, and we'll move him out as soon as possible."

A torrent of thoughts collided in Vonnie's mind: Dominic, dead refugees, a police investigation that might include her. And now this—a dying stranger would be moving into her house, and people would be crawling all over the place, intruding on her privacy. She struggled to maintain her composure.

"So, when can I expect my guest to arrive?" she asked in a shaky voice.

Ana could see her friend's distress—Vonnie was sweating, and her hands were trembling. Her living conditions would be exposed, but it couldn't be helped.

Ana softened her voice. "Vonnie, I'm sorry, but we don't have another alternative. A man's life is at stake. I'll give you time to prepare. Call me when you're ready, and I'll come up and inventory the room; we'll have to move some of the furniture out."

Vonnie nervously looked at the group and sighed. "I appreciate all of you. Thanks for all you do, and again, I apologize for my comments." Then she looked directly at Ana. "Give me a few hours, I'll do whatever you want."

# 25

# AAPO

The Vasquez family dinner had been a fiasco, and Aapo was livid as he paced the floor of his bedroom.

*I've had it with Humberto; this is all his fault. All he had to do was keep his mouth shut about the missing money and let me handle Papa, but instead, the treacherous bastard squealed like a three-year-old. I need to stop him before he gives those numbers to Papa. And those miserable toy soldiers at the Puerto Maria warehouse who allowed Chance Moore to escape are going to regret the day they were born.*

Aapo quickly checked his cell phone for service, dialed the number for the one person who could resolve his issue, and scheduled a meeting for eleven that night. Then he went to the window and nervously peeked through the drapes. It was dark outside, and moonlight shone on the quiet, still lake. In the distance, lights glowed in the houses that dotted the lake's edge. Two bodyguards with automatic rifles stood talking and smoking cigarettes on the boat dock below.

He picked up the house phone, and a female servant answered.

"Yes, Mr. Vasquez, how may I assist you?" she asked in a pleasant voice.

Aapo examined the fingernails on his right hand. "Tell Stella to come to my room." he demanded.

"Mr. Vasquez, I'm sorry, Stella has left for the day. She'll be back tomorrow. Is there any way I can assist you?"

Furious, Aapo spoke through gritted teeth. "Call and tell her I expect her here within the hour. And have someone bring me a scotch on the rocks." He slammed the phone down.

At 11:00 p.m. sharp, in the back of a dark, dingy bar, Aapo slid an envelope across the table to a tall man with long blond hair and a baseball cap pulled low on his forehead.

Two days later, he was using a straight razor to carefully remove the stubble under his chin when his cell phone vibrated on the vanity countertop. He lowered the razor and tapped the icon to read the text message. The text displayed one word: "Done."

Aapo took a deep breath, rinsed the razor, and continued his shave.

* * *

The sun beamed down in the afternoon's cloudless blue sky. A green translucent donut-shaped inflatable supported Aapo as he floated in the pool, his head tilted back, sunglasses on, hands and feet dangling in the tepid water. In his peripheral vision, he noticed Alex striding toward him.

Alex stood at the pool's edge and looked down at Aapo. "Excuse me, Aapo, something important has come up; we need to talk." There were several newspapers tucked under his arm.

Aapo lazily removed his sunglasses and squinted at Alex. "What's up?"

"I think it's best if we talk on the veranda. I'll have someone bring you a drink." Alex walked to a wrought iron table with an umbrella, put the newspapers down, and spoke quietly into a wall phone. Then he sat and waited for Aapo to join him.

Aapo sauntered to the table, drying himself with a towel. A servant appeared with his drink on a small tray.

Sipping his drink, Aapo asked, "What's going on?"

Alex calmly slid the stack of newspapers toward Aapo. "I regret to tell you this, but Humberto is dead."

Pretending to be surprised, Aapo quickly picked up a newspaper from the stack. "When? What happened? Who killed him?" Then his eyes went wide with shock at what he was seeing. "And what the fuck is this picture on the front page?"

"Haven't you received any calls from the captains or lieutenants today? They've been trying to reach you."

"No cell service," Aapo said, lying as he madly flipped from one newspaper to the next. "I can't believe every fucking newspaper in this country would print these pictures on the front page."

Each newspaper displayed color photographs taken from different angles. The most potent images showed two nude men in bed, their genitals blacked out, bullet holes in their bodies, and bedding saturated in blood.

"It's big news; the coverage will run for days," Alex said.

"So how did this happen? Where were his bodyguards?" Aapo asked, manically shuffling through the newspapers.

Alex leaned back and crossed his arms. "The bodyguards were also killed. The police are positive someone moved the bodies and staged the pictures; the bullet wounds, blood trails, bloodstains—nothing matches up."

Aapo continued to riffle through the papers. The discarded pages littered the floor around the table. "So, how did the police and media find out before our guys?" Aapo asked, bringing a page closer to his face.

"We don't know. But by the time our men arrived, the police and the press were swarming the place like roaches. Of course, they found weapons and drugs—the usual stuff." Alex sighed. "Your father doesn't know."

Aapo stopped fumbling with the newspapers and looked at Alex. "So, when should we tell him?"

"The sooner the better. I withheld the newspapers and asked the nurse not to turn on the TV."

"I forgot about the TV," Aapo said, standing and pushing back his chair. "I'm sure the coverage is pretty dramatic." He moved around, gathering the papers. "Contact the newspaper publishers and warn them that if they print another picture, we'll blow them the fuck up. It's embarrassing. I'll get changed and meet you in Papa's room in fifteen minutes."

"Make it an hour," Alex said, standing and handing Aapo a folded newspaper page.

Standing at his father's bedroom door an hour later, Aapo took a deep breath, squared his shoulders, knocked softly, and stepped inside. The heavy drapes were closed, and the subdued light from the lamps made the room look gloomy. There was an adjustable hospital bed with side rails and an IV pole with a bag of fluid. A male nurse in dark-blue scrubs was fluffing the pillows and tidying the bed. A thick ornamental carpet covered the floor, slippers were tucked under the bed, and a walking cane leaned against an armchair.

Alex stood with his back to the door in front of Eloy. When Aapo entered, Alex looked at him over his shoulder, then stepped aside. Dressed in baggy blue striped pajamas, Eloy sat in an over-stuffed, upholstered chair, hunched over a mobile tray table, eating soup. He looked up, surprised to see Aapo. "What do you want?" he asked.

Alex placed a chair in front of Eloy. "Sit down, Aapo." Then to the nurse, he said, "Give us some privacy."

The nurse hastily left the room and quietly closed the door.

Aapo gulped, lowered himself into the chair facing Eloy, and tightly clutched the refolded newspapers in his lap.

Suspicious of Aapo's presence, Eloy glared at him. His voice was cold. "What is this? Why are you here?" he asked.

Aapo timidly reached for his father's arm. He could feel Eloy's body tense at his touch. "Papa, I came to tell you that Humberto is dead."

Eloy's eyes went wide with shock, and his hands trembled. The spoon fell, clanking against the bowl. "What are you telling me—my son is dead?" He looked up at Alex. "Is this true?"

"Yes, patron, it's true," Alex responded softly.

Aapo placed the newspapers on the tray table, ensuring the photo of Humberto and his lover was on top. "I wanted to tell you before you saw these disgusting pictures in the newspapers."

Eloy glanced down at the newspaper and began breathing heavily. His eyes bulged. Aapo tightened the grip on his father's arm. Then, rushing to get the words out, he said, "Papa, I'll find the dogs who did this, and when I do, I'll make them pay with their lives. I'll handle this. I'll handle everything—don't worry; they won't get away with it."

Eloy jerked his arm away from Aapo's grip and flung the bowl of soup in Aapo's face. The overstuffed chair and the tray table impeded his attempt to stand. Irate, he thrust the tray table away from him toward Aapo.

"YOU... YOU..." he bellowed, struggling to formulate a sentence. Those were the only words he uttered before his eyes rolled back and foam bubbled from his mouth, running down his chin. He writhed in his chair, his body convulsing uncontrollably.

Aapo jumped up from his chair, knocking it and the tray table over as he struggled to wipe soup from his eyes.

"NURSE, NURSE," Alex yelled as he wrestled Eloy to the floor.

The nurse rushed into the room, dropped to his knees, and immediately assisted Alex.

"He's having a seizure. Call the doctor." Alex instructed.

The nurse sprang for the phone on the bedside table. And fearful of the scene unfolding before him, Aapo ran from the room.

Back in his bedroom, Aapo ripped off his shirt, cursing, rushed to the bathroom, snatched a towel from the rack, and roughly wiped the soup from his hair, face, and hands. Then he hurled the towel against the wall.

"I hope he dies." he snarled.

The police investigation into Humberto's death was perfunctory; none of the neighbors heard or saw anything unusual, and there were no suspects. Nevertheless, reporters and camera crews gathered at the Vasquez family's lake house with interview requests.

Secretly pleased with the attention, Aapo pretended to be distraught while willingly giving statements to the press, proclaiming to work with law enforcement to apprehend the criminals who killed his brother.

Two nights later, a caravan of five black vehicles left Lake Izabal and snaked through the countryside toward the Vasquez family estate near the town of San Rosa, fifty miles north of Guatemala City. The estate also served as Eloy's official seat of power, and Humberto would be buried on the estate in the family cemetery.

The lead vehicle carried two bodyguards and Humberto's casket. In the second vehicle were four bodyguards. The third was a van with Eloy, Alex, the nurse, Eloy's doctor, and two bodyguards. Aapo, a bodyguard, and his chauffeur rode in the fourth, and another group of bodyguards was in the fifth.

Aapo sat alone in the dark back seat of the chauffeur-driven Mercedes. He tried to relieve a pounding headache by squeezing the bridge of his nose. The cell phone lying on the seat beside him consistently vibrated with incoming calls and texts that he refused to acknowledge. The previous night, someone ransacked the New York offices of PIIE. Papers and files littered the floors, furniture was broken, electronic equipment smashed, and everything was doused with gasoline even though nothing was set ablaze. It was a warning message.

He loudly exhaled with relief as familiar landmarks marking the entrance to the Vasquez estate came into view. A mile-long driveway wound its way through sprawling grounds of manicured lawns, rows of hedges, topiary, and flower gardens and stopped at a fifteen-foot, ornamental wrought iron gate. Beyond the entry gate, a spacious tiled courtyard spread to the bottom of a broad set of steps that led up to massive, carved double doors. The ambient glow of spotlights situated among the landscaping illuminated the majestic four-story, Spanish colonial-style mansion.

On the day of Humberto's funeral, Aapo was the shining sun while a universe comprised of politicians, business leaders, celebrities, and select members from Central American crime families revolved around him. He preened and pretended to be overawed by the thoughtfulness of the mourners. Everyone expressed their condolences as if the Vasquez family were any other highly esteemed members of society. Armed security guards patrolled the grounds, and plainclothes security men discreetly circulated among the guests. When asked about his father, he told them Eloy had taken to his bed, overcome with grief over losing his youngest son.

The Vasquez family's wealth was on full display. Aapo gave tours of the house's grand interior, outdoor living spaces, the expansive multi-car garage filled with vintage automobiles, and four thoroughbred racehorses in a custom-designed barn. He reveled in the attention and acted as if it were a giant cocktail party rather than his brother's funeral.

* * *

The Vasquez group had been at the mansion for a week when Alex stuck his head inside the spa. "Excuse me for interrupting, Aapo, but I have some news that might be of interest to you."

The scent of lavender was heavy in the dimly lit room. Soft music with the sound of trickling water and Japanese flutes drifted from hidden speakers. Aapo was lying face down on a massage table; a sheet covered his lower body. The masseuse, a young, attractive, dark-haired woman, was kneading the muscles in his back. "Can't it wait?" he mumbled, irritated by the interruption.

"There's news about your hacker." Alex said, settling himself in a chair.

Aapo quickly looked up from the face cradle. "It's about time. Did they get him?" he asked.

"Unfortunately not, but they came close. The soldiers shot him near the Belize border, but he eluded them again. The captain thinks he may have crossed the border."

Aapo hurriedly sat up and pulled the sheet around his waist. The masseuse backed away from the table and stood quietly, watching the scene.

"So why didn't they go after him?" he asked, angrily jumping to his feet and pulling the remainder of the sheet off the table.

"In case you've forgotten, it's an international border. So, imagine what would have happened if Belizean border security discovered our men carrying automatic weapons," he said in a voice dripping with sarcasm.

"Like I give a fuck," Aapo spat. "I want that man caught and brought back here immediately. Send me the men who were tracking him. I want to talk to them."

"Your father reassigned them to help with the turf skirmishes in the Southeast."

"WHAT? He took my men?" Aapo yelled.

"They aren't your men," Alex said in a dry, calm voice. "Eloy is the leader of this organization, and directly or indirectly, everyone reports to him."

Adrenaline surged through Aapo's veins. His eyes flashed with anger. "How can he be in charge? He's almost dead," he yelled, tightly gripping the sheet around his waist.

Unintimidated, Alex stood, walked to the door, and turned back to look at Aapo with a smirk. "Your father isn't dead yet. If you have a problem with his decision, I recommend you talk to him."

Aapo wanted to scream. It had been almost two weeks since the earthquake, and because his father had usurped his authority over the cartel soldiers, no one was searching for Chance Moore. He yanked off the sheet, flung it across the room, and paced the floor naked, his hands balled into fists.

"Excuse me, sir." It was the masseuse, her voice almost a whisper. "Do you want to continue with the massage, or would you prefer I return later?"

Aapo stopped pacing, placed both hands on his hips, and looked at the woman. She dropped her eyes and looked at the floor.

His lips curled into a menacing smile. "Take off your clothes," he demanded sharply.

Her head came up instantly. "What? Sir, I..." she stammered, frightened.

"Take off your clothes, or I'll rip them off," he snarled, slowly advancing like a lion locked on its prey.

She backed away from him, eyes brimming with tears. Her voice quivered. "Sir, please... don't do this," she pleaded.

Aapo lunged, grabbed her by the arm, and slapped her hard; she screamed.

"When I give you an order, you follow it. Do you understand?" His face was so close to hers that their noses almost touched. Then he screamed, "Now take off your clothes."

Terrified, racked with sobs, and fingers trembling, the woman hastily undressed.

An hour later, physically gratified from the sex with the masseuse, Aapo lay naked in the spa's steam room. The strong eucalyptus scent and the hot steam filled his lungs as he languidly drifted, thinking about his new dilemma. Chance Moore had to be caught and brought back to Guatemala by any means necessary. The Specialist hired to handle Humberto never failed; it was time for a new assignment.

* * *

The next night, Aapo and the Specialist met in the parking lot of an old, abandoned warehouse. The Specialist, the bib of his baseball cap pulled low, leaned against an old, dented Nissan Sentra smoking a cigarette when Aapo arrived in a black Mercedes.

"This is going to be a complicated job," the man said, blowing cigarette smoke in Aapo's direction. "It might take a while to find this guy, then figure out how to get him back across the border alive and undetected. It would be easier to kill him and leave him there."

Annoyed, Aapo fanned the smoke away and handed the man an envelope. "Well, you can't kill him. I need him alive and in one piece; it's okay to rough him up if you need to, but don't do any real damage. Is that clear?"

"Yeah, I got it," the man said. The cigarette dangled from his lips as he examined the envelope's contents. "This isn't enough money to pull this thing off. I can't do it alone; I need help."

"You're on the clock, and time is ticking. Let me know how much more money you'll need. I don't give a fuck about how you handle it."

"You're the boss," the man said, giving Aapo a two-finger salute.

Aapo turned to walk back to the Mercedes, then stopped. "And this time, get in, get out, and no funny business-like last time. I don't like it; it causes problems."

A questioning look crossed the man's face. "What are you talking about?"

"Your last job is what I'm talking about... staging Humberto's body, taking pictures, and notifying the police and media. What were you thinking? Why draw that type of attention? It's the last thing either of us needs."

The man blew out a long stream of cigarette smoke, tossed the butt to the ground, and stepped on it. "I don't know what you're talking about. I didn't move the bodies. I left them where they lay. I checked to ensure everyone was dead and left them where they were. You paid me to kill them, and that's what I did. No more, no less."

Aapo was confused. "Are you sure you weren't being watched or followed? No one else knew that you were going to kill him except the two of us."

The man stiffened, and his eyes locked on Aapo. "So, what are you insinuating... that I told someone something? You'd better think twice about what you're saying because I don't like what I'm hearing."

Aapo took a step back and held up both palms. He was dealing with a dangerous man and had to tread carefully. "Hold on, hold on, don't get defensive. So, you're telling me that you killed them, left the scene and someone else showed up, moved the bodies, then anonymously called the police and media?"

"Look, I'm a professional. I don't play games or make stupid mistakes. You paid me to do a job, and I did it. End of story; case closed. Anything that happened after I left didn't involve me" the man said gruffly. Then he got into his car and slammed the door.

"But somebody knew, and they had impeccable timing. The coroner estimated Humberto had only been dead for two or three hours before the police found him."

The man quickly rolled down the driver's side window. "As I said, I did what I was supposed to do and nothing else," he said, cranking the car and gunning the motor. "I'll be in touch as soon as I assemble a team." The tires on the Nissan screeched as it sped out of the parking lot.

The bodyguard opened the rear passenger door of the Mercedes and waited for Aapo to return to the car. Too stunned and confused to speak, Aapo stood for a long moment watching the taillights of the assassin's car leave the parking lot and turn into traffic.

# 26

# VONNIE

Vonnie carried two mugs of coffee as she walked to the bedroom where the stranger was recuperating. The security guard, a brown-skinned, muscular young man in his late twenties, wore a white golf shirt with the Hollister Plantation security logo on the front, tan cargo pants, and tan military boots; a handgun rested in a holster on his waist. He sat beside the bedroom door, scrolling through his cell phone, then immediately stood when he saw Vonnie approaching.

"Good morning, Miss Hollister." he said, smiling and accepting a mug of coffee.

"Good morning," Vonnie responded, quietly glancing into the room. An IV pole was at the head of the bed; tubes extended from a bag of fluid into the patient's arm, and various medical utensils were on a tray on the bedside table. A crumpled blanket and pillow lay in a recliner across from the bed.

Ana was standing at the head of the bed, a stethoscope in her ears, checking the blood pressure of the unconscious man. Vonnie waited until Ana stepped back from the bed before entering the room.

"How's he doing?" she whispered, handing Ana the remaining coffee mug.

Sipping the warm black liquid and looking down at her patient, Ana said, "He's slowly coming to the surface. He's murmuring and moving around; he'll be fully conscious soon. His vitals are still shaky because of the malaria, but the medication is helping."

"Can you step out for a quick second? I want to talk to you about something," Vonnie asked.

"Sure, give me a few minutes, and I'll meet you in the kitchen" Ana responded, setting the mug on the bedside table.

Vonnie was drinking coffee at the kitchen counter when Ana came in and sat across from her. Vonnie thought her friend looked tired and had lost weight. The stress from treating COVID-19 patients and the man down the hall was evident. She reached across the counter and took Ana's hand.

"Ana, I love you. You mean more to me than you'll ever know, and I want to apologize for how I've treated you. I've been a royal bitch, and I'm sorrier than you'll ever know." Her voice quivered and tears welled in her eyes. "I should have listened to you when you told me about Dominic. I've been nothing but an old fool." The tears flowed, and she dropped her head in shame.

Ana lifted Vonnie's chin so she could see her face. "It's okay, Vonnie. You've been through a lot over the past few years. You've done nothing but move from one heartbreak to another without a chance to heal. I knew you would understand why I didn't want you involved with that man once you saw the news."

Vonnie moved around the counter and wrapped Ana in her arms. "Please forgive me. I don't know what I'd do without you. You're all I have."

Ana looked at her friend and smiled. "Vonnie, all is forgiven. I'm not mad at you. I was disappointed you ignored my advice, but you're my sister; I want what's best for you." Then Ana took a deep breath. "Vonnie, I know the signs, and it's obvious that you're struggling with depression. You've been distant and unavailable ever since you came back. It's like you're a different person. I was hoping we could discuss it, but after we argued over Dominic, you cut me off. Regardless, I want you to know depression is nothing to be ashamed of; I'm here for you, so let me help. You don't have to face the battle alone." Ana reached across the counter and handed Vonnie a dish towel. "Here, wipe your nose; you're getting snot on my top," she said, smiling.

They laughed. Suddenly, they heard yelling, a loud crash, and a heavy thud coming from the bedroom. Both women ran toward the room. The security guard was on the floor, struggling to subdue the angry patient fighting him. The IV pole banged against the floor, and blood spurted from the man's arm.

"Stop fighting. Stop fighting. We're trying to help you" Ana yelled, rushing into the room.

The man's eyes were wide with terror. He panted heavily, looking from one face to another, kicking with his uninjured leg while wildly swinging his free hand. The security guard moved behind him, pinned his arms, and held him in a bear hug. Blood ran down the man's arm as he continued to struggle.

"Stop fighting. You're safe and we're trying to help you" Ana yelled again in frustration. She immediately dropped to her knees, quickly removed the adhesive tape that held the IV needle in place, and applied pressure on the injection point to stop the blood flow.

"Who are you? Where am I?" the man asked in a panic-stricken voice, straining to free himself from the security guard.

Ana's voice was stern. "We'll talk after you calm down. You're safe here. No one is going to hurt you. But we must get you back in bed so I can treat you. Are you going to cooperate, or do I have to give you a shot to knock you out so I can do what I need to do?" she asked.

"Okay, okay, I'll cooperate. No shots" the man said, rapidly weakening from the struggle.

"Good," Ana said, getting up from the floor.

The security guard released his grip and assisted Ana in placing the man back in bed. Vonnie rushed to gather cleaning supplies to clean up the blood.

The man was quiet; beads of sweat dotted his brow. He closed his eyes and breathed heavily. Ana looked at the security guard, who anxiously watched her place the stethoscope in her ears. "Call Hadwin and John; tell them our patient is awake."

* * *

An hour later, Hadwin, John, and Vonnie stood around the bed, all with severe expressions on their faces. Ana sat in the recliner across from the bed.

Calmly, John waited for the man to speak. The stranger looked afraid as his eyes darted from one person to another. Finally, when he didn't say anything, John initiated the conversation.

"I'm John Ramirez, chief security officer here at the Hollister Plantation; this is Hadwin Lopez, principal operations manager of the plantation; his wife, Dr. Ana Lopez; and Miss Yvonne Hollister, owner of the plantation, and in whose home you're currently a guest. Naturally, we have questions for you, and I'd appreciate it if you'd introduce yourself."

"Where am I... I mean, what country am I in?" the stranger asked.

"You're in Belize. Where did you come from?"

"Guatemala" the man said, closing his eyes. Relief covered his face, and he released a long exhale.

John and Hadwin exchanged glances.

"Are you an American citizen? We noticed your tattoos," John asked.

"Yes," the man responded, with his eyes still closed.

"Well, that's a coincidence; Miss Hollister is also from the US. So, what's your name?"

The man raised his head and looked at Vonnie. "You're from the US? What part?"

"I'm from North Carolina; how about you?" Vonnie asked, folding her arms across her chest.

"Born and raised in Louisiana," the man said, with a weak smile.

"And your name is...?" John interjected.

"Moore... Chance Moore."

"Well, I can't say it's a pleasure to meet you, Mr. Moore, because we have concerns about how you ended up on our doorstep, especially considering your physical condition. Let me tell you how we're going to proceed. First, I'll collect your basic information, then I'll call the police, who will interview you and assume responsibility for you. Got it?" John said.

"Do I have a choice?" Chance asked.

"Not really," John said, shrugging. "A lot depends on what you tell me before I make the call. I'm hoping we can have an honest, candid conversation. We didn't find any papers on you, so until you can prove otherwise, you're currently in the country illegally, regardless of how you got here. You were shot and in possession of an illegal firearm. I'm required, by law, to report you to the police. So why don't you tell us what happened to you?"

"I'll get us some chairs" Vonnie said.

Chance told them a story of a retired FBI agent vacationing in Guatemala City. There was a late night with too many drinks in a local bar. Thugs kidnapped him as he walked back to his hotel, stole his passport and identification, and were intent on holding him until they finished draining all the cash from his credit cards. He spoke of his escape during the earthquake, walking the road east, and evading the kidnappers, who eventually shot him as he was running away.

Ana noticed beads of sweat on Chance's forehead, a glazed look in his eyes, and slurred speech.

"Okay, everyone. Enough for now, take a break," she said, standing and stretching. "Mr. Moore isn't going anywhere. It's time for his meds, and he needs to rest. You can come back later."

"Good idea. I need a break myself," John said, standing. "That's quite a story, Mr. Moore. I hope you're telling us the truth because it's the same story I'll tell the police chief when I speak with him."

"So, what do you think they'll do to me?" Chance asked, concerned, unconsciously rubbing his wounded leg.

"I can't say. The police will send someone to take your statement and contact the US Embassy. We'll be back when they arrive" John said, picking up his chair and moving toward the door.

Vonnie and Hadwin followed John out of the room with their chairs in hand. The three formed a triangle on the back porch.

"So, what's up, John? I can see those wheels turning in your brain. Do you believe him?" Hadwin asked.

"His story is plausible. Sometimes rich foreigners get reckless and don't take their security seriously. But something about his story doesn't feel right. I need to think about it. It's a good thing I have this," John said, smugly waving his cell phone.

Surprised at seeing the phone, Hadwin asked, "You recorded him?"

"And that's not all. I took fingerprints and a blood sample the first day Ana started working on him. I have several military and law enforcement contacts in the States, and we exchange favors from time to time. So, now that I have his name, or what he says is his name, and demographic info, I can send it to them and see what turns up."

Vonnie nervously bit her bottom lip. "Is that legal? I mean, can you do that? Shouldn't we wait for the police or let the embassy obtain that information?"

John looked toward Hadwin to intercede.

Hadwin put a hand on Vonnie's shoulder. "Vonnie, we still don't know who this guy is. All we have is a story that might or might not be true. Remember, there may be people who haven't given up searching for him. If John has US resources that can help speed things up, let him use them."

Vonnie crossed her arms over her chest, dropped her head, and sighed. "This is all too much," she said, shaking her head from side to side.

Irritated, John said, "Vonnie, my goal is to get this guy out of here as soon as possible. I know he appears trustworthy and respectable because he worked for the FBI, but none of what he told us has been confirmed. You said you'd let me handle this, so let me handle it. Trust me."

Vonnie could see the frustration mounting on John's face. "Okay, okay, I trust you. Do whatever you think is best" she said timidly, hoping to appease him.

# 27

# CHANCE

Early the following morning, Chance lay still. The soft bed and clean linens felt luxurious after endless days of walking and sleeping on the damp ground. Too weak and sore to move, he cautiously opened his eyes and surveyed the semi-dark bedroom. The recliner beside the bed where the nurse usually sat was empty, but he could hear the young nurse, Alicia, and the security guard whispering outside the open bedroom door. Sighing heavily, he closed his eyes and thought about his predicament.

*Right now, Aapo is in the middle of a major meltdown. He went through a lot of trouble to smuggle me out of the US, across Mexico, and into Guatemala, only to have me escape without returning a dime of the money I stole from him. Now this thing between us is about more than money. His pride is at stake. I've made him look like a fool. He's not going to stop until he finds me. And then, there will be hell to pay.*

Ana interrupted his thoughts when she briskly entered the bedroom and snatched open the drapes. Sunlight immediately flooded the room.

"Good morning, Mr. Moore. A police officer is due in an hour to interview you. Vonnie is fixing your breakfast. How did you sleep? Are you in pain? Are you having any new symptoms I need to be aware of?" she asked in a single breath while scanning his forehead with a digital thermometer and taking his pulse.

Alicia was hastily wrapping his arm in a blood pressure cuff on the other side of the bed.

"I've felt better; nothing new to report" Chance mumbled, squinting in the bright sunlight.

Ana pulled back the bed covers and gently removed the bandage from his leg.

"You're healing well, but you still have a low-grade fever, which makes me feel concerned, so I intend to continue the antibiotics."

"Thanks, Doc. Whatever you say. I'm in your hands" Chance said, yawning, watching her fingers as she probed around the wound. He looked up as Vonnie entered the room carrying a food tray. His eyes lit up, and a smile appeared on his face. "Wow, real bacon, eggs, orange juice, and coffee? I must be in heaven."

At ten o'clock, the original group of four and a police officer sat around Chance's bed, listening to him retell the story of how he ended up on the plantation. The officer was a serious-looking man of about thirty and dressed in a heavily starched, well-pressed khaki-colored uniform. He rapidly scribbled notes as Chance spoke.

The officer smiled when the story ended. "Well, Mr. Moore, it sounds as if you've had quite an adventure. Unfortunately, many foreigners in your situation aren't as lucky as you."

"I believe you, and I can't believe I ended up in a place like this. But I'm an uninvited guest here and want to leave as soon as possible. What's the next step in this process, and how can it be expedited?" Chance responded, noticing the sign of relief spread across John's face.

The officer crossed his arms and stroked his chin. "Well, your case presents something of a dilemma for us. First, I'll submit my report to the chief; he'll contact the US Embassy, who will confirm your information, conduct a background check, et cetera. And unless there are extenuating circumstances, they will eventually issue another passport. Unfortunately, the US Embassy is providing limited services due to the pandemic, and the Belize government intends to suspend all international flights within the next week. So, all this will take additional time, and even with your passport, it may be a while before you can leave the country."

"So where does he go until you get this resolved?" John asked.

The officer looked from John to Vonnie. "Well, that's another part of the dilemma. He can't move freely about the country without official identification, and thus far, we have no reason to arrest him. There are no reports of any criminal activity involving Americans, and he's not a refugee. He requires medical attention but can't be admitted to the hospital because they're all over capacity with COVID-19 patients."

John leaned toward the police officer. "I sympathize with your dilemma, but we're not running a bed-and-breakfast for wayward tourists. I expect you to take possession of him. Where you put him is up to you."

The officer looked pleadingly at Vonnie. "Miss. Hollister, the chief wanted me to ask if you would consider allowing Mr. Moore to remain here until we hear back from the embassy. Your plantation has the resources to secure him and provide medical care. And you will be reimbursed for all expenses incurred for the inconvenience."

Vonnie nervously looked from Hadwin to John. "Well... I don't know..." she said.

John abruptly stood and barked at the officer. "Are you ignoring what I said? This man isn't our responsibility. Come with me. Let's call the chief, NOW!" The two men quickly exited the room.

Ten minutes later, John and the police officer returned. John looked mildly deflated. "Okay, I don't like it, but I've agreed with the chief's recommendation. Typically, authorities detain people in Mr. Moore's position in prison or a refugee camp. But COVID-19 is ravaging both places, and holding him in either location could be a death sentence because of his physical condition." John looked at Chance with a steely expression. "As a show of compassion, he can stay until the embassy reissues his passport."

Then John looked at Hadwin and Vonnie. "In the meantime, the chief will contact Border Patrol and ask for additional surveillance in this area. This guy should never have crossed the border undetected." Finally, John addressed Vonnie directly. "Do you have a problem with any of this?"

"No problem. Whatever you think is best. I'll stand by your decision" Vonnie said with relief.

"Thanks, John. I appreciate you allowing me to stay. I'll leave as soon as my passport arrives," Chance said.

The officer smiled broadly and put on his hat. "Good, then it's all settled. I'm glad we worked it out." He was the only person smiling as the group left the room.

Alone, Chance lay in bed drenched with sweat, head pounding, exhausted but relieved the interview was over.

*The best option is to regain my strength as quickly as possible, get my passport, and leave before anything tragic happens. If Aapo discovers me here, he'll unleash the hounds of hell on this place. These are innocent people, and I don't want to see them hurt trying to help me.*

* * *

For the next two weeks, Ana and Alicia tended to Chance's wounds, distributed medications, and Vonnie prepared his meals and assisted him in maneuvering around the house. An armed security guard sat outside his bedroom door twenty-four hours a day. Everyone was friendly, and the food was incredible. Finally, there was a sense of normalcy and safety in his life.

Since they were both from the US, Chance and Vonnie quickly bonded. He hobbled around the house on crutches, telling jokes and funny stories that kept her laughing. There were friendly arguments about US politics and the better NFL or NBA sports teams. They also exchanged personal histories. He liked to cook, so leaning on his crutches, he assumed control of the kitchen, but they washed and dried the dishes together. After dinner, they settled down to watch a movie or sat on the back porch talking until long after dark. Then each morning, Vonnie came downstairs to a ready-made pot of coffee, and they sat together rocking on the back porch, watching the plantation come alive.

One tranquil, starlit night, while rocking on the back porch, Vonnie's voice quivered as she told him about the deaths of her loved ones, the crushing depression, and her decision to sell the plantation.

"I've never lived here full-time. Unlike my parents, who considered the plantation their primary residence and North Carolina as the place where they worked, for me, this place was more of a vacation home. The success of the plantation and the part my ancestors played in building the country is my family's legacy, and I'm proud of it. But I'm not getting any younger, and I'm tired of mourning every day. It's time to move on and create a new life before I'm too old to enjoy the time I have left. This place makes me feel like I'm stuck in quicksand. The more I struggle to be free, the deeper it pulls me down."

Unlike Charlotte or women he dated in LA with surgically enhanced bodies, perfectly veneered teeth, and botoxed faces, Chance found Vonnie unpretentious and down-to-earth despite her privileged upbringing and wealth. There were multiple Hollister family photographs in his bedroom. A portrait of a man, woman, and teenage girl hung on the wall opposite the bed. On top of the bureau and accent table were smaller photos. The girl in the pictures was undoubtedly Vonnie at different stages of maturity. Hers was the first face he saw in the morning and the last one he saw each night.

* * *

Chance had been on the plantation for three weeks when John entered the bedroom and found him and the security guard playing dominos. The security guard quickly left the room, and John sat in the vacant chair, leaned back, and crossed his arms.

"Your background check came back clean, and the embassy is expediting your passport. Ana says your leg is improving, but you're still experiencing malaria symptoms. How do you feel about your situation?"

Chance pushed the table to the side. "I'm ready to go, John. Ana has me on crutches, so I'm moving around. The malaria symptoms aren't as bad as they were; the drugs are working. I'm not up to full speed, but as soon as I have my passport, I plan to check into a hotel in Belize City, and I'll be out of your hair."

"Ana is reluctant to let you go until your fever stops spiking. If you leave, she's concerned that you may not be able to receive immediate medical attention since all the medical services are wrestling with COVID-19."

"Well, I appreciate Ana's concern; she's been awesome. But I'll take my chances whether I'm a hundred percent or not. The embassy referred me to a lawyer who's going to assist me after I leave here. So, you have nothing to worry about."

John stood and quietly closed the bedroom door. A stern expression covered his face, and he spoke in a low, threatening voice. "I'm going to remove the guard, but I want to clarify one thing. I don't care how clean your background check is, for as long as you remain in this house, you will respect Vonnie in every sense of the word. Do you understand what I'm saying?"

Chance was surprised at John's tone and demeanor. "John, I know you don't know me personally, but I'd never do anything to disrespect Vonnie or any of you. I owe you my life, and I don't take what you've done for granted." He extended his hand for John to shake.

John's grip was too tight, but Chance matched it. The two men stared intensely at each other before John released his hand. "Good, that's what I wanted to hear."

* * *

Chance's passport still hadn't arrived after five weeks, and he grew increasingly anxious. Even though he tried to appear upbeat during the day, at night there were recurring nightmares of him running for his life through the rainforest, the decapitated head and bodies of the men he killed, and of being brutally tortured by a vengeful Aapo. In the middle of the night, the horrific dreams made him awake in a cold sweat. Each morning, Ana assumed the damp bed sheets and pajamas were from night sweats caused by malaria.

Eager to express his gratitude and make himself useful, he worked with Hadwin's IT team and created several programs that spewed production analytics that made Hadwin grin from ear to ear. Ana replaced the crutches with a cane and reduced her daily hands-on examinations to once a week. But when she and Chance were together, they had long conversations about her challenges of treating COVID-19 patients without the proper protective equipment or supplies. The rapport established with Vonnie, Hadwin, and Ana didn't extend to John. John remained aloof and strictly professional.

One Thursday night, when Chance and Vonnie were having dinner, Hadwin called and extended an unexpected invitation for Chance to join a boy's night poker game in the mechanic's shop. After he and Vonnie put away the dinner dishes, Chance hobbled across the grounds toward the shop. It had rained that afternoon, and the scent of fruit and flowers was heavy in the warm, humid evening air. The plantation's residents were outside; those sitting on their porches waved as he passed by, and three women smiled at him while they were on their evening walk. In a far-off playing field, a group of teenage boys kicked a soccer ball, and children shouted and squealed with laughter as they chased each other through the yards.

As he neared the mechanic's shop, Chance began to feel uneasy; something wasn't right. The hair prickled on the back of his neck, so he stopped and slowly surveyed the surroundings but saw nothing unusual. Three security vehicles were parked close to the entrance of the shop. He opened the door and stepped inside.

Immediately, someone grabbed him, putting him in a chokehold. He struggled with his attacker, trying to remove the vicelike grip from his neck. Then, shocked, he saw John glaring at him with a face distorted with rage.

John punched him hard in the gut. The man holding him released his grip, and Chance crumpled to the oil-stained cement floor, gasping for breath. Next, a security guard roughly rolled him onto his chest and zip-tied his hands behind his back. Then, two guards pulled him up and forcefully sat him on a three-legged metal stool. Bent over, Chance tried to catch his breath. His left leg blazed with pain.

After a few seconds, he saw Hadwin, a hateful look on his face, arms folded, leaning on a metal equipment shelf.

John towered over him, breathing like a mad bull. "What the f—" was all Chance could say before John backhanded him hard across the face, knocking him back to the floor. Stunned, head pounding, with searing, red-hot pain in his leg and the taste of blood in his mouth, Chance moaned.

John pressed his boot down hard on Chance's cheek. "You fucking lied to us, Chance" John said in a dark, menacing tone, pushing the boot down harder. "You didn't think we'd find out, did you?" Then, stepping back, he barked at the guards, "Sit him up."

The guards jerked Chance up and sat him back on the stool.

His eyes were closed, his head drooped, and he breathed heavily. His mouth hung open as saliva and blood dripped from his cut lips.

"You see, Chance, my sources in the US came through for me. Of course, those embassy assholes only ran a simple background check on you, but what my folks found worries me. And I don't particularly appreciate being worried. So, this time, I want the truth."

A guard handed John a short, thick rubber hose.

John slapped the hose loudly in his palm. "Here's what we're going to do, Chance. I'll tell you about the information I've gathered, and you'll fill in the blanks. And, if I think you're lying, I'll bust your wounded leg wide open. Got it?" he said with a sneer.

"Got it. You won't have to use the hose. I'll tell you what you want to know" Chance responded, looking up at John with a defeated expression.

"Good, then I'll start. You left the FBI shortly before a financial scandal involving your late wife surfaced in the media. You had lost everything, and instead of staying and facing the music, you ran away like a coward. Several weeks later, you show up in beautiful, sunny California and begin an exciting new life.

"Then there's the social media scrub. My folks discovered you and a former FBI coworker, Mack Owens, were big party animals in LA. Boy, you guys were living it up with elaborate parties, private jets, yachts, and supermodels everywhere. It makes one wonder how two retired ex-FBI cybersecurity experts funded such a fantasy lifestyle. The interesting part is that you went from having nothing to paying off well over two million dollars of debt in less than a year and without a job."

John waved a document in Chance's face. "According to this missing person's report, you've been missing from California for almost three months. Your neighbors became concerned because your garage door was up, your Jeep was unlocked, and camping equipment was lying around your Jeep, and the police discovered the home security alarm was still activated. Unfortunately, no one came looking for you. It's a small town, so the report has been sitting in the police station gathering dust.

Meanwhile, the LA police found the dead, tortured body of Mr. Owens a week before you went missing. But the LA coroner said he'd been dead for several days before anyone discovered the body. I have copies of the crime scene pictures on my laptop; they're horrible.

Finally, my people could find no record of you flying on a commercial or private airline anywhere in the past three months, and my Guatemalan government contacts had no idea you were ever in the country. So, this time, Chance, tell us the true story; we're all ears."

Chance dropped his head back, looked at the ceiling, and exhaled loudly. "Whoever your sources are, they do good work." His head was spinning; the taste of blood and vomit filled his mouth; and his wounded leg was on fire. Reluctantly, he told version two of his story, which was much closer to the truth.

It included the inadvertent hack of Aapo Vasquez's bank account, the abduction, and being smuggled out of the US and into Guatemala. The descriptions of his escape and ending up on the plantation remained the same.

"Look, I was running for my life. When I ended up here, I thought it was a miracle. I never imagined I'd be here this long. I've been hounding the embassy for my passport so I can leave."

Hadwin's eyes were like daggers, and his voice was cold. "The cartel is still looking for you, aren't they?" he asked.

Chance dropped his head and shook it. "I don't know, and that's the truth," he said.

"I'd say YES," John said. "If the Vasquez Cartel smuggled you out of California, across Mexico, and into Guatemala, they wouldn't think twice about coming to Belize. We're right next door. Do you realize you've put the lives of innocent people in danger because of your lies? Those cartel motherfuckers will rain down holy hell on this place if they find out you're here."

Hadwin stepped forward. "John, we need to put Vonnie on a need-to-know basis. She doesn't need to know all of this. Hopefully, Chance will be out of here in another day or two. In the meantime, hire as many additional resources to augment your security team, as necessary."

"I agree about not telling Vonnie. We don't want her to freak out. I'll call Border Patrol and the local chief and tell them there is cartel activity in the area." Then, John looked down at Chance with disdain. "Is there anything else you haven't told us? Because if I find out there's more, you won't need a passport when I'm through with you."

Shifting on the stool, Chance looked from Hadwin to John. "That's it, guys. I've told you everything."

John turned to Hadwin. "I want him out of The Big House tonight. I don't want him anywhere close to Vonnie; it's too risky."

"You're right," Hadwin agreed. "I'll have a space cleared out here in the back of the shop, and I'll make up something to tell Vonnie so she won't get too suspicious. That part will be hard; she'll have a million questions because she likes this asshole." He glared at Chance, slapped John on the back, and walked toward the door. "Let's get out of here. We need to talk."

In a flash, John whirled around and kicked Chance in the chest, knocking him off the stool. Chance lay on the floor, struggling to breathe.

"Cut him loose" John yelled to the guards as he followed Hadwin out the door.

# 28

# CHANCE

The day after the altercation in the machine shop, as the workday was over and the plantation was quieting down, Chance was sitting under a tree beside the shop in a metal folding chair, his sore leg propped up on an upturned five-gallon plastic bucket. There were scratches and bruises on his face. He had a black eye and a cracked and swollen bottom lip. Another large bruise spread across his chest from John's final kick, and his entire rib cage hurt every time he took a breath. He saw John's bodybuilder physique rapidly striding in his direction and his body tensed.

A scowl covered John's face as he tossed an envelope at Chance. "I hope this is your passport."

Chance hurriedly tore open the envelope and extracted a small, navy-blue booklet with a gold seal on the cover. "Yep, this is it," he exclaimed, sighing with relief as he flipped through the pages. "I'm officially free to get out of your life."

John reached into his shirt pocket and handed Chance a bus ticket. "In the morning, I'll have one of my men drive you to the bus station in Punta Gorda. The ticket is to Belize City. From there, you're on your own."

Chance pushed himself up using his cane. "John, I apologize for lying to all of you, but I was vying for time, hoping I could get out of here without anyone knowing how bad my situation was. I appreciate everything everyone did for me. I'll never forget it." He stretched out his hand for John to shake.

John glared at Chance and spat, almost hitting his foot. Then, as he strode away, he looked back over his shoulder. "Fuck you, Chance."

Humiliated, Chance returned to the shop and waited for someone to bring him his dinner. After dinner, there was nothing to do but count the slowly passing hours. He lay on an old army cot in the dark, wearing Bermuda shorts, unable to sleep in the oppressive heat. There was a laundry list of things to do once he arrived in Belize City, and he was ready to go. The sooner he left, the safer everyone would be, including himself.

According to a little digital clock on a metal desk across the room, it was 2:34 a.m. when ear-splitting sirens from the plantation's emergency alert system began wailing. Confused, Chance fumbled for the flashlight on top of an upturned cardboard box beside the cot. Then, barefoot, he hurried to the door and stepped outside. The odor of something burning hung heavy in the hot, moist night air.

In the distance, lights flickered on in the houses; people were pouring out into their yards, running, hollering, gesturing. He looked to his right to see glowing flames in the banana groves.

The fire was massive.

Rushing back into the mechanic's shop, he hastily pulled on a T-shirt and shoes, grabbed his cane, and joined the chaotic crowd headed toward the groves.

* * *

Vonnie tossed in bed, trying to get comfortable. A heavy, unfamiliar odor wafted through the open balcony door, disturbing her sleep. She instantly awakened to the sound of the screeching emergency alert sirens, swung her feet to the floor, and rushed to the balcony. The sight was unbelievable—the banana trees blazed like torches in the night.

She returned to the room, turned on the bedside lamp, and called Hadwin. He didn't answer. Then she called Ana. "Ana, what's happening?"

Ana's words came fast. "We don't know how it started. Hadwin is organizing everything. The fire department is on its way."

"Good. I'll be right down," Vonnie said, frantically tossing discarded clothes piled on a chair. She was pulling a dirty T-shirt over her head when there was a loud crash downstairs. "What the hell...?" she said, running into the hall and looking down the dimly lit stairwell. There was a sound of rapid gunfire, men yelling in Spanish, and then an explosion, which sent a fireball of light past the bottom step. Silhouetted in the light of the fire was a man holding an automatic rifle.

Terrified, Vonnie sprinted back to her bedroom, locked the door, and ran to the balcony. Unfortunately, it was too high to jump from there, and everyone around appeared to be racing toward the fire in the banana groves. Her hysterical cries for help went unnoticed and were drowned out by emergency sirens.

The intruders yelled at one another; there were footsteps on the stairs. Frantically searching for a way to protect herself, her eyes fell upon the large armoire beside the door. She strained to push the heavy furniture in front of the bedroom door to block it. Horrified, she realized she might be safe from the intruders but trapped in the burning house.

* * *

Chance stood amid a nervous, agitated group of people watching the fire in the banana groves light up the night sky. Questions darted from one person to another. "How did it start? How could it spread so fast?"

Then the realization hit him like a thunderbolt—the fire in the groves was a diversion. He turned and looked back toward The Big House. The glow of fire flames danced in the first-floor windows, and no one was paying attention. There was a sinking feeling in the pit of his stomach. Aapo's men had come for him. They must have covertly conducted surveillance on the plantation and mistakenly thought he still lived in The Big House.

Vonnie was alone.

Chance limped and hopped toward The Big House. As he got closer, there was the unmistakable sound of gunfire. Finally, he rounded the front of the house in time to see John running up the steps and disappearing through the broken front door. More gunshots.

Lowering himself, he crawled up the steps and peeped through the front door. He stayed on the floor, crawling, avoiding the flames, and using the furniture for cover. Smoke and toxic fumes filled the air; flames crept up the drapes and papered walls. A dead man lay prone on the dining room floor.

Still crawling and dragging himself across the floor, he saw John lying at the bottom of the staircase; blood covered his chest. Chance quickly moved to him. "John... John," he whispered, lifting his head.

John moaned, barely opening his eyes. "There's two of them upstairs... Vonnie's up there. Here, take this." He handed Chance a Glock 9mm pistol.

Chance cautiously crawled up the stairs, controlling his breathing, trying not to cough as the rising smoke burned his throat and eyes. Nightlights along the baseboards dimly outlined the floors on the second and third landings. When he almost reached the second floor, he heard heavy, hurried footsteps, and paused. A man, swinging an automatic rifle from side to side, emerged from the hall and started toward the steps. Chance fired three shots. The man's body jerked, and he fell backward, dead.

Chance waited, straining not to cough, and pulled the neck of his T-shirt over his nose. John said there were two men. Was the third man hiding on the second floor, or was he already on the third floor? Finally, unable to wait any longer, Chance continued moving upward. Unable to control himself any longer, he coughed several times as he squinted through stinging, watering eyes, as he looked for the third assailant. Finally, gripping the doorframe of Vonnie's room with one hand, he struggled to stand up. He turned the doorknob but was unable to open the door. "Vonnie, it's Chance; open the door."

* * *

Vonnie was on the balcony, hysterical, and on her cell phone talking to Ana. From the balcony, she could see flames and smoke billowing from the lower level of the house.

"Try to stay calm. I promise you—we'll get you out," Ana said, urging.

"But how, Ana? There are men in the house with guns, shooting up the place. The first floor is on fire. I'm going to die in here," Vonnie screamed into the phone.

"Vonnie, I have to go, but please, please, please pull yourself together. The men will get you out. They just brought John in with a gunshot wound." Ana disconnected the call.

Vonnie stepped back into the bedroom, trembling. Her heart raced. But then, she heard the beating on the door and Chance calling her name.

* * *

Bullets sprayed the woodwork on the right side of Chance's head, and he quickly dropped to the floor. The smoke was so thick he couldn't see the shooter. Then he heard several more gunshots and a loud thud.

"Chance, I got him. You're clear. Get Vonnie, and let's get out of here" Hadwin yelled from the second landing.

* * *

When the bullets tore through the wall, Vonnie screamed, fell to the floor, and covered her head with her arms, too terrified to move.

* * *

Chance pounded on the door. "Vonnie, open the door. We have to get out of here. We can't wait much longer," he shouted between coughs.

Hadwin raced up the stairs to Vonnie's door and pounded hard. "Vonnie, it's Hadwin. Open the damn door" he barked.

* * *

Vonnie scrambled to her feet, pushed the armoire back to its original position, and unlocked the door. Smoke immediately filled the room, making her cough.

Hadwin roughly grabbed her hand and quickly pulled her down the stairs. Chance followed, limping, gripping the railing for stability while keeping a hand on Vonnie's shoulder.

"I can't see," Vonnie whined between coughs as she pulled her T-shirt over her nose.

Everything on the first floor appeared to be in flames.

"We're trapped," Hadwin shouted. "I can't see a way out."

Between hacking coughs, Chance yelled, "Vonnie, is there another room with a window low enough for us to use?"

"Follow me," Vonnie whimpered, lowering herself to the floor and crawling toward the hallway that led to her father's study. Down on all fours, Hadwin and Chance followed her. After scrambling several feet, Vonnie stopped and tossed aside the oriental floor runner.

"The hurricane shelter," she gasped as she released a latch embedded in the hardwood floor.

Hadwin and Chance eagerly assisted her as she struggled to open the heavy hatch door. Vonnie descended the ladder, flipped on a light switch, and helped Chance down. Hadwin closed the hatch door behind him.

The men coughed and wiped their eyes as they looked around the space. The air was dank, and the mildew odor was heavy; thick cobwebs hung from low beams on the ceiling. Dull gray paint covered the cement walls. A set of wooden bunk beds, chairs, and a small table were on the left side of the space. Wall cabinets and shelves, a wooden countertop, and an old porcelain sink with dead insects sprinkled across the surfaces were on the right.

Vonnie walked to a shelf filled with old, dust covered canned foods and pulled down a plastic-wrapped twelve-pack of bottled water. She ripped open the package and handed bottles to the men.

Hadwin struggled to clear his throat between coughs. "Wow, I'd forgotten all about this place. I haven't been down here since we were in high school."

Vonnie gulped the water, poured some into her hand, and wiped it on her face. "Let's get out of here."

Exhausted and downcast from their ordeal, the three emerged from the rear door of the hurricane shelter. Everyone on the plantation was outside. The banana groves were still burning, and so was the house. A crowd surged forward when they recognized the three people stumbling down the hill. There was loud cheering, whooping, and hand clapping.

Just as the three reached the service road, fire trucks, police cars, and emergency vehicles, all with sirens wailing and lights flashing, pulled onto the grounds.

"It's about damn time," Hadwin growled as he trotted toward the fire trucks. Then, over his shoulder, he yelled back at Chance. "Take her to Ana."

Vonnie turned and looked up at the house. Portions of the exterior and first floor windows were ablaze. Her knees buckled, and she crumpled to the ground shaking, tears streaming down her face. Chance immediately helped her stand up. She put her arms around his neck, buried her face in his chest, and wept.

The sea of onlookers grew solemn and quiet as Chance limped toward the clinic supporting Vonnie. They parted, clearing a path. Sad, sorrowful eyes followed them to the clinic's door.

* * *

Ana rushed into the clinic's waiting room where Chance sat with his arm around Vonnie's shoulder and her head resting on his shoulder. Ana sat beside Vonnie and pulled her into her arms as uncontrollable sobs racked her body. She looked over Vonnie's shoulder at Chance. "I'm going to give her something, then take her to my house and put her in the spare bedroom. I don't know when Hadwin or I will be home. I have to care for John" she said.

"How is he?" Chance asked, ashamed to admit that he had forgotten about John during the chaos of trying to rescue Vonnie and escape the burning house.

"He'll survive; the bullet went through his shoulder. I need to finish patching him up," Ana said, reaching into her breast pocket, extracting a syringe, and injecting Vonnie. "These are for you" she said, handing him two orange medicine bottles. "One is for malaria; the other is an antibiotic."

Ana's demeanor, her stoic expression, and the look in her eyes were telling Chance more than goodbye. She knew about his lies, and everything that happened tonight was his fault.

In Hadwin and Ana's spare bedroom, Chance sat by Vonnie's bedside, holding her hand quietly until the sedative administered by Ana finally put her to sleep. Then he lightly kissed her forehead and quietly left the house, his head and shoulders weighed down with remorse and shame.

Three dead men were lying in a row on the front lawn of The Big House, and the police wanted an explanation. So, he slowly made his way toward the array of flashing blue and red lights parked on the service road.

* * *

It was dawn before the crowd of weary, exhausted plantation dwellers returned to their homes. Small fires still burned in the banana groves even though workers had spent the night throwing dirt on smoldering ashes hoping to save what they could.

Depressed and guilt-ridden, Chance sat on his cot in the mechanic's shop, elbows on his knees, both hands covering his face. The sun was up, promising another hot, sweltering, humid day.

A security guard abruptly entered the shop. "Ready?" the unsmiling man asked.

Chance slowly walked past the guard and entered the white SUV with the Hollister Plantation logo on the door.

"No luggage?" the guard asked as he climbed behind the steering wheel.

"Nope," Chance said gravely, looking out his window so the guard couldn't see the tears welling in his eyes. "Let's go."

The entire plantation was eerily subdued and quiet. The stench from the burned and scorched banana trees filled the air. Sadness and gloom saturated every person, house, tree, and blade of grass the truck passed as it moved down the service road toward the plantation's exit gate.

Chance swallowed hard. The firefighters had successfully extinguished the fire in The Big House. It stood on the hill with its white exterior charred and blackened.

Intentional or not, the devastation was his fault. These people had saved his life and showed him nothing but kindness. And in return, he had lied to them and brought Aapo's wrath to their doorstep.

As the security guard turned onto the highway, Chance closed his eyes and sighed; he had never felt such crushing guilt, disgrace, or shame in his entire life.

# 29

# ALEX

It had been two and a half months since Humberto's murder. With Humberto dead, the cartel's ground operations fell into disarray because Alex's covert schemes to extinguish the cartel had picked up pace. Aapo was still embezzling from the cartel's coffers but, due to the chaos within the ground operations, income was significantly reduced.

Since being made aware of Humberto's death, Eloy was sequestered in his bedroom, heavily medicated, unable to make decisions, give orders, or entertain visitors.

Aapo hadn't visited Eloy's room since the day he told him Humberto was dead. He was impatient for his father to die. Instead of trying to resolve the mountain of issues impacting the cartel he lounged by the pool, played golf, and entertained a host of select businesspeople, corrupt politicians, and prostitutes.

As soon as his father died, he intended to liquidate all the remaining assets and move forward with building his synthetic drug facility. Until then, his primary focuses were evading the disgruntled investors to whom he owed money and recapturing Chance Moore.

* * *

It was one in the morning when Alex finally closed the lid of his laptop. Then he stood up and stretched. In two days, decades of documentation including photos, emails, texts, voicemails, and recorded phone calls would be automatically transmitted to trusted government and law enforcement officials and media outlets in the US, Mexico, Guatemala, eight countries in Europe, and five in the Caribbean. He was closing the last chapter of the Vasquez Cartel's horror story.

He slipped silently into Eloy's bedroom. A small lamp sat on an accent table, dimly illuminating the room; an upholstered chair was beside the table. Soft symphonic music played in the background. Eloy snored peacefully in his hospital bed. There were various medicine bottles, a blood pressure machine, and a metal water pitcher on the nightstand beside the bed. An almost empty IV bag hung on a pole at the head of the bed, and the tube snaked down into Eloy's arm.

Alex looked down at the sleeping tyrant with contempt. He quickly pulled up the bedrails and locked them in place. Velcro ties were hastily wrapped around Eloy's wrists and ankles and secured to the bed rails.

The flurry of activity woke Eloy. Confused, frowning, he looked up at Alex, blinking to focus his sleep-filled eyes. "What's...?" he said in a weak, groggy voice. Then, anxiously, he looked from one hand to the other. "What are you doing?" he asked, tugging at the Velcro straps raddling the metal bed rails.

Alex extracted a syringe from his breast pocket and injected the contents into the IV bag. Then he shook the bag, mixed the fluids, and increased the flow rate.

Eloy's eyes were wide with fright as he watched, realizing what was happening. "What are you doing?" he asked, struggling against the restraints and shaking the bed.

Alex calmly walked to Eloy's mahogany liquor cabinet and perused the contents. Then he settled into the upholstered chair with a bottle of Louis XIII cognac and a Baccarat crystal whiskey glass.

Eloy continued to shake the bedrails. His nostrils flared; his eyes bore into Alex. "I'll have you killed for this; who do you think you are?" he shouted. Then, terrified, he lifted his head and looked toward the closed bedroom door. "GUARDS, GUARDS, SOMEBODY... HELP."

Alex lit a cigar, puffed until the end glowed, then blew smoke toward the ceiling. He sipped the cognac and looked at his lifelong oppressor. "Stop shouting, Eloy. No one will come to save you. I've set them all free. They're no longer slaves to be used and abused by you and your sons. So, it's just you, me, and Aapo, and he's fast asleep. A sedative in his nightly scotch on the rocks. He won't wake up until long after you're dead."

Eloy's face glistened with sweat, and his head fell back onto the pillow, worn out from struggling. "You've betrayed me, Alex. You were nothing... a nobody until I took you in." He snarled through clenched teeth.

Alex sipped his drink, gingerly placed the glass on the side table, and flicked the cigar ashes onto the floor. "It might be hard for you to accept, Eloy, but I'm the real puppet master. Not you. You see, knowledge is power. I know everything about you, the cartel, and those two half-breed mongrels you call sons. I control everything. I own the telecom; every network, phone, laptop, text, and email is manipulated as I see fit. And I know where the money is and where it isn't. And you wondered why your precious organization was falling apart." He puffed on the cigar, and placed his right ankle on top of his left knee.

"I knew Aapo would kill Humberto, and I could have prevented it. But why would I? I tried to kill Humberto several times, but he always escaped. Then Aapo stepped in and saved me the effort. But I was responsible for the pictures of Humberto and his lover appearing in the newspapers. I did it to humiliate you in front of the world."

Drenched with sweat, Eloy moaned, "Why, Alex? I treated you like a son. I gave you everything. I trusted you."

Alex looked at the Apple watch on his arm as he poured himself another drink. He inhaled deeply on the cigar, leisurely blew out a long stream of smoke, and sipped the liquor.

"It's revenge, Eloy. Pure and simple. A wise man once said, 'Knowledge makes a man unfit to be a slave.' So, if you trusted me, that was your mistake. In the next twenty-four hours, my life's work will be complete. I will have fulfilled the promise I made to my father on his grave to avenge what you did to our family."

Suddenly, Eloy's body lurched upward, but he was held in place by the restraints. He thrashed, convulsing so hard that the bed shifted and thudded on the carpeted floor. Gurgling sounds rose from his throat, and blood streamed from the corners of his mouth. A foul stench filled the room when his bowels exploded. The soft music continued playing as Alex closed the door and walked away. Throughout the mansion, there was only stillness and silence.

The crystal chandelier hanging in the foyer glimmered as Alex casually descended the spiral staircase with the cigar in his mouth, the drink still in his right hand, and the laptop tucked under his left arm. His footsteps echoed as he crossed the marble floor and stepped outside into the calm, tranquil night. Outside, the mansion glowed from the lights hidden among the shrubs and plants. The sky was clear, filled with stars, and a light fragrance from the flowers surrounding the courtyard wafted in the warm breeze.

Alex stood on the top step, coolly blowing smoke rings. There were no waiting limousines or luxury cars parked in the courtyard. Instead, a battered, white Toyota Corolla waited patiently at the bottom of the steps. The house and the grounds were empty of staff and security guards. They had all been handsomely paid and discharged. And they all knew the consequences of divulging any information.

As he drove away from the mansion, the Apple watch vibrated with an incoming text. The remainder of his plan was in motion—a cargo ship had docked at Port Champerico. Six men had disembarked and left the port in two black SUVs.

A horde of media outlets would flock to the mansion in two days. Then, like rabid dogs, the cartel captains would rip one another apart, grappling for control and territory, and rival gangs would take advantage of the chaos. In six months, the Vasquez Cartel would be a memory.

Alex smiled as he took a final puff on the cigar, tossed back the last of the cognac, and turned up the volume on a Rolling Stones CD. Then he pressed hard on the little car's accelerator and roared down the driveway into the night.

Two days later, he stood by his father's graveside as workers replaced the small wooden cross with a five-foot gravestone. After a tearful goodbye he walked away content in knowing that the work started by his father, was finished. The reign of the Vasquez Cartel was over, and he was leaving Guatemala forever.

He exited an Uber in front of a single-story house in an upscale Phoenix, Arizona, suburb. It had been thirty-nine years since he had secretly smuggled his family out of Guatemala, and he hadn't seen them in-person since then. But through the years, there were communications. Another encrypted folder on his laptop contained pictures and emails from them. They were now US citizens. His mother, Adriana, was in her late eighties and lived with his sister, Catalina, and her family. Alex's younger brother, Bruno, and his family lived nearby.

The front door to the house opened as he stepped onto the sidewalk, and Adriana, her white hair pulled back into a bun, stooped, and leaning on a cane, shuffled to greet him. An excited, cheerful crowd flowed out of the door behind her. Then, with tears in her eyes and a broad smile, she dropped the cane and reached for him. Alex rushed into her arms and wept.

# 30

# AAPO

The morning after Eloy's death, Aapo threw back the bed-covers, sat up, yawned, stretched, and looked at the bedside clock.

*Damn, how did I oversleep? I was supposed to play golf this morning. I thought I set the alarm for seven thirty. Now I've missed my tee time.*

Still yawning while scratching his head, he shuffled to the bathroom and turned on the shower. While observing himself in the vanity mirror, Aapo picked up the house phone on the bathroom wall. But there was no response from the staff. So, he tried again, waited through five rings, and finally slammed the receiver back in its cradle.

As hot steam filled the bathroom, he sighed as his thumb nimbly keyed in his cell phone's access code. Nothing happened. He wiped his hands on a towel and tried again. And again, nothing happened. Frustrated, he turned the phone off and back on and roughly wiped it with the towel only to obtain the same results. "Fuck it" he said, putting the phone aside and opening his shaving kit.

The straight razor glided effortlessly through the foamy lather on his cheek. The phone not working meant a few minutes free from his investor's daily threats. Due to his inability to repay them and the exorbitant interest rates on the loans, the payments ballooned, and the total amount owed was staggering. The investors no longer believed his lies. Earlier in the week, the Russians sent him drone shots of the drug facility's abandoned construction site. Weeds surrounded idle backhoes and earth-moving equipment, giant spools of dusty blue and yellow cables, unfinished buildings, and piles of unused building materials partially covered by rainforest vegetation. They knew there was no synthetic drug facility, and the work had stopped. As much as he hated being in Guatemala, it was safer than returning to New York. Guatemala was the seat of power for the Vasquez Cartel; he was protected here.

The only call Aapo was interested in receiving was from the Specialist hired to retrieve Chance Moore. It had been weeks since the capture team had crossed the Belize border and finally tracked Chance to a banana plantation. Chance was under surveillance, and the team was planning the abduction. But something was wrong because all communication had stopped since then, and there were no responses to his calls or texts.

After dressing, Aapo went to the kitchen. There was no cell phone service, and none of the staff responded to his calls on the house phone. And there was no update on Chance Moore. He fumed as he forcefully pushed open the kitchen door, prepared to vent to the first servant he encountered. The large restaurant-style kitchen was clean and orderly, but no staff.

"HEY, where is everybody?" he yelled as he walked across the kitchen, exited the back door, and looked around the service entrance with his hands on his hips. All the parking spaces were empty.

Irritated, he punched Alex's extension on the kitchen phone. "Alex, better have a good explanation for this," he mumbled. Finally, after five rings and no answer, he hastily left the kitchen and walked toward the elevator. Aapo scanned for servants along the way, a maid dusting the furniture or arranging flowers, but no one was around. Something wasn't right; it didn't make sense. It was as if he was the only person in the mansion.

*Where the hell is everybody? This isn't a holiday, and even if it were, somebody would be here.*

His father, had his father also left? Anxiously, Aapo entered the elevator and pushed the button for the fourth floor. The elevator doors opened to a foul odor that filled the hallway. Aapo scrunched up his face.

*What the hell is that smell?*

The disgusting odor became more intense as he got closer to his father's room. He held his breath and leaned in, placing his ear close to the door. Symphonic music played on the other side of the door.

Alex's suite was next to Eloy's. The door was open, but Alex wasn't there, so Aapo returned to his father's door. With one hand covering his nose and the other trembling as he slowly turned the knob, he peered inside.

The overpowering stench hit him like a wave, and he gagged as his eyes took in the gruesome scene. Eloy's lifeless, bloated body lay in the hospital bed, his protruding arms and legs secured with straps to the bed rails. The ghastly face was turned to the side and stared at him with open, bulging eyes; the mouth open as if frozen in the middle of a horrible scream. A dried, dark, brown fluid spread from the open mouth, down the chin, and pooled on the pillow.

Aapo's stomach lurched, and he slapped a hand over his mouth in a failed attempt to stop the vomit gushing from his mouth. Then, overcome with the horror that was his dead father, he staggered from the room.

Terrified, he ignored the elevator and stumbled down the stairs back to his bedroom on the second floor. With his back against the locked bedroom door, Aapo fought to organize his thoughts. The house was empty of servants, Alex was gone, and someone had killed his father.

Snatching his car keys from the credenza, he jerked open the nightstand drawer to retrieve his pistol; it wasn't there. Someone had taken the gun. He left the bedroom in a flash, clumsily ran down the spiral staircase, and dashed to the trophy room on the first floor.

Aapo dropped his head, pinched the bridge of his nose, and slumped against the doorframe. There was no reason to search the room; any weapon that would have been useful was gone. The gun racks were empty, and displays of antique weaponry—spears, swords, and knives from all over the world—had vanished. Ice-cold fear crept slowly up his spine.

The urgency of the situation sent a surge of adrenaline through his body. Retracing his steps, he rushed back to the foyer, threw open the massive door, stepped outside, and halted. There were no vehicles in the courtyard.

*Maybe the valet took the Mercedes to the garage to be cleaned.*

His racing heartbeat pounded in his ears as he sprinted to the customized garage that housed Eloy's collection of antique and luxury cars. Sweat trickled down his face, and his mouth gaped open as he stood in the garage doorway, speechless—the cavernous space was empty. There was no use in going to the horse stables.

The realization of what was happening to him struck him like lightning. Someone had planned this. His father was brutally murdered in his bed; Alex, the entire staff, and the bodyguards were gone, so there would be no witnesses. He couldn't defend himself without a weapon, and there was no way for him to escape. He was alone and vulnerable.

Physically and mentally drained, Aapo staggered back through the foyer and out of the house.

*If I can get to the highway and stop a passing car, I can pay the driver to take me to Guatemala City.*

Halfway across the courtyard, he saw two black SUVs speeding toward the fifteen-foot wrought iron gate. Aapo raced back into the house. The first vehicle crashed through the gate without slowing down. The screeching sound from the bending and buckling of the metal gate was deafening as the SUV plowed its way into the courtyard. The second vehicle followed close behind.

Aapo looked from left to right, desperately trying to find the perfect hiding place, but there was no time. The pursuers shouted to one another as they quickly exited their vehicles.

Panting, sweating profusely, he lumbered back up the staircase to his bedroom and hastily barricaded the door with furniture. Then, bullets from an automatic rifle tore through the wooden door. Aapo crawled into the bathroom and locked the door.

Gunfire continued shredding the bedroom door and the furniture blocking it. The shouting voices grew louder; furniture scraped against the hardwood floor as the assailants pushed against the door. He was trapped. Soon his assassins would be in the bedroom, and there was nothing with which to barricade the bathroom door.

Bullets peppered the bathroom door, ricocheting off the mosaic tiles, shattering the glass shower stall and vanity mirror. Plaster and glass fragments filled the air and rained down on Aapo, who was crouched in a ball with his arms covering his head. The contents of his shaving kit lay strewn about the floor. The half-opened straight razor was within arm's reach.

Aapo whimpered, taking short, gasping breaths as tears streamed down his cheeks and snot dripped from his nose onto his lips. His chin quivered, and his hands shook as he picked up the razor and slowly pressed the lever to extend the blade.

Hard kicks landed on the bathroom door until it splintered and broke off its hinges. One man entered the bathroom, rifle braced against his shoulder, ready to kill anything that moved.

But Aapo didn't move; he lay slumped against the wall, his chin touching his chest. The bloody straight razor was inches away from his fingertips. Blood from the slit in his throat streamed down the front of his shirt.

# 31

# VONNIE

It had been three weeks since the fire at the Hollister Plantation. John had given Chance a one-way bus ticket to Belize City, and no one had heard from him since then, nor did they want to. Hadwin focused on the cleanup operation in the banana groves, and John was on sick leave, recovering from the gunshot wound in his shoulder. Ana was conducting video and house calls and treating patients in the clinic. Vonnie was living with Hadwin and Ana and suffering from severe depression.

The accumulated weight of all the serial tragedies crushed Vonnie mentally and emotionally. Her stash of opioids and anti-depressants were abandoned during the fire, so at night, Ana gave her a special herbal tea that helped her sleep, and during the day, there was a nasty tasting brew to relieve the hip and knee pain and, finally, another concoction to sooth her anxiety.

Vonnie's days were spent lying on the sofa, channel surfing, or napping until she pulled herself up to prepare lunch for Hadwin. After lunch, Hadwin returned to work, and it was back to the sofa until late afternoon when she'd straighten the house and prepare dinner. When Hadwin and Ana arrived home she'd have a cursory conversation, then return to bed.

Nine months before the fire, selling the plantation as quickly as possible, moving on, and not looking back were all that mattered. But the fire made her realize the plantation meant more to her than she had ever imagined.

Whenever she stepped onto Hadwin and Ana's front porch, the scorched remains of her family's beautiful, stately home glared down at her from its perch on the hill. The groundskeeper hadn't mowed the lawn. Energized by the constant rain, high temperatures, and humidity, weeds and creeping vines had overtaken the once-immaculate landscape.

After the fire, firefighters shut off the electricity, and at night, silhouetted by the moonlight, the structure looked exceptionally foreboding. Every time she looked at the house, it was as if the boarded-up windows and blackened frame screamed at her: "You didn't care, you didn't want me; you were going to sell me to the highest bidder."

But there were no bidders. The last potential buyer had backed out, not wanting to move forward with a significant expenditure during the pandemic.

* * *

It was almost 9:00 p.m. Ana was still at work, and Hadwin and Vonnie sat at the kitchen table, huddled around Hadwin's laptop. Insurance papers, spreadsheets, and other documents covered the dinner table. Vonnie could tell Hadwin was quickly running out of steam and ready to wrap up the discussion.

"It looks like the fire was good in some ways and bad in others," Hadwin said, leaning back in his chair and rubbing his eyes. "The fire destroyed several areas with newly planted trees, but it also wiped out a section showing signs of the Panama Disease fungus; the remainder of the crop looks healthy. The bad news is we can't replant Cavendish trees in the sections previously infected with the fungus. Vonnie, we're losing the war against the disease. It's time we become more aggressive about diversification and reducing our Cavendish dependency. We shouldn't continue using Cavendish bananas as our sole source of income. Let's look at this as an opportunity."

Vonnie rested her chin in her hand and leaned closer to the laptop screen. "Hadwin, you're the eternal optimist who always finds a way to make lemonade. Where everyone else sees a disaster, you see an opportunity" she said with a faint smile.

Hadwin used a pen to point to figures on a spreadsheet. "The plantation has always done well financially, but the pandemic has boosted our bottom line because people eat at home versus going to restaurants. In the US, bananas must be on everyone's grocery list because we can't grow them fast enough. I figure we'll still be in the black even without the money from the crop insurance."

Vonnie pretended to listen but couldn't focus because her mind kept wandering. She stared at the spreadsheet. The pages of cells with tiny numbers were too complicated; it was all a blur. "Well, that's good news; move forward with whatever you think is best." Then she took the mouse, clicked on another spreadsheet, and scrolled through the rows. "Now, what about the house? Have you received estimates for the repairs?"

Hadwin stood, put his hands on his waist, and bent backward, stretching. "That house was built to withstand hurricanes. The exterior is a wooden facade, but the overall structure and the foundation are a mixture of stone, cinderblock, and cement. It will take some work, but you have to decide what you want to do before we start obtaining estimates."

Vonnie leaned back and folded her arms. "I don't know what I want."

Hadwin looked at his longtime friend; his brow furrowed with concern. "Vonnie, I know you're hurting, but it's been three weeks, and you haven't gone anywhere near The Big House. Of course, you're welcome to stay with Ana and me as long as you want, but the house issues aren't going away.

"I had the men board it up to keep the weather out, but something must be done with the remaining personal items before any work starts. You can afford to do whatever you want to fix it up; insurance will cover it, and as I said before, the plantation is in the black. Just let me know when you want to talk with an architect."

"Thanks, Hadwin. I appreciate how well you're handling everything. Find some time on your calendar for us to tour the house; I'll go, ready or not." Vonnie reached out and laid a hand on Hadwin's arm. "And thanks for letting me stay here. You and Ana are all I have. I don't know what I would do without you."

Hadwin placed his hand on top of hers. "Ana and I are here for you. We wouldn't have it any other way. You're family."

Then he stifled a big yawn and walked toward his and Ana's bedroom. "I have a long day tomorrow. I'm going to bed."

Vonnie watched him walk away. "I'll wait up for Ana."

She powered off the laptop, entered the living room, and curled up on the couch. The house was quiet except for the ticking of a large, ornamental wall clock that hung over the TV. Gold-colored plastic spikes encircled the round clock face, resembling the sun. Unlike The Big House, which was built as a semblance of wealth and grandeur, standing on a hill for the world to see, Ana and Hadwin's house was a family home.

Family photos covered the walls and tables throughout the house. There were multiple photos of Ana and Hadwin with their two sons on vacation, at college graduations, and at their weddings. Ana, holding her three grandbabies. Craft paper with colorful kid-size handprints to Grandma and Grandpa were stuck to the refrigerator door with plastic fruit magnets. Their house was worn, clean, comfortable, and oozing with love.

The crunching of car tires on gravel and a slammed car door broke her thought pattern. It was 9:30 p.m., and Ana was finally home. Vonnie went to the kitchen and selected a bottle of wine. The cork popped just as Ana walked through the door.

Ana looked disheveled. The gray in her hair was more prominent. It hung loose as if she had forgotten to comb it. Her face had a tired, weary expression. The blue scrubs were wrinkled and baggy on a body that was at least twenty-five pounds lighter than it was two months ago. Ana always showered and changed clothes at the clinic before coming home.

"Yippee, wine. Use the big glasses and bring the bottle," Ana said, half-heartedly tossing a laundry bag to the floor and flopping heavily in Hadwin's recliner. She kicked off her shoes, put her ankle across her knee, and massaged her foot.

Vonnie brought the wine and placed Ana's glass on top of a stack of magazines on the table beside the recliner. She assumed her place on the sofa and sipped her wine.

"Another bad day?" she asked, knowing the response.

Ana drank three big gulps of the wine before speaking.

"Vonnie, I'm sixty, and I don't know how much more of this I can take. The days get longer and longer, and my patients keep dying. I'm so exhausted I can hardly put one foot in front of the other."

"Well, you've done an excellent job here on the plantation. We still haven't had an outbreak. So that's something you can be proud of."

"Thanks for the compliment. I've been overly strict with the folks here. Behind my back, they call me the COVID Cop, but I don't care. An outbreak would devastate this place. We have fifty-three people over sixty-five, and they all live in multigenerational households."

Ana swirled the wine in her glass, took another gulp, and held her glass out to Vonnie to refill.

"I'm ready to retire. Running myself ragged isn't even close to what I'd planned to be doing at this age," she said, switching feet and continuing the massage. "Hadwin made reservations at a resort in Placencia and is forcing me to take the weekend off. He's concerned about me, and I am too; my body and mind are break-ing down."

Suddenly, she perked up. Her eyes sparkled. The wine glass was almost to her lips.

"Did Hadwin tell you about the huge donation we received today?" Ana asked, smiling broadly.

Vonnie smiled, pleased to see the relaxing effect the wine was having on her friend.

"No, all Hadwin wants to do is look at spreadsheets, talk about that banana fungus, and decide how we should diversify crops. What donation?"

Ana was animated, grinning from ear to ear. "We received a giant truckload of PPE, N95 masks, gloves, digital thermometers, face shields, hand sanitizer, and COVID testing supplies—a whole truckload. And I don't mean one of those small box trucks; I'm talking about an eighteen-wheeler.

"You should have seen Alicia and me when Hadwin called us to come to the receiving dock. We went crazy, jumping around, laughing, crying, and screaming like four-year-olds on Christmas morning. There's no way I can store it all in the clinic; Hadwin will secure it for me."

Vonnie quickly uncurled her legs and sat up. "Wow, that's awesome! Who donated it?"

Ana drained her wine glass. "I have no idea; it was an anony-mous donor. I searched the paperwork. It specified me as the recipient, but nothing identified the sender."

"And you don't think it was from the government?"

Ana stood and kicked her shoes to the side. "Someone from the Ministry of Health would have notified me. We would never have received anything on this scale from them. The delivery address was the Hollister Plantation. I plan to share it with the other clinics, but these supplies were for me" she said, beaming.

A puzzled expression crossed Vonnie's face. "There's a critical shortage of medical supplies within the entire country, but you receive a truckload from an unidentified source. That's more than weird. I wonder how whoever sent them could acquire supplies the government couldn't?"

Putting her hands on her hips, Ana twirled around and strutted toward her bedroom, swinging her hips from side to side like a fashion model. "I don't know who it was, and I don't care. I have a guardian angel somewhere in the universe, and he loves me."

* * *

Monday afternoon, Vonnie and Hadwin walked to the front of The Big House. A large piece of plywood stood beside the open, battered front door. Hadwin handed Vonnie an N95 face mask.

"You didn't steal these masks from Ana, did you?" she said, laughing as she pulled the elastic straps over her head.

"I certainly did; she won't miss them," Hadwin responded slyly. He looked up at the house, then at Vonnie. "I asked the men to remove some boards to give us light and let in some fresh air. The fire marshal taped off all the unsafe spaces, but I want to warn you that it's hot inside, and there's plenty of mold and mildew."

Although there was no clear proof, the police reasoned the fire in the banana groves was created as a distraction while shooters entered The Big House searching for Chance. The fire marshal surmised the fire started in The Big House when bullets hit the cans of flammable liquids Vonnie had carelessly left sitting around the family room when she was redecorating.

Vonnie took a deep breath, steeled herself, and followed Hadwin through the door. Instantly, time slowed down as if they were moving through a slow-motion movie scene. All sound disappeared. She was floating as if in an eerie, silent dream. Hadwin's mouth moved, but she couldn't hear the words.

Hadwin pointed to issues and features; one moment he was looking up at the ceiling, and the next he was bent over, looking at something on the floor. Quiet and stoic, Vonnie drifted along behind him. She felt like she was in an ancient museum full of broken, charred relics, and Hadwin was the docent conducting the tour.

It was interesting to see how her family's elegant matriarchs had perfectly camouflaged the stone walls and cement floors. The hand-carved, pristine white crown molding was discolored from smoke. The arms of the crystal chandelier, which had been shipped from Austria, were tarnished and twisted; shards from the crystal pendants had been swept in a pile to make way for foot traffic. Even though the walls were burned, in several places, Vonnie could see the chips in the mortar made by the bullets and bullet holes. Blackened skeletal remains of custom-made chairs and tables, Arabian carpets purchased on vacation in the Middle East, and drapery fabrics from Morocco were all unrecognizable. They were now remnants of 150 years of accumulated artifacts that made up her family's history. And it had all been reduced to useless debris.

The outside temperature was a scorching 102 degrees, and no breeze flowed through the broken windowpanes on the second floor. Vonnie gently removed a photograph from a shattered frame lying on the floor in the hall. It was of her great-grandfather standing beside a high-backed chair where her grandfather sat; her two-year-old father was sitting in her grandfather's lap.

In this photo was her legacy—the proud, hardworking, intelligent men who had not only built the plantation but also helped shape the country. Then without warning, her heart broke. It was as if the eyes of the three men were looking into her very soul. They had worked their entire lives to pass a priceless torch to her, the last person in the Hollister lineage, and she was going to sell it. The shame and guilt were overwhelming.

She felt herself sway as the suppressed emotions came flooding to the surface. Sweat streamed down her face and into her eyes. She wiped her forehead with the back of her arm; the elastic straps on the N95 mask irritated her face.

"Hadwin, I've seen enough for today," she called out in a shaky voice. With one hand, she fanned herself with the photograph and, with the other, rapidly pulled the top of her T-shirt in and out, trying to circulate the hot air around her face. "Send the blueprints to whichever architect you think is best. I'll meet with him and come up with a plan." She turned and quickly started down the stairs.

Hadwin stepped out of a bedroom into the hall with a questioning look. "What? But we're just getting started. You haven't seen the entire house; we still have the third floor," he said, watching her descend the stairs.

She looked at him over her shoulder. "I've seen enough." Then she hastily left the house and snatched off the N95 mask. She paced back and forth on the porch, crying and hyperventilating until Hadwin appeared.

Hadwin immediately noticed Vonnie's emotional distress. He walked to her and placed his hands on her shoulders. "Vonnie, calm down. I know this is hard, but you have Ana's and my support. You don't have to do it alone." He hugged her and allowed her to cry into his chest. "Take all the time you need; come back whenever you feel ready."

They were walking beside the service road when a Hollister Plantation security car stopped beside them; John grinned widely from behind the wheel. The sling on his left arm was visible through the driver's side window. "I know, I know, I'm not supposed to be here; please promise me that you won't tell Ana," He said, smiling sheepishly.

Vonnie and Hadwin laughed out loud. "I won't tell her, but you'd better not let her catch you," Vonnie said.

"That's why I'm leaving as fast as I can. By the way, Hadwin, did you read that email from Chance?" John asked.

Hadwin put both hands in his pockets and smiled. "Yep, I read it; it looks like we can finally breathe in peace" he responded.

"I'm just glad it's over. I've already released the extra guards I hired and put my team back on their regular schedules."

Vonnie no longer smiled as she looked from one man to the other. "What email? What's over?"

The two men looked at each other guiltily, remembering that after Chance's confession in the mechanic's shop, they had agreed to put Vonnie on a need-to-know basis. She didn't know all the details about Chance's situation. Their smiles disappeared. John spoke up.

"Chance sent us an email late last night. It contained web links to three different Guatemalan newspaper articles. The man that sent the three gunmen here to recapture Chance is dead" John said.

Hadwin quickly inserted himself into the conversation. "That means we don't have to worry about anyone else coming here in search of Chance. He's gone, and so is the man who was trying to find him."

"Right," John said. "After the fire, Chance Moore was the last person I ever wanted to see again, but I was happy to get that email." He wanted to get away before Vonnie asked more questions. "I need to get out of here before Ana sees me. I'll see you in a few weeks."

Vonnie stepped closer to John's car. "John, hold on a minute. Not so fast. I have a few questions for you. First, how many extra guards did you hire while Chance was here?"

John looked at Hadwin, unsure of the abrupt change in Vonnie's attitude. "Three."

Vonnie folded her arms. "So, nine guards were on duty the night of the fire?"

John looked at Hadwin again, but Hadwin shrugged, indicating he was also confused. "No, six guards were on duty when the fire started; three were off duty. They'd worked a ten-hour shift, but they came as soon as I called them. So, what's the problem, Vonnie? What's your concern?"

Suddenly, Vonnie became livid. One hand went to her hip, and the other waved back and forth, clutching the photo. She leaned toward John. "My concern is, I don't think six security guards are enough to protect the plantation. I don't want what happened on the night of the fire to happen again. I want top-level security. You said it yourself; we have over two thousand acres with no physical border. Six security guards can't protect two thousand acres twenty-four hours a day, seven days a week.

Do you foresee the refugee situation improving in our border countries? I don't. Do you think there will be more skirmishes like the ones you experienced over the past five years? I do. We need more guards.

And what about technology? Shouldn't there be security cameras, scanners, or something like that? What about guard dogs? I want layers of the best security money can buy. This property won't be defiled again as long as my name is on the deed. If a monkey tries to steal a banana, I want it shot on sight!"

Hadwin and John looked at one another, shocked, blown away by Vonnie's tirade.

"Okay, Vonnie, you're the boss, and frankly, I think it's a good idea. Hadwin and I will discuss it, but I don't want you to freak out when I present the cost estimates," John said, anxious to leave.

Vonnie softened her tone. "Don't worry about the budget; we'll make it work." Then, looking inquisitively back and forth between Hadwin and John, she asked. "So, where is Chance?"

Shame-faced, head down, brushing nonexistent lint from his slacks, John said, "The government banned all international flights two months ago; he's probably in Belize City."

The three chatted a few minutes longer, then John drove off, and Vonnie and Hadwin silently continued their walk across the grounds. Vonnie took slow, deep breaths and tried to calm herself. Just moments before, the picture of her ancestors had shaken her to the core, and she was still in a heightened emotional state from the torrent she unleashed on Hadwin and John. So, she decided to lighten the conversation with Hadwin.

"Hadwin, how are the boys doing? Have you talked to them lately?"

Hadwin brightened immediately. "Oh, the boys are doing well. Did Ana tell you they both plan to leave the States, move back home, and work with me?"

Vonnie fanned herself with the photograph as they walked. "Really? I'm surprised. I thought they liked living in the big city."

"They did before they married and had kids; neither wants to raise kids in the city. Junior has his MBA, and Michael has a master's degree in tropical agriculture. I'm thinking about the next five years. I want to retire, and those boys have helped me around this place since they were in diapers. It was all arranged for them to move down this year, but the pandemic hit, and now everything is on hold," he said disgustedly. "Ana is heartbroken but thank God for video chats with the grandkids."

They were standing at the fork in their paths. "Thanks again, Hadwin. I don't know what I'd do without you and Ana, and I apologize for my overreaction about the security," Vonnie said.

"No problem, Vonnie; we all went through a lot during the fire. We're lucky to be standing here. But your concern is valid. John and I will handle the security upgrades."

Vonnie turned to walk toward his house, then stopped. "Oh, Hadwin, send me a copy of the email you and John received from Chance."

# 32

# DOMINIC

Dominic Castillo sat on the soggy ground, propped against a tree as night descended upon the rainforest. He was sick; the fever, throbbing headache, bone-rattling chills, and body aches were getting worse.

The shoulder-length dreadlocks were gone, hastily chopped off to alter his appearance. His salt-and-pepper hair was bushy and dirty, and gray-and-white stubble covered the lower part of his face. His clothes were damp and filthy.

Forty feet away was a group of five Nicaraguan refugees. The men were walking north through Belize to the Mexico border. And Dominic had been hovering on the fringes of the group for two days.

Traveling was excruciatingly slow because of the constant need to hide from the Belize military patrols. If the soldiers discovered the group, they would be deported and forced to return to the nightmarish circumstances they were trying to escape. And he would be arrested, convicted, and sentenced to death.

Each night, the group constructed a makeshift shelter from tree branches where they slept together, shielded from the rain and protected from the animals that crept through the forest at night. They did not invite him to join them.

One of the refugees shared morsels of his food with him the day before, but tonight, when he approached and again begged for food, the entire group turned hostile. Huddled together in front of their shelter, around a campfire, they whispered, casting disparaging glances in his direction.

Frightened and humiliated, Dominic looked longingly at the fire as his aching body shivered. The insects and mosquitos were intolerable. Sores and raw skin from the bites and his vigorous scratching covered his body. Leaning his head against the tree, he thought about his deplorable condition and the phone call that started his demise.

* * *

The call came while he was at the resort in San Ignacio with Vonnie. It was the middle of the night, and he was returning from the bathroom when he stopped to take in the scene before him. The door to the bedroom's secluded patio was open. It had rained earlier in the evening, and a humid, refreshing breeze streamed into the room along with the dim glow from the accent lights around the patio. His prized big game fish, Vonnie, was splayed naked on the bed, snoring like a hog, fucked into oblivion. Dominic lit a cigarette, climbed into bed, put one hand behind his head, and blew smoke at the ceiling fan.

*Before this weekend is over, I'll make sure she won't be able to live without me. I'll propose and convince her to have a quick, private wedding next month. Then, with my connections, a cargo ship to Panama. Once I'm out of the country, fuck the cartels and all the leeches who have been sucking my pockets dry for years; they can all kiss my ass. With access to all that Hollister money, I'm going to live the life of the rich and famous.*

Then, the dream disintegrated when his cell phone vibrated on the nightstand; a text message displayed "911." It was the emergency code used by his men to notify him when something was wrong and required his immediate attention.

* * *

As Dominic watched, the number of men around the fire dwindled; they were settling down for the night. Stiff and sore, he shifted his position, reached around, and scratched his back. Luckily, his fingers closed around the insect and squeezed it between his thumb and forefinger. He yearned to lay down and stretch out, but the ground was too wet. So, instead, he rocked and hugged himself, straining to find relief from the gnawing hunger and pain.

Vile thoughts of those who had abandoned him crossed his feverish brain. As soon as the story about the Honduran refugees dying in the back of his truck hit the media, he'd become a pariah, an outcast. The police swarmed his business and home, interrogated and threatened his employees and associates, and froze his assets. None of the business partners responded to his plea for help. And of all the women who previously welcomed him into their beds, only two girlfriends in remote villages had allowed him to stay for several days. But eventually, they both turned him out, afraid someone would call the police.

Turning himself in wasn't an option. When David Mendez, deputy commissioner of the Belize Law Enforcement Bureau, had summoned him to the Christmas Mass at St. Matthew's Cathedral, he warned him about what would happen if anything went wrong with one of the shipments. Three people died in the back of his truck. So, the money he paid Mendez and his cronies for protection meant nothing. Mendez would sit back and watch him hang.

Embers glowed in the campfire, the refugees slept, and the night creatures called and responded to one another. The forest vegetation rustled and moved with the activity of invisible animals. In the dark, tracking the scent of a jungle rat, the venomous fer-de-lance viper slithered across the forest floor. Unaware of the danger, Dominic placed his hands on the ground to adjust his position against the tree. The bite was delivered with lightning speed, and searing white-hot pain raced up his arm.

The following day, just as the first glimmer of dawn lightened the morning sky, the kick from a heavy boot failed to arouse the man lying at the base of a tree. After a closer examination, the soldier realized the man was dead. Forty feet away, other soldiers searched the remains of the abandoned Nicaraguan campsite.

## 33

# VONNIE

The air in the basement of The Big House was much cooler than upstairs. But it was also damp and musty. A battery-powered, industrial spotlight illuminated the space. A yellow bandanna protected Vonnie's hair from the dust and drooping spiderwebs. Her sweaty T-shirt was smudged with stains, as were her jeans and sneakers. An N95 face mask dangled from her fingers as she slumped in an antique chair, scanning the immense trove of unexamined objects stacked on shelves and sitting on the floor.

Since the walkthrough of the house with Hadwin and retrieving the old, sepia photograph of her family's patriarchs the previous week, clearing out the contents of the house in preparation for its restoration had become not only a mission but therapeutic.

The photograph of her great-grandfather, grandfather, and father leaned against the lamp on her bedside table as a reminder of the courage and tenacity it took to overcome adversity and build something from nothing. The accumulated weight of indecision, stress, and pressure of selling the plantation and moving on with her life was gone. The pandemic was raging worldwide; no one wanted to buy the plantation, but she was safe and healthy and had everything she needed to take her time and let life work itself out one day at a time.

Since she no longer lived in The Big House and instead lived with Hadwin and Ana among the plantation's residents, there was rarely a day when one or a group of her former playmates didn't stop to chat as she trekked back and forth across the grounds. For the first time, she was meeting their spouses, adult children, grandchildren, and, in several cases, great-grandchildren. Evenings were spent sitting on porches, sipping limeade, laughing about the old days. The renewed relationships gave her a sense of peace; these people were her family, and they cared about her.

Even though she started early each morning, working in the sweltering heat in a house without air-conditioning was grueling. But a plan was taking shape in her mind about how to preserve her family's legacy. Every closet, drawer, nook, and cranny had been examined, and unknown parts of her family's history were revealed. Decades of letters, diaries, photos, and other memorabilia previously considered old, useless junk were now precious.

It had taken three weeks to clear most of the first, second, and third floors, and now she was in the basement. Her body agreed that all the stooping, lifting, pushing, pulling, and sweating were better than a gym membership. Vonnie hadn't taken an anti-depressant or pain pill since the night of the fire. And even though Ana's secret potions tasted like stale monkey piss, they significantly eased the withdrawal symptoms.

A box of hand-embroidered bed linens sat at her feet. Next to that was a chest filled with lace tablecloths and napkins. Vonnie pushed the chest aside with her foot, climbed the steps back to the main floor, and left the house, imagining a long, hot shower and a chilled bottle of wine.

It was Friday afternoon, and the plantation was shutting down for the weekend. A line of cars and pickup trucks crept toward the exit gate; migrant workers were boarding vans, and the plantation dwellers walked between and around the vehicles toward their houses.

At the bottom of the front steps was a commercial-size, portable dumpster overflowing with burned and discarded items protruding over its sides. A few feet away was a portable storage container with its door retracted. While closing the container door, Vonnie felt her cell phone, tucked in the back pocket of her jeans, vibrate.

Two days later, on Monday, at 7:00 p.m., she strode across the Belize Hilton's elegant lobby past the reception desk, her head high, chin up, back straight, and her hair in an updo. A face mask temporarily hid the conservative but attractive makeup. She wore a sleeveless turquoise silk A-line dress. The ruby and diamond earrings, matching pendant necklace, and bracelet were gifts from her grandmother. A red leather bedazzled purse was clutched in her hand, and red leather pumps graced her feet.

The sun's scorching rays were finally slipping below the horizon, and a moist breeze blew lightly across the water as she entered the hotel's outdoor restaurant overlooking the harbor. Strands of string lights sparkled above the restaurant's guests. Sailboats and yachts bobbed in the water, moored for the night. Vonnie navigated between tables covered with white tablecloths and small votive candles flickering in the middle of glass centerpieces surrounded by white flowers.

She was startled at the transformation of the man sitting at the table on the far side of the restaurant. When she first laid eyes on him, he was barely clinging to life, and now he was healthy, handsome, and polished. His mixed-gray hair and beard were cut close and neatly trimmed. And he wore a black linen blazer, crisp white shirt, and light tan slacks.

As she approached, Vonnie quickly reminded herself that this man had lied to her and everyone who tried to help him. Because of those lies, he had nearly destroyed everything she and her family held dear for 150 years.

His eyes lit up, and he stood when he saw her approaching. "Vonnie, it's good to see you again" Chance said as he quickly moved around the table to seat her.

Vonnie smiled politely, still trying to come to terms with his appearance. She noticed a slight limp when he moved to her side of the table. "When both my realtor and my lawyer call on the same day and inform me that you, of all people, want to buy my plantation, the least I could do was meet with you in person and talk things through. It's not as though we're strangers." She removed the face mask and placed her hands in her lap to hide her uneasiness.

Chance motioned for the waiter. "You're right, and I'm glad you wanted a private meeting. I was concerned you would prefer working through a third party," he said, smiling. "I'm happy to see you; you look nice."

The waiter appeared, and they ordered drinks.

"Thank you, Chance, but I prefer to skip the small talk and get down to business. We have a lot to discuss."

Chance folded his arms on the table and leaned in. "I agree, and if you don't mind, I want to say something before we start the business discussion. John and Hadwin forbade me to see you again after leaving you at Hadwin's house on the night of the fire. So, I couldn't apologize for the horrendous mess I caused before leaving the plantation the following day. Considering all that occurred, I didn't think it was appropriate to call you and say I'm sorry over the phone. And frankly, I thought you'd hang up on me."

Vonnie's face and voice were stern. "You're right; I wouldn't have spoken to you. I appreciate you risking your life to save mine, but if it hadn't been for you, I wouldn't have needed saving in the first place," she said. She sipped her wine and tried to relax. "I'm surprised and confused by your offer to purchase the plantation. It isn't something I expected, especially from you. So, why are you doing this?" she asked, twirling the stem of her wine glass between her fingers.

Chance tasted his whiskey and gently sat the glass down. "One, because I can; I have the means to do it. And two, I want to make amends. I owe you, and I couldn't live with myself if I didn't at least try to make things right."

Vonnie took a deep breath. "While you were recovering, John and Hadwin insisted I let them handle things related to your situation. And I did because I knew they would do whatever it took to protect me, the plantation, and everyone who lived there. But then, they abruptly moved you out of the house, the fire happened, and it was apparent there was a lot about you they never intended for me to know.

"I read your email to John and Hadwin and visited the links to the Guatemalan newspapers. And it blew my mind to think that you were so important to a cartel that they would not only chase you into another country but were ready to kill anyone who prevented them from recapturing you. So, it was easy to conclude that the only reason they were after you had to do with money and lots of it. And, when a cartel is involved, the money is always dirty."

Vonnie glared at Chance and leaned closer. "I'm concerned, Chance. You've told so many lies, I don't know what to believe. Those are my people on that plantation. I'm responsible for their livelihood, well-being, and protection. I will not see them harmed or compromised in any way, at any cost. Can you look me in my eyes and truthfully tell me they'll be safe and what happened during the fire won't happen again?"

"Vonnie, my situation with the cartel was one long nightmare, but it's over: in the past. I'm a free man; no one is chasing or trying to kill me. That's why I sent the email to John and Hadwin with the newspaper links. And I swear this is a legitimate transaction; your lawyer and banker can attest to that. So, there's nothing for you to be concerned about."

He leaned across the table and took both of her hands in his. "Vonnie, I promise you, the plantation and its people will be fine; you don't have to worry."

Vonnie pulled her hands free from his and sat back. "Chance, you know nothing about growing bananas. So, what do you plan to do with a two-thousand-acre plantation?"

"I'm going to give it to Hadwin," Chance responded coolly, finishing his whiskey and signaling to the waiter for a refill.

"WHAT," Vonnie shouted. The other diners curiously looked in her direction. Then she lowered her voice and leaned toward him again. "You're going to give it to Hadwin? Are you serious?"

Chance grinned. "You're right; all I know about bananas is that I like them in my cornflakes," he laughed. Then, his expression and voice became more serious. "Hadwin and Ana deserve it. They saved my life. I couldn't have asked for better medical care than what Ana gave me. And Hadwin killed the gunman who was trying to kill me when I was trying to rescue you. You might own the plantation, but it's Hadwin's heart and soul; it couldn't be in more perfect hands."

Vonnie's head dropped, and she used her napkin to dab at the tears in her eyes. "That's unbelievable; it's such a wonderful thing to do. It's so perfect" she said with a sniffle.

"Then we have an agreement? You're going to sell it to me?" Chance asked.

Vonnie looked at him, her eyes shining with tears. "Yes, we have an agreement."

"And do you forgive me for all of the problems I caused?"

"How could I not forgive you, Chance? You could have left Belize and not looked back, but you stayed, stepped up, and did the right thing. Thank you."

* * *

Wednesday morning, at 9:30 a.m., Hadwin was in his office keying numbers into a spreadsheet when Vonnie called. "Hadwin, I'm in Belize City, and I've sold the plantation. I need you and Ana to meet me at my lawyer's office on Friday at one o'clock to review the paperwork."

"YOU DID WHAT?" Hadwin shouted, not believing what he'd just heard. "You sold the plantation without consulting me? I can't believe you'd do such a thing without saying anything to me." He jumped up from his chair, his anger mounting. "Vonnie, we agreed that I'd be in on any negotiations, and now you're telling me you went ahead without me?"

Vonnie laughed. "Calm down, calm down. Don't worry, everything is fine. We got everything we wanted and then some."

"Vonnie, I'm pissed. I trusted you, and you went behind my back. Why didn't you at least talk to me first? Please tell me you haven't signed anything yet."

"Hadwin, it's fine, and no, I haven't signed anything, but I have verbally agreed to the terms. That's why I want you and Ana to be here."

Hadwin fumed. "What's Ana got to do with this? I'm the one who needs to be there. And which corporation is it? I need to research them so that I can prepare."

"Hadwin, please do what I ask," Vonnie begged. "And bring Ana. You don't have to do any research. I'll see you on Friday, and I promise everything will be okay."

"Vonnie, you've blindsided me, and I don't like it. So, on Friday, I'm warning you that if I disagree with anything, I will raise hell; you can count on it" he said, disconnecting the call and angrily flinging the phone onto his desk.

* * *

On Friday, Hadwin and Ana arrived promptly at one o'clock at the Ackerman and Jenkins law offices. The office was in an immaculately restored Victorian house in the North Side District of Belize City. Hadwin wore a long-sleeved white shirt with the Hollister Plantation logo on the pocket and black slacks. Ana's hair was gathered in a bun on the back of her head. She wore Hadwin's anniversary diamonds in her ears, a black-and-white paisley sundress, and black strappy kitten-heel sandals.

A female receptionist escorted them to the conference room where Vonnie, Chance, and Mr. Joseph Ackerman Sr., Vonnie's lawyer, awaited them. The conference table was rectangular with six chairs, a single chair at each end and two on each side. Mr. Ackerman sat at the head of the table, farthest from the door, and Chance and Vonnie sat together on his left side.

Confused and shocked expressions showed on Hadwin's and Ana's faces when they saw Chance sitting beside Vonnie. Hadwin stopped inside the door. "What's going on? What's he doing here? I thought we were here to discuss the terms for selling the plantation."

Vonnie smiled brightly, walked over, kissed Ana on the cheek, put her hand on Hadwin's back, and gently nudged him toward the conference table. "Come in, come in, sit down. "We'll discuss everything," she said, assuming her place beside Chance.

Hadwin steered Ana to the two seats on the opposite side of the table, closest to the door. Ana's eyes darted suspiciously from one person to another and finally stopped at Chance. "Chance, you look well. How is your leg?" she asked.

A broad smile covered Chance's face. "I'm great, Ana, thanks to you." He walked around the table and squeezed Ana's shoulder, and to Hadwin, he extended his hand to shake. "It's good to see you, Hadwin."

Hadwin's demeanor didn't change, but he reluctantly shook Chance's hand. Then he stretched across the table and shook the lawyer's hand.

Vonnie took a deep breath and cheerfully announced, "I'm selling the plantation to Chance; we've discussed it, and he's agreed to my terms."

Hadwin was flabbergasted. He blinked several times and stared at Vonnie. Wide-eyed, Ana looked from one face to another and stopped at Vonnie's.

"I don't understand," Hadwin said, crossing his arms over his chest. "It doesn't make sense."

"Well, it makes sense to me. He's giving me my asking price, and there won't be any changes to the living situations of the residents. Although, there will be changes to the plantation's management," Vonnie said.

Hadwin's face tightened, and his nostrils flared. He brought his arms down under the conference table and clenched his fists in his lap. Ana gently placed her hand on his thigh. "What type of changes are we talking about?" he asked.

Vonnie turned to Chance. "Chance, I'll let you explain."

Chance could see the tension in Hadwin's face and the uncertainty in Ana's eyes. "Hadwin, I owe you and Ana a debt that money could never repay. I wouldn't be here today if it weren't for you. So, I'm giving the plantation to you and Ana. I hope you'll accept it as a sign of my appreciation for all you've done for me."

Hadwin's mouth dropped in disbelief. Ana's nails dug deep into his thigh, and he slowly regained his composure. "You're buying the plantation from Vonnie and giving it to me?"

"I'm giving it to you and Ana. Don't leave her out; she saved my life first" Chance said, laughing.

Ana covered her face with both hands and began to cry. Vonnie grabbed a box of tissues from the sideboard and went to her friend. She pulled Ana from her seat and wrapped her in her arms, and they cried together.

Hadwin looked at the women, then at Chance. "Chance, are you serious? So, you're giving us everything, all of it. No strings attached?"

"All of it, my friend. No strings attached."

Hadwin's voice trembled. "Chance, I don't know what to say; you have no idea..." He struggled to remain calm. "Has all of this been documented?"

Mr. Ackerman beamed. "Everything is ready for your review." He placed his hands on top of a stack of blue binders. He looked at the women still huddled together, then at Chance. "I think it would be appropriate to give Mr. and Mrs. Lopez. private time to discuss matters and review the paperwork. Why don't we reconvene at three o'clock?"

Chance rose from his seat and went toward Hadwin. Again, he extended his hand for Hadwin to shake. "If anything in the paperwork doesn't suit you, just let me know, and I'll make it right."

Hadwin's eyes were moist as he stood on unsteady legs and firmly gripped Chance's hand. "Chance, thank you. You have no idea what this means to Ana and me."

Chance walked over to Ana and wrapped her in a big hug; she sobbed into his chest. Then, still wiping her eyes, Vonnie handed the box of tissues to Hadwin and pulled him into a hug.

# 34

# CHANCE

After signing the papers granting Hadwin and Ana ownership of the plantation, the lively party of four went to Chance's house to celebrate. The rented two-story, three-bedroom villa rested on a bluff overlooking Belize City. A retractable glass wall extended across the first floor, separating the interior and exterior spaces; the exterior space included an expansive patio with a hot tub and lap pool.

Chance was ready for the celebration and quickly popped the cork on the first bottle of Dom Perignon as the group settled into a private chef-prepared dinner.

There was a crescent moon and star-filled sky above, and the city and harbor lights glowed below. After dinner, in the interior portion of the house, Chance and Hadwin reclined on oversized, cushioned lounge chairs, drinking liquor and smoking cigars while watching the women in the hot tub on the exterior patio.

Chance removed a cigar box from the side table and handed it to Hadwin. "Here, give this to John."

Hadwin looked quizzically at Chance. "So, John gets a gift too?" he asked, smiling and swirling the ice in a third vodka and tonic.

"It's his pistol; he gave it to me after I found him on the floor during the house fire. I kept it because I had no other source of protection after leaving the plantation, but I don't need it anymore, and it's illegal for me to have it."

Hadwin opened the box, looked at the Glock 9mm, then closed it. "He never mentioned it. I guess he thought he'd never see it again; I'll make sure he gets it." Then Hadwin slouched lower in his seat. "Chance, I want to ask you a few questions... just between us; it won't go further. And if you don't want to answer, it's cool," he said, shrugging.

"What is it?" Chance asked while taking in the view of the harbor far below.

"I'm curious... what did you do after leaving the plantation, and how did you find out those guys in Guatemala were dead?"

Chance sipped his drink and looked at Hadwin. "After leaving the plantation, I couldn't assume the hunt for me was over because we killed those three men during the fire. Aapo Vasquez was desperate, and I'd made a fool of him by stealing his money and escaping. I knew he wouldn't stop trying to recapture me. So, after arriving in Belize City, I contacted the embassy lawyer, who helped me find a place to stay off the beaten path; my first apartment was nothing like this. Then, I bought a laptop and other computer equipment and focused on finding a way out of the country. While searching for a way to get out of Belize, I also researched Aapo and the Vasquez Cartel."

Chance walked to the bar across the room to freshen his drink. "You didn't hear me say it, but some internet research wasn't legal. I hacked into every law enforcement agency in Guatemala. As a result, I had access to all the police information related to the Vasquez Cartel. Eventually, I found out about the deaths of the patriarch of the cartel, Eloy, and his sons, Aapo and Humberto. It was headline news in every media outlet in the country. That's why I sent those emails to you and John. I wanted you to know the search for me was over, and the plantation was safe."

"Damn, you're one lucky son of a bitch," Hadwin said, shaking his head from side to side. "Okay, next question... during that night in the mechanic's shop, you told us the cartel was after you because you stole money from them. Is that the money you used to buy the plantation?"

Chance thought before responding. During the altercation in the mechanic's shop, he knew John wouldn't kill him or bust his leg with the rubber hose; John only intended to intimidate and scare him. John and Hadwin only needed to understand why the cartel was chasing him and enough information to protect the plantation. He had no intention of ever telling anyone about all his and Mack's illegal hacking activities.

"Don't you think it's appropriate that the cartel pay for the suffering and damage they caused?" Chance said, puffing his cigar, hoping the response was sufficient. He had no idea whose money paid for the plantation. The money in his offshore bank accounts was one big pot of soup.

"Well, all I have to say is, FUCK 'EM," Hadwin said, his speech slurring.

Chance looked at his friend and smiled; Hadwin was drunk.

"Okay, the last question; I already know the answer, but I'll ask anyway. You bought that truckload of PPE for Ana, didn't you?"

"It was the first thing I did once I got settled," Chance responded. "With enough money, a person can buy anything on the dark web, even COVID supplies during a pandemic."

* * *

On the exterior patio, Vonnie lay back, eyes closed, her mind drifting. The force of the hot tub's jets pounded her body, making her never want to move again. Chance coming forward to buy the plantation and giving it to Hadwin and Ana was so wild and wonderful that she couldn't believe it at times. Her heart was so light it floated on the steam rising from the bubbling water. She was finally free to move on with her life, and her family's cherished legacy was now in the hands of someone her father loved and trusted. It was magical.

Ana sat opposite Vonnie in the hot tub. Leaning forward, lowering her voice to a whisper, she asked, "Vonnie, have you seen the news?" She eyed the men lounging several feet away, not wanting them to hear the conversation. It had been two weeks since the story of the Belize military finding Dominic's body appeared in the media.

"Yep," Vonnie responded with her eyes closed. "I've seen the news on TV, on my laptop, on my phone, and I've read the newspapers." She sat up, reached for a towel, and wiped her face.

Ana sipped champagne while closely watching her friend. "Can you believe what happened to Dominic?"

"Yeah, it's hard to believe, but the entire incident was tragic; three people died because of him." Vonnie had no intention of telling anyone she was with Dominic when the refugees were found dead in the truck. It was a secret she would take to her grave.

"Just think, a snake killed another snake; it sounds like justice to me," Ana said, draining her glass. "You know how I felt about him." She reached into the ice bucket, grabbed the neck of the champagne bottle, and emptied it into her flute. "So, what are your plans now that you've sold the plantation?"

Vonnie sipped her drink. "Well, I've already separated the personal things I want to keep; I intend to give the rest away."

Ana's eyes widened in surprise. "Give it away? Wow, Vonnie, there are a lot of antiques and expensive things in that house. So, who are you giving it to?"

"The people who live on the plantation. Their labor made it possible for my family to buy all that stuff; I don't need it. So, I plan to have a big cookout and give it all away, then I'll say goodbye to everybody."

Ana immediately sat upright. "Goodbye? Where are you going? You don't have to move out just because you sold the property; you can stay with Hadwin and me as long as you want."

Vonnie reached out for Ana's hands. "Give me your hands, Ana, because I know you'll cry," Vonnie said, smiling. "Chance has been working with the embassy, and as long as we test negative for COVID-19 before leaving Belize, we can enter the US."

"How? There are no commercial flights or cruise ships any-where right now," Ana said, her eyes watering as she tightly gripped her friend's hand.

Vonnie retrieved the towel and handed it to Ana. "Chance is going to charter a plane."

"When?" Ana whimpered, clutching the towel.

"After the cookout. Chance says he's in no rush; he'll wait until I'm ready to go."

* * *

The Gulfstream G550 jet gleamed, and the engines softly purred as it sat ready for flight on the tarmac of the Belize International Airport. In the blazing sun, airport workers stood in small groups, ogling at the aircraft. A male flight attendant stood at the base of the stairs to the plane's entrance, waiting to assist his passengers.

Smiling and walking beside Chance toward the plane, Vonnie said, "Wow, I feel like a rock star. I wasn't expecting anything like this." She wore her hair in a ponytail, light makeup, sunglasses, a long white maxi-sundress, and sandals; a multicolored, grass-woven tote bag rested in the bend of her elbow.

Chance wore sunglasses, a peach-colored polo shirt, navy-blue Bermuda shorts, and navy loafers without socks. "This is a special occasion; we deserve it," he said, stepping aside and allowing Vonnie to ascend the stairs.

They sat on opposite sides of the aisle during the flight, facing each other, animatedly chatting, drinking martinis, and eating lunch, then they grew quiet, each looking out the window, lost in thought.

Watching the clouds drift over the blue water of the Gulf of Mexico, Chance thought about the past, beginning with Charlotte's death and the series of events that led him to where he currently sat—the last eight months had reshaped his vision of the type of future he wanted and how he wanted to spend the rest of his life.

Across the aisle, Vonnie thought of how she intended for the legacy of the Hollister family to live on in Belize. In four days, she had an online meeting with representatives from The University of Belize to discuss the creation of the Hollister School of Tropical Agriculture. An official invitation to join the university's board of governors was forthcoming. Her new position meant periodic visits to Belize, and while there, she would stay with Hadwin and Ana, their two sons, and their families in The Big House. She was genuinely excited about something for the first time in years, and impatient to start the project. Determined to continue turning her baby steps to recovery into strides, an appointment with a doctor to restart counseling was scheduled for later in the week.

Chance and Vonnie's thoughts were interrupted when the flight attendant told them to prepare for landing.

Surprised, Vonnie looked at Chance and said, "I thought this was a five-and-a-half-hour flight."

Chance laughed. "It's five-and-a-half hours if you're flying Delta."

Chance exited the plane first and held out a hand to assist Vonnie as she stepped onto the tarmac at RDU airport.

Vonnie turned to him. "Chance, we're friends, and I don't want to lose that friendship; we've been through too much together. So, tell me—no, promise me—you'll keep in touch, and we'll see each other again."

Chance put his hands on Vonnie's shoulders and kissed her forehead. "Vonnie, I feel the same way. But don't worry. I promise to stay in touch with you and the folks in Belize. We're more than friends; we're family now."

* * *

Four hours after Vonnie's goodbye, Chance deplaned in Vera Cruz, Mexico, and walked to a white Cadillac Escalade. The smiling driver promptly opened the back passenger door and stored his luggage. The two men spoke Spanish; the friendly driver pointed out interesting features as he drove through the historic city.

Finally, about twenty-five miles past the town, the driver turned onto a steep, narrow road and eventually stopped at a square, one-story yellow house with a flat roof. Mixed-colored blossoms overflowed the window boxes on each side of a turquoise-colored door. A small, well-manicured lawn and a cement walkway led to the front of the house.

Chance exited the vehicle and stretched. The elevation was much higher than he had expected; the smell of the ocean filled the air, and palm trees fluttered in the wind. He nervously rang the doorbell several times and waited patiently, but there was no answer. So, he followed a trail of steppingstones to the back of the house. The backyard was high above the ocean, and the sound of ocean waves crashing against the rocks below rode on the wind.

His cyber skills made it easy to find her, but the fear of rejection was nerve-racking. Soliciting the courage to contact her had taken days. Since then, there had been long phone calls and video chats in which they both agreed that life was short and time too precious to waste.

She stood at the far end of the backyard with her back to him, looking out at the ocean. The luxurious hair blowing in the wind was now a shiny gray. A multicolored shawl was wrapped around her shoulders. The lower part of her long white dress fluttered in the wind, exposing her calves; she was barefoot.

Chance stopped after a few feet, not wanting to startle her. His voice was shaky and uncertain. "Conswaylo?"

Conswaylo turned to face him, and the decades of separation disappeared on the wind. She had been widowed for over ten years. Her mature beauty was striking; the years had been kind. There were no wrinkles in the brown, suntanned face, a youthful sparkle twinkled in her eyes, and she stood straight with a confident sensuality. The full lips parted into a warm smile, she opened her arms wide, and Chance rushed toward his future.